Hot
and
Hairy

A Day in the Life of a Hairdresser

A Novel
by
Gloria Jean

Hot and Hairy
A Day in the Life of a Hairdresser

A Novel
by
Gloria Jean

Published by
Glamour City Press
P.O. Box 28104
Fresno, California 93729

Library of Congress Catalog Card Number: 93-91559

ISBN 0-9636506-1-0

Copyright ©1993

First Printing November, 1993

Book Cover Design by Gloria Jean

Printed in the United States of America

To Hairdressers everywhere.

I honor your creativity
and
I thank you for making this world
a more beautiful place to live in.

Chapter 1

"Run into the light."

Lola shook her head and hoped to shake the memory of her dream from the night before. Again, she repeated the words that echoed in her mind.

"Run into the light."

She shuddered, remembering the terrifying feeling of being chased. Never before having experienced such a frightening nightmare, she was perplexed, unable to understand the symbolism of her dream. The meaning of the words, "run into the light," eluded her. She rationalized that the champagne she had drunk the night before at the art gallery opening had caused her nightmare. After trying to fool herself, she instinctively knew there was more to her dream than she could comprehend.

Driving down Main Street in her candy-apple red convertible, Lola felt the warmth of the sunshine on her tanned face and arms. Her diamond bracelets glistened.

Above her, blowing tufts of white floated through the aqua blue sky, kindled with the special magic of glorious springtime.

Lola caught a glimpse of the nearby sea and saw gulls rise in a cloud of white wings. The water was quiet with calm subdued little waves that broke close to the beach. The early-morning ocean breeze misted her face. She brushed blonde strands of Bombshell Beige, Clairol #102 from her forehead, then ran her fingers through her long curls that danced in the wind and prayed that the heaviness in her heart could blow away that easily.

She thought everything would be all right, if only her tyrant landlady would sign another six-year lease for Contemporary Hair Design, the successful beauty salon she and her friends had worked so diligently to create.

Tension eased, and her pretty face relaxed when she contemplated the day's coming events and smiled. The long-awaited Saturday had arrived, April Fools' Day. Five-thirty was the time she and her employee Raquel had set to even the score with Derrick, the prankster who won every time. Lola remembered how she and Raquel had brainstormed weeks earlier to come up with one sure-fire scheme to get back at Derrick, the womanizing hair designer. Now it was just a matter of hours before they would have the pleasure of carrying out their trick. This would even things up with Derrick, at least for a while, until his sharp mind came up with another clever plan. Lola bit her lip and hoped that Raquel would behave herself for a change and not play any of the radical jokes that she had earlier threatened to play on Derrick.

In or out of the salon, the practical jokes they played on each other never stopped. Laughter in the beauty salon was so much a way of life that regular customers expected it and looked forward to the entertainment. Even though Lola knew that it was against California law to have animals in the beauty salon, she fondly remembered the old eccentric lady who could not find a baby-sitter for her adorable little monkey. The lady had hidden Roscoe in her large purse. Lola found out about Roscoe when he jumped out of the purse on the floor and climbed up her leg under her dress. Lola shuddered when she thought back to the hair-pulling fight scene between a woman who found out that the shapely dish sitting next to her in the hair dryer was her husband's mistress. The wife had scurried out of the salon with some of Lola's rollers still in her hair. Lola never saw either the rollers or the women again.

Back to reality, Lola slammed on the brakes, screeching her car to a halt in her parking space behind the salon. Her landlady, 390-pound Bertha Sanders, was sweeping leaves around the garbage area of the old building. Grumbling loudly, a permanent scowl was etched on Bertha's moon-shaped face. Lola knew she should take this opportunity to try, for the millionth time, to persuade her widowed, hermit landlady to agree to a renewal of her lease. Lola slipped on her cushioned gold slippers, then approached Bertha cautiously and forced a smile.

"Good morning," Lola said. "How are you today?"

Bertha continued to sweep, ignoring Lola.

"Have you considered my latest offer?"

Bertha growled, looked Lola up and down, dwelled on her perfectly made-up face, then answered in her low, crackly voice, "If I've told you once, I've told you a thousand times, you hotsy-totsy hairdresser, I'm going to tear down this decrepit building and make a parking lot out of it."

"But Bertha, please... I love having my salon here in Venice. You've watched me work day and night to build up my business."

Her voice saturated with grief, Lola's heart pounded wildly as she spoke.

"So what else is new?" Bertha said, sounding like a witch. "You're nothing to me."

Lola's eyes began to tear. She had never felt so helpless in her life and she feared losing hold of the familiar. Lola had, from their first meeting, been kind to Bertha. Even though she did not always approve of Bertha's actions, she did respect and abide by her rules. For once, she wished that Bertha would treat her like a human being. Lola was not willing to give her salon up just yet. Desperate, she would fight for what she wanted until the last minute, which would be midnight that night.

"Bertha, you'd be better off collecting rent and continuing to live upstairs. It's not your style to live in that senior citizens' complex. You've lived upstairs for sixty years. Don't allow this place we love to become a newly-paved parking lot. It's your home; the salon is my second home. It's where both of us belong and you know it."

"I don't want to hear another word out of you. Ever."

Bertha threw the leaves in the garbage can, grabbed her broom and like a shuffling shadow lumbered up the stairs to her back door, tugging on the iron handrail at each creaking step.

Lola looked up to Heaven and prayed for a miracle. Opening her gold lamé purse, she reached in and found her ring of keys. Familiar smells of the beauty salon greeted her when she opened the door, hair spray mingling with permanent wave solution. Automatically, she flipped on the light to the well-stocked supply room, looked at the haircolor bottles of Clairol and the tubes of Majarel, L'Oreal hair spray, and boxes of Zotos permanent-wave solutions neatly filling the shelves. Lola had no intention of leaving her salon. The abundance of beauty supplies was a symbol to herself that she would not have to move to another salon. Hurt emerged over her frustration of not being able to communicate with Bertha.

Nearby, a Chippendales' calendar hung on the wall over the porcelain sink. Lola flipped the page over to April.

"How time flies. It's April Fools' Day already. Let's see what today brings," she said. "May it be filled with goodness."

Plastic tint bottles, frosting caps, hair brushes, and styling combs lay clean and dry in the dish rack. She put her purse in the cupboard under the sink, then opened the refrigerator door and squeezed her sack lunch between the orange juice and brie, hoping she would have a minute later in the day to take a bite of her turkey sandwich.

Glancing at the clock, she saw it was 7:30 a.m. She knew the salon would be in full swing by nine. Saturdays were chaotic. She couldn't bring herself to face the fact that this could be her last Saturday in her salon.

Warm memories of Lola's hairdressing career raced through her mind while she prepared the shop for the day. She pressed the button on the stereo. Music entered the room like a graceful swan skimming the lake, each note clear and bright. A cool breeze blew in from the ocean, and the far away sound of waves washing ashore sounded peaceful. In the morning light, Lola stood strong and breathed in deeply the soothing crisp air, filling her lungs. Slowly she exhaled and relaxed into the comfort of her vital body.

Lola, enjoying her aloneness in one of her favorite environments, became more serene. Coffee was brewing; candy dishes were filled with chocolate kisses, lemon drops, and peppermints. Clean, white towels were neatly stacked in the cupboards above the shampoo bowls; Nexus shampoo and hair conditioner bottles were filled. A broad assortment of magazines, which satisfied her wide range of clients, lay neatly on the coffee table like fallen dominoes; ashtrays were emptied, and a boxful of freshly baked muffins were placed beside the flowered porcelain teapot.

Lola stood in front of her work station. With the marble on the vanity cold beneath her fingertips, she stared at the photograph of herself and Rick. She remembered that night at the lively luau in Hawaii when that colorful picture had been taken. It had been their first vacation together. More good memories than bad crowded her mind. A yearning for his arms to be around her again filled her heart, and she missed the warm feeling of her head on his muscular chest. Part of her life seemed so empty without him. She found herself staring at his face in the photograph, seeing nothing else. Lola sank into the chair and cried. Instantly, as a saving grace, her grandfather's words sprang into her mind.

"There are worse things than loneliness."

She wiped a tear from her cheek, gently put the picture in the drawer, and retrieved her framed autographed picture of Elvis, putting it on her work station.

"Just you and me again, Elvis. That's all right by me."

Lola settled down comfortably in the chair behind the antique mahogany reception desk. A pile of mail lay in front of her. She leafed through it, separating the bills from the junk mail.

Unconsciously popping her bubble gum and twirling her curly hair around her finger, she flipped through the pages of the *National Enquirer*. Totally engrossed, she lapped up the fascinating scuttlebutt.

Lola, still fatigued from fourteen hours of bending hair the day before, stretched her weary legs and aching feet up onto the desk. Rolling the sleeves of her white silk blouse up to her elbows, she sipped mint tea and breathed in the cool sea breeze blowing through the opened etched windows. She rubbed moisturizer on her chemical-damaged hands while glancing around the room. Her salon was a personal space, she thought, a comfortable area she had created for herself and her clients. Her stomach sank at the thought of losing it all. The consideration of a new beginning terrified her. She consoled herself by remembering that, no matter what happened, nothing could take away her special memories of her magical haven.

It was quiet and peaceful now, but Lola knew that within the hour it would be a ramble-scramble zoo. Tired or not, she was ready. She knew she had to be. The show goes on. Beauty must be made. That was the reality of hairdressing.

Like never before, Lola's eyes slowly scanned the room. She felt that just in case this was her last day in her salon, she wanted the details of everything to be embedded in her mind forever.

She was still enticed by the beauty of the multi-colored floral fabric covering the tufted furniture she had carefully chosen for her avant-garde salon. Hearty plants hung from the ceiling. Lush ferns potted in wicker baskets and Italian cloisonné bowls set on the floor creating a jungle effect. Laughing aloud, she remembered how the florist had joked, saying that plants loved hair spray, especially Lola's favorite brand.

Even though the building she leased was one of the oldest wooden ones in Venice, she had elegantly decorated around its short-comings. The interior had been designed to be warm and inviting, funky with luxurious touches. Intricate hand-carved cherry wood frames surrounded the mirror at each of the four work stations.

Bouquets of baby's breath, peace roses, and delicate fern were artistically arranged in imported lead crystal vases on marble vanities beneath the mirrors. The shiny black-and-white checked linoleum had been walked on and danced on by thousands of clients throughout the years.

Lola knew that Raquel, more than herself, was grateful that the walls could not talk, particularly the walls of the mirrored facial room.

Lola glanced at Nattie's work station, neat as could be. Nattie was the open book—the big-mouthed, old-time, glamour-girl hairdresser who could not care less what type of environment she was in as long as there were good-looking men around. Lola knew that behind Nattie's abrasive exterior was a generous, caring human being with a well-oiled disposition.

She perceived that Derrick was totally oblivious to his surroundings, except for the facial room that gave him complete privacy for his rendezvous with his clients, especially the married ones.

Lola had become fast friends with Derrick and Raquel while attending beauty school in Hollywood. They had shared her same dream of building distinguished reputations as innovative stylists and wanted to teach their cultivated creativity at hairstyle shows nationally and abroad.

With a ten-thousand-dollar loan from her parents, Lola had bought the salon from Nattie. Their contract stipulated that Nattie could work every Friday and Saturday for as long as she wished.

Lola was gratified that they had accomplished their goals. Contemporary Hair Design was one of the most up-to-date, happening, well-known salons in Southern California. The salon's address book was brim full of exciting clients who were sophisticated thinkers, talented, and successful.

Wallpapered walls of yellow, gold, and white stripes complimented brass shelves which held the trophies and plaques she and her co-workers had won at hairstyle shows throughout the world. Lola's mind flashed back to the day at a hairstyle show in Paris when the internationally famous hairdresser Etienne performed his magic on several top models' hair, making them look more ravishing than they were. It had amazed Lola how adeptly Etienne moved his hands so quickly as he styled their hair. His hands had appeared to be a blur of electric light that moved in an exotic dancing motion. Etienne was one of Lola's role models. She respected and admired him for his artistic ability, humility, and his desire to share his knowledge.

Lola's lease would be up in a matter of hours and she had not been able to find another building to rent in the area. Fate had botched up every salon deal she had tried. She dismissed her feeling that something beyond herself was controlling her destiny and interpreted it to be a positive omen that she would stay in her salon. Several times before when Lola had been backed up against the wall, things had turned out in her best interest. She felt deeply in her heart that this situation would be like that, too.

Living and working in Venice was her way of life. At thirty-two, she was not willing to give up the career and lifestyle she had worked so hard to build. She knew the decisions she would have to make if she lost her business would alter her life forever. It was a forced gamble.

The ring of the telephone brought Lola out of her contemplation.

"Contemporary Hair Design. May I help you?" Lola listened with delight to the gentleman on the other end. "Well, congratulations, Ralph. I'm pleased to know that everything went OK with the delivery. Tell Mary the baby's first haircut is on the house, and no... please don't worry about having to cancel at the last minute like this."

Actually, Lola was relieved that her first appointment had canceled. The quiet time would be a welcome lull before the usual Saturday storm.

The front door creaked open. A sweet, gracious granny dressed in a pink jogging suit with matching tennis shoes entered the reception area and handed Lola a box of homemade brownies.

"Good morning, Gracie. Thank you. Your brownies are the best. How about telling me your secret ingredient?"

"I melt marshmallows in them while they bake." Her smile lit up her face, accentuating her rouged cheeks. "My Grandma Bessie from Louisiana taught me that trick. I caught my two husbands with that recipe."

"Did your being adorable have anything to do with it?" Lola teased.

"Oh, yes. You know how men like lovable, soft women," Gracie winked. "Just like us."

"You're too much. By the way, how was your trip back East?"

"Fabulous, I had such a good time traveling and enjoying our great country that I've booked a one-month excursion to the Orient."

"Sounds wonderful. Nattie will be here shortly. I'm sure she'll give you advice and one of her famous haircuts for that trip, too."

"I'm sure she will."

Lola inhaled the aroma of the brownies and quickly took a scrumptious bite all the time stamping checks from the previous day.

"Make yourself at home, Gracie."

"Thank you. You know I always do. That's part of the joy of coming here."

"That pleases me. People like you make my life a pleasure."

Lola watched Gracie pour herself a cup of coffee and settle comfortably into the love seat.

"I'm glad you made the coffee today, Lola. I don't mean to complain, but Nattie's coffee is so strong that it wrinkles my wrinkles."

"I know... It's like acid. We should smear it on our wrinkles and use it as a facial peel. It would probably make them vanish."

"Either that, or we could wish them away." Gracie bent over and smelled the pink carnations on the inlaid mosaic coffee table. She picked up a *National Geographic* and began to read an article while waiting for Nattie.

If there was one thing Lola knew about Nattie, it was that she was always on time. For forty years Nattie had been a real professional dedicated to her clients and to the beauty business. Lola got a kick out of how Nattie boasted and prided herself on being a martyr who had survived the traumas of life. She loved Nattie's far-fetched stories claiming that she had seen, done, and heard it all, and still lived to tell it. Lola accepted that Nattie was a concerned controller who loved taking the time to solve everyone's problems, and even though she wasn't the best haircutter in the world, she was a genius when it came to hair coloring and taking care of business. Nattie was smart enough to hook clients in by giving them a soothing therapeutic massage during their shampoos. Lola remembered Nattie's story about when she was a young girl and how she had been taught by her Japanese neighbor the art of Shiatsu. Lola shifted her thoughts as the telephone rang.

"Good morning. Contemporary Hair Design." Lola patiently waited for the person to speak.

"Where are you, Raquel? I thought you'd be here by now."

Lola rolled her eyes and sighed.

"Are you nuts?"

Lola was used to Raquel giving her excuse after excuse, but today was the last day she would have thought Raquel would pull such a stunt.

"What do you mean you won't be in today? Look, I know it's a beautiful day, and I'd like nothing better than to sun myself on the beach too, but a lot of people are depending on us. Girl, you must be crazy. For once, I'd like to know that you're reliable. We're booked solid and you're going to take a siesta? Please... Don't get my blood pressure up. Your first appointment is due at nine. She's a bride. You can't leave her stranded on her special day."

While listening, Lola scribbled on the note pad, sharp pointed doodles. Lola broke the lead on her pencil, then quickly grabbed a pen. Today was one day she expected cooperation from her co-workers. Biting her tongue, she continued to listen to Raquel's song and dance.

"I can't help it if you were up till 4 o'clock in the morning. I'm the one who needs more beauty sleep. I tossed and turned all night long, had a nightmare, and barely slept a wink. The dark circles under my eyes are dulling my emerald greens."

Lola continued to listen.

"Don't you darlin' me with your Southern charm. You're lying like that pretty red rug in your hall. Who'd you pick up last night?"

Lola crumbled the top page of the notebook into a tight ball. She needed to know that she could trust her friends in her time of need.

"Please, spare me the details." Lola pushed the chair back and stood up. "I've spoiled you all these years and covered for you. And now you have the nerve to ask me to squeeze in a bride's hair and make-up. I'm tired of wearing my body out doing both your work and mine. Besides, you need the money to keep up your over-extended lifestyle."

Lola's mouth hung open after Raquel's next statement. Her erratic doodling with the red pen became more frantic. She sat down.

"Two thousand dollars by noon? You're scaring me. What kind of trouble did you get into this time? Are you down at the police station again?"

Lola gave a long sigh of frustration.

"But you just bought a new car three months ago. I'm the one who needs a new car. The one I bought last year has turned out to be a real lemon."

Lola held the receiver away from her ear; Raquel's wailing cry echoed through the air. A curious Gracie looked up from her magazine with an inquisitive expression.

"Don't beg, Raquel. Please calm down. Don't beg. You know I hate it when you beg. Just come on in. We'll discuss it then."

There was an extended pause. Lola pushed the note pad across the desk, an astonished look on her face.

"Darn you anyway. How could you pull a stunt like this on me? No... No you don't. I'll get you for this one. You can be sure of it."

Lola hung up the phone and sat in silence, shaking her head, a smirk on her face.

"What's wrong?" Gracie asked. "What did Raquel say?"

"Raquel is something else. After all that stupid, idiotic conversation, she yells out 'April Fools' Day! I'll see you around nine.' Can you imagine her doing this to me with what I'm facing and all? Oh Gracie, I have a gut-level feeling that it's going to be one of those days."

"Making history, like last New Year's Eve day?"

"Yeah."

"Don't tense up and fight it, dear. Flow with it. You'll never hold back the river."

A smile came to Lola's full lips. She wondered if she would ever fall for one of Raquel's pranks again or if she had finally learned her lesson.

The back door slammed. Lola heard Nattie whistling "Oh What a Beautiful Morning" and knew the sound of the refrigerator door opening and closing would be next. She figured Nattie must have brought pizza in again. Like clockwork, every Friday night, oversexed, sixty-three-year-old Nattie ordered pizza for dinner and dessert. Nattie hated pizza, but her young handsome pizza man really did deliver. Thanks to Bertha though, none of the pizza ever went to waste. Shrewd Nattie swapped the pizza for a choice parking space behind the salon.

Lola watched Nattie perform her regular sashay up to the reception area. Her torch crimson hair was artificially arranged, ratted high into an inverted bowl shape with barrel curls. She pointed her forefinger at Gracie.

"I'll be with you in a minute, girlie," Nattie said in her low, raspy voice. "Relax, I'll let you know when I'm ready for you."

The short, sexy, geriatric cutie handed Lola a tube of moisturizing creme, then propped her elbows up onto the desk.

"You've given too many permanents this week, babe. This will help heal the cracked skin on your hands."

"Thanks, Nattie. You have an uncanny way of knowing what people need before they do."

"Yep. That comes from being an ultra-sensitive individual and working so closely with people for forty years. Just part of the territory. Hey, did you hear from your honey yet?"

"No, and I won't either."

Lola's voice became an extension of her broken heart.

"Babe, don't give up yet. Rick will see the light. He'll be back soon."

"I don't want him back, and he knows it. I mean it."

"Call it like it is. You two are crazy about each other."

"You're not hearing the message I'm trying to convey." Lola reached over and rubbed Nattie's ears. "Now, read my lips. Just because two people love each other doesn't mean they're good for each other. Anyway, I deserve better than a womanizer who can't commit."

"But, babe, he's got mega bucks."

"He's a good lay, too. So what? Without trust and harmony I have nothing. There's no way we could have a good future together."

"You're a dreamer, babe." Nattie shook her head. "Wake up and fly right."

Lola realized it was difficult for Nattie to understand that money could not buy everyone off. Lola knew she and Nattie were from different worlds, different time frames, but somehow they managed to respect each other and get along well. Lola knew Nattie had a heart of gold under her harsh exterior. She had demonstrated it time and time again throughout their years of working together. Nattie proved her true friendship and had been especially loving and nurturing during the time of Lola's mother's illness and death.

"I took Bertha out for dinner Thursday night," Nattie continued. "It cost me an arm and a leg, but it was worth it. I have never in my life seen anyone eat so much food at one sitting, except for Dorothy, of course. It's like she's in love with food. She pants like a dog until the waiter brings her plate. It's embarrassing to be seen with her."

"What did she say? Did she mention the lease?"

"Rest assured that the lease is in the bag. I know how to handle her. You know me... I could talk a person out of their birthday. Remember, Bertha was my landlady for thirty years."

"I wish I could believe you, but Bertha treated me like a non-entity again this morning. I've been more kind and friendly to her than anyone else. You'd think she'd at least return the respect and treat me with a little civility."

"Trust me, babe. Have I ever let you down?"

"No."

"Well? Just remember, Bertha has the sensitivity of a bulldozer. She's stubborn because she was raised on goat's milk. Now relax, it'll be OK."

The phone rang. It was Sam, the film maker Lola had done free-lance work for the last five years. He needed a favor, someone to do make-up for a last-minute television commercial that afternoon.

"I'm sorry Sam. There's no way Raquel or I can get out of the salon today and meet you on location, but if Francois will come here around noon, Raquel can get him ready for the shoot by one."

Sam hung the phone up before Lola could say good-by.

"I love the way he says 'thanks... Ciao, baby.'"

"Sam's a fun guy, lots of class." Nattie put three sticks of bubble gum into her mouth. "Gives fabulous parties, makes the best chili in the world."

"Raquel's going to think she's died and gone to Heaven when she feasts her eyes on Francois. He's such a good looking hunk, and a great dancer, too."

"Yeah he is. Moves smooth like a real pro." Nattie shimmied. "I remember him from the Chamber of Commerce party. He was wearing a white tuxedo, white vest, and no shirt or socks. Wow! Looking at that gorgeous chest and long legs is enough to make any woman drool. Va, va, va voom! The guy is a dreamboat." Nattie wiggled her hips. "And... We all know I know a good-looking man when I see one."

"He's just Raquel's type. You know how she loves sophisticated European men."

"She'll put on that Southern accent and charm of hers and melt him down in a jiffy."

"He's a real man. And that incredible face! She'll be beside herself."

"I'm waiting to see that. She's so cute when she drools." Nattie turned and barked at Gracie. "Well, are you going to keep it parked, or do you want a haircut now?"

Gracie stood to attention, purse in hand, and followed the slinky redhead back to the shampoo bowl. Nattie's high-heeled white boots clanked on the floor, and her short gathered mini skirt swayed with the exaggerated movement of her narrow hips. Black fishnet stockings hugged the fine definition of her curvy legs. Lola shook her head while watching the youthful spring in Nattie's step. Being in Nattie's presence was like experiencing an action-packed movie. Never a dull moment.

"Oh, another Saturday... And April Fools' Day, at that." Nattie pushed up the raglan sleeves of her over-sized silk blouse. "Ho, hum... I have a feeling."

"You too?" Lola asked.

"Yep. But don't fret. We'll live through it. We always have before."

"But, Nattie, it's different this time."

"No it isn't. Just a different set of circumstances."

Lola could see that Nattie was ready to take on her work day as Nattie smacked her lips and blew her bubble gum while putting the towel and drape on Gracie.

"I'm glad you don't dress like a little old lady any more, Gracie," Nattie bellowed at her petite client. "We've got to keep up with the times. It's better to push seventy than to have seventy push us. It's not the years, girlie, it's the miles."

"You and I are close in age."

"Yeah, thirty-nine plus. Thirty-nine is their business, the plus is ours."

"You're in top form today."

"You've got that right, babe. Great sex will do it every time. At our age, good circulation is a must. Our hearts need more than garlic all day long. You know how it is."

"Oh, I remember it well."

"Remembering isn't half as fun as doing. Get out there and get a guy. Come and play golf with me. There's tons of fun guys at the clubhouse. Take your pick, and I'll set it up."

"Thanks for the invitation, but for now, I'll take a rain check."

"Suit yourself, babe." Nattie popped up the handle of the foot rest. "Here, let's go for comfort."

"Whoa... You really know how to make a person feel at home." Gracie's feet flew up, then rested comfortably as she lay back in the shampoo chair.

"Yeah, we're real professionals. We like to spoil our clients."

"Nattie, there seems to be more cracks in the ceiling."

"Long as they're not in my face."

Lola watched steam from the hot water rise up and envelop the eyeliner around Nattie's fake eyelashes. Black smudged the wrinkles under the corners of her eyes. Lola had given Nattie several eyeliners that would not smudge, but Nattie stuck with the same brand she had used for the past thirty years.

"Your scalp's as tight as a slab of cement. Too many stressful years of teaching, sis. Trust me, I'll work these knots out of your neck right now." Nattie's arms moved with the rhythm of a fine-tuned machine.

"That's why I come to you. Thank you."

"Don't thank me, babe. I'm just doing my job."

During the ten-minute shampoo, Nattie's magic fingers pressed every muscle and pressure point to relieve the tension in Gracie's neck. Nattie was quite a talker, but she knew to be quiet while her clients enjoyed their relaxing shampoo.

A yellowed picture of a 1940's Revlon girl hung on the wall at Nattie's work station next to her prized possession, an autographed picture of her with her favorite movie star, Clark Gable. Lola knew that Nattie's pencil-thin eyebrows and painted on Joan Crawford lips were from a happy time, long past.

"How about a glass of wine, Gracie?" Nattie asked while walking to her styling station. "I've got a new French Colombard that will make you sizzle."

"Thank you, but I think I'll pass, Nattie. It's a little too early for me to start on wine. This coffee will be just fine."

"You call that unleaded stuff coffee? Hell's bells, it isn't even strong enough to stain a blouse."

Nattie pressed her foot on the pump to lower the styling chair for Gracie.

"Hop up, babe." Nattie held her arm. "Put a little pep in your step."

"Beautiful day today, Nattie," Gracie said as she got comfortable.

"What's so good about it?"

"Well, the sun is shining, and the birds are singing."

"I hate the sun. It gives me a rash. And those darn birds messed up my clean car." Nattie lit a cigarette and set it in the ashtray to burn. "Lola brought bran muffins in today. Would you like one?"

"Yes, thank you."

Nattie handed Gracie a napkin and a muffin speckled with raisins and filled with cream cheese.

"I hate that health food crap." Nattie twitched her nose. "They call it food but it all tastes like cardboard to me. You know what, Gracie? At our age, we need all the preservatives we can get."

Lola cringed as she watched Nattie drop eight sugar cubes into her coffee cup, plus three extra teaspoons of instant coffee.

"Nattie, why did you put so much sugar into your coffee?"

"That reminds me. I forgot the Jack Daniels." Nattie reached into her cupboard. "My friend will warm up my day."

"Did you have an enjoyable week, Nattie?" Gracie sat calmly.

"It was terrible. I had company who stayed too long. Boy! Benjamin Franklin was right when he said fish and visitors stink after three days."

Nattie grabbed her scissors and comb and began to cut Gracie's gossamer hair.

"I'm going to give you the haircut of your life."

Nattie randomly threw the hair between snips. One wet piece flew onto the wall and stuck to the wallpaper. Nattie, definitely having a flamboyant style of her own, was the only hairdresser Lola had ever seen flail hair into the air while she cut.

Nattie reached for her jeweled cigarette case and pulled out a Camel. With her long fingers, she inserted it into a three-inch-long mother-of-pearl cigarette holder. She flicked the gold lighter, studded with rubies and sapphires, and inhaled deeply.

"Damn! Will you just look at this flame?" Nattie said. "It's a no-win deal to turn this torch down low. I've tried every way imaginable." She blew smoke into the air. "This lighter is a work of art, just look at the gems. I'd hate to give it away just because the flame is so big." Nattie puffed again then turned toward Gracie. "You didn't go on that trip back East, did you?"

"Yes, I did."

"I told you you're too old to travel and take a long trip like that. Your young cousins should have come here to visit you. You could have died on that long trip. Kaput! Fini!"

"In a minute, I would do it again, thank you very much. I wouldn't have missed this trip for the world. It's not every day that a retired teacher like myself gets honored at the White House."

"Yeah, but with your health the way it is you could have died. You've got to learn to go easy on yourself."

"Hey, life is to enjoy. Besides, I'm not one to stagnate and lose myself among the grandeurs of my past. I loved seeing my cousins again. They hadn't visited California in several years."

"Did you do like I told you?" Nattie pushed her sleeves up again.

"Well..." Gracie looked away.

"Well, what?" Nattie said as she wrapped her lips around her cigarette, took a deep drag, then raised her chin in the air. Her tongue pointed through her circled lips like a snake peeking out of a hole. She touched her tongue to her lips and blew out smoke rings, watching them enlarge and fade as they floated away. "I've had that trick down pat since I was twelve years old," Nattie said as she moved her hands up and down her shimmying hips to the fast beat of the music. "I've still got it, baby. I'm a first-class filly with thoroughbred legs."

Remembering Nattie's World War II stories, Lola laughed to herself as she pictured Nattie on the docks in San Diego, razzle-dazzling the sailors. Lola realized that Nattie had missed her calling as an actress, but she knew Nattie had made up for it by entertaining from behind her styling chair. That stage guaranteed her a captive audience.

"Well, did you fly out on Ace Airlines like I told you?" Nattie asked. "They're the best, you know. I warned you that Global West has a terrible reputation."

"No, I kept my flight reservations on Global West. It was very pleasant. They kept on schedule, and their food was absolutely delicious. Plus I enjoyed a wonderful conversation with a very attractive golfer. Theodore and I are flying up to golf at Pebble Beach next weekend."

Gracie handed Nattie a stack of photographs. Nattie shuffled through them, then pushed them towards Lola with a patronizing "Nice... Theodore is a good looking guy."

"He sure is." Lola straightened them out. "I love looking at photographs, especially ones of our beautiful country. America the Great."

"Oh, yes. It was a splendid vacation." Gracie explained each picture while Lola looked at them. "Everything was so marvelous."

"Pictures are a terrific remembrance," Lola said. "Looks like you had an exciting trip."

"You must have gotten a Nikon like I told you to," Nattie butted in. "Your little Kodak camera is nothing but a toy. It never could have taken pictures this good. Those Japanese cameras are the best. See, you trusted me and now you have great pictures to show for."

"I took these photos with my old Kodak," Gracie said.

Lola was willing to wager that Gracie's patience was running thin. From past experience, she knew it would not be long before Nattie put her foot in her mouth.

Nattie puffed on her cigarette. Smoke came out of her mouth and nose. Some of it got caught in her ratted barrel curls, her archaic hair-do from the 60's.

"Did you at least do yourself a favor and stay at the Garden Hotel like I told you?"

"No, Nattie, I kept my reservations at the Billings. Theodore stayed there, too. It's a charming, old hotel with efficient room service. And I had a spectacular view of the White House."

Lola listened as Gracie told them the highlights of her trip to the Capitol and the fascinating places her cousins had taken her to see.

"My holiday was a long-time dream come true. It was a great honor to be at the White House. It's so majestic, a very special place to experience. Lunch with the President and his wife was the high point of my trip. There were one hundred educators from around the country. I have my plaque hanging above my mantle."

"Couldn't your cousins find better company to entertain you?" Nattie asked, then gulped her brew.

"Your necklace has turned your skin green," Gracie said, staring at Nattie's neck.

"Twenty-four carat gold does that to me."

"Jewelry made of tin foil does that to me."

Nattie continued to puff on her cigarette while putting finishing touches on Gracie's hair.

"Almost done," Nattie said.

Lola, feeling the tension build, quietly turned and walked up to the front desk when she heard Nattie demand, "By the way, Gracie, just exactly what did the President have to say to you?"

"Uh..." Gracie sat still, pausing a moment too long to suit Nattie. She continued with, "Ahem..."

"Well, out with it," Nattie demanded. "I insist you tell me every word of your conversation."

"Well, Nattie... The President reached over... Put his hand on my arm in a comforting way and said, 'I don't know how to tell you this, Gracie, but you have the ugliest haircut I have ever seen in my life.'"

Lola buried her face in a towel while she tried to contain her laughter. She admired Gracie for many things, but mainly for her subtle cleverness which transcended the mundane. Lola thought how Gracie was so much more grand a person than she seemed.

Another of Nattie's clients, Mrs. Clardy, came in while Nattie collected money from Gracie. Lola knew it would not be too long before Nattie and Mrs. Clardy engaged in their weekly dysfunctional communication.

Nattie greeted her with, "Where's my birthday present, Clardy? You're a week late."

"You'll get it when I'm good and ready to give it to you. No sooner. No later. Now... Did that register in that so-called brain of yours?"

"At least I have a brain," Nattie said, glaring at Mrs. Clardy. "And let me add that I hate your old-lady hair-do. Those curls on your forehead look like horns. This is the nineties, babe. You're a blue-rinse mama. When the hell are you going to let me update your do?"

"If I was stupid enough to leave it to you, you'd pour that wild hellcat red on me. I'd have to rinse my hair with Tang just to tone it down."

"Except for a good man there ain't nothing on this earth to tone you down."

"Don't start in on that. You're the only person I've met in my entire life that needs to get laid three times a day."

"You should have seen me in my teens. The sailors didn't nickname me 'Lightening' for nothing." Nattie shrugged her shoulders. "Where's your cute limousine driver today?"

"He's running errands... And staying away from you. Keep your vulgar, octopussy ways to yourself."

"I'm definitely giving you a new hair-do today; one your limo driver can run his fingers through."

"Ugh!"

Lola, knowing the exact words of Mrs. Clardy's rebuttal, watched her take her usual erect stand with her orthopedic shoes eighteen inches apart, book under her arm, and shoulders and head straight forward. Her carved cane waved in the air. She stared into Nattie's eyes with her penetrating gray eyes which had faded with age.

"Look, you're an Aries ram, and I'm a Capricorn goat, and I'll lock horns with you any day. You give me what I want, or I'll beat you with my cane. And don't you make that towel too tight on my neck again."

"I'd need a bath towel to fit around that bull neck of yours."

"How dare you insult me like that. You know I don't like anything tight around my neck."

"You were probably hanged as a horse thief in a past life. No wonder you don't like anything around your neck."

"I don't even like horses!"

"Case closed." Nattie rubbed creme into her hands. "Take that diamond and emerald necklace off. How many years will it take you to learn to not wear an expensive necklace when you come in to get a permanent?"

"I beg your pardon," Mrs. Clardy said in a huff. "I'll wear what I want to wear, when I want, and how I want."

"You're nothing but a damn show-off. That solution could ruin your jewelry." Nattie looked closely at Mrs. Clardy's scalp. "Well, no vermin today."

"How dare you suggest such a thing," Mrs. Clardy gasped. "You know darn good and well that I'm an immaculate fanatic."

"Yeah, sure... And I know that nobody's above anything."

"Well, I never..."

"That's for sure. You never, never, never. That's why you have a sour puss. Why, the only difference between you and a baboon is lipstick."

"Flattery will get you nowhere. Now hop to it, Nattie. I'm not going to wait one more minute. I demand that you start on my hair right now, and you watch that foul mouth of yours today, or I'll wash it out with soap and pepper it good."

"Yeah? You and who else?"

"I have my sources. Don't you start threatening me."

"Blah. Blah. You're just a bunch of hot air," Nattie said. "Put a wiggle in it, get the lead out, and stroll on back. I'll meet you and your diamonds back at the shampoo bowl."

Lola knew that Nattie's and Mrs. Clardy's verbal exchange would never alter. Nattie had told her years earlier that Mrs. Clardy was the type of person that craved to communicate by arguing. Lola, coming from a loving, gentle home environment, found this expression to be irritating and foreign.

Chapter 2

Lola hung up the phone with her client Janice, glanced at the clock and saw it was 8:30, then continued doing paperwork for her salon. The creak of the door brought her out of her concentration. A mystical, serene feeling accompanied the elderly Oriental woman who entered the salon. Her face benevolent, her body short and plump, she wore a crocheted vest over her royal blue dress. The solemn look on her face reminded Lola of an Egyptian statue she had seen at the Getty Museum in Malibu. This mysterious woman glided toward Lola, her aura tranquil with unfamiliar vibrations. Her piercing gaze transfixed Lola. Overwhelmed with this woman's charisma, an eerie feeling encompassed Lola, and she rubbed the goose bumps on her arms. With old-world knowledge, the Oriental woman exuded power and strength, yet was peaceful and still.

"I want haircut now." The woman's voice was a soothing mono-tone, thick with an accent. Her eyes did not blink when she repeated, "I want haircut now."

"I'm sorry I can't give you a haircut right now," Lola said, covering her uneasiness with a smile. "I'm booked solid all day long. Maybe someone will have time later."

"I know you have time." The woman stretched her arm out and pointed her finger into Lola's face. "I need haircut now."

Lola felt that her space had been invaded because instinctively she knew she could not hide her innermost feelings from this woman.

Changing her course of action, Lola asked the woman to take a seat near the shampoo bowl.

"I don't want head washed." Motionless, her face immobile, the woman said, standing erect, "I just want haircut."

Lola was accustomed to cutting hair when it was wet and clean, but under the circumstances, she succumbed to the woman's wish.

The woman followed Lola to her work area and then climbed into the white leather styling chair.

"Now cut," she said.

"How would you like your hair to be styled?"

Lola was nervous and could not understand why she was uncomfortable with this woman.

"Whatever you want."

"I'll style it to compliment your features," Lola said.

Feeling the coarseness and texture of her hair, Lola admired the tones of blue that shot through its blackness. It was so glossy it threw off the light with a gleam. After putting the plastic drape around her neck, Lola began to snip the straight strands into a short, geometric, layered cut. Although the woman exuded unfamiliar vibrations, Lola was not repulsed by touching her.

Lola tried small talk, but the woman remained silent and stared into the mirror in front of her while keeping penetrating eye contact with Lola as often as she could.

Unfamiliar feelings came over Lola. Like standing stark naked, Lola felt that this woman had stripped her of a protective veil and had made a direct path to her heart. Lola whipped the scissors around and snipped as fast as she could to quickly finish the haircut and send the woman on her way.

"Every soul has to withstand great pressure and be tested," the woman began to speak. "It is part of life's path. Do not be foolish and allow what torments you to overpower your life."

"Excuse me?" Lola said, feeling invaded. "Where did this come from?"

"When you come against difficulty and confusion, go to innermost sanctuary. Follow light as it breaks in your heart. Learn from experience you created," the woman advised.

"What do you mean 'I have created'?" Lola said, folding her arms.

"It's your reactions to daily events and to conditions of life that bring attunement, achievement," the woman continued. "Many times life has proved to you there is a higher power than you. Your dreams guide and teach you. Do not be frightened by them. Divine intervention has occurred many times in your life."

"What are you talking about?" Lola said, tapping her foot.

"You cannot deny what I say."

Lola knew that the woman was speaking the truth. Comfortably, she relaxed her arms, her mind flashed back to one time, in particular, when she had walked into her mother's bedroom in the middle of the night and saw gilt-winged angels beside her mother's bed a few hours before she had died.

"I know about the angels. Can you deny what I say?"

"No," Lola said, her heart fluttering. Bewildered, Lola felt the supernatural powers that surrounded the woman and she felt safe in them. Lola knew for a fact that her father was the only person who had known about the angels.

The compassion this woman emanated touched Lola's heart deeply. Confused, overwhelmed with emotion, tears ran down her cheek. Lola did everything she could to keep from crying out loud.

"Go within," the woman said softly in a gentle tone. "Pray... Meditate. They are powerful things to do. Answers and solutions come in many different ways. Desire truth with all your heart. Truth is freedom. Expect abundant health, wealth of knowledge, and understanding of nature's law, and you will feel divine love emanate from beauty of all living things on our emerald earth."

"You make it sound so easy."

"It is when you remain without arrogance. Continue to humble yourself. If you don't, life will do it for you. It is easy to be stirred and emotionally upset by contact with inharmonious people and conditions. Keep emotions stilled, in right place, and you will not have far to go to attain more enlightened realm of goodness."

Unable to comment, Lola continued snipping the black silk.

"You looked in mirror this morning, and you cried," the woman continued. "The stress you feel makes you think your youth and beauty are gone forever. It is gift from God to have your type glamour; few are born with it. Cherish yourself. Do not allow misery to take beauty and happiness away. If you choose misery, it will be yours. It is better to have happiness as companion. Exercise free will wisely."

The woman's words touched Lola's soul. She fought to hold back her tears while remembering how she had sobbed those hurtful droplets filled with grief earlier that morning while brushing her teeth. She had glanced up into her bathroom mirror, awestruck. While looking at herself in the mirror, Lola saw she had lost the joyousness in her youthful face. Lola felt that because of the stressful heartaches in her life at that time that she had aged and had lost her beauty forever.

She accepted the fact that her beauty had been altered, and she was grateful that she had been able to enjoy glamour in her youth.

"You think life stripped you of love, beauty, and security. Security is within. Good feelings will return physical beauty. Be assured you will know true love in your lifetime."

"Really?" Lola clung onto her words.

"You know man you will marry."

"What?"

"It will happen in own timing. Everything happens at right moment, acceptable time of universe. Life has taught you to not force issues," the woman said. "Reality of life is illusion to most eyes. Keep desires strong and everlasting."

Lola, speechless, leaned forward, her scissors slowing their pace as she hung on to the woman's every word.

"It is natural occurrence in life to have new beginnings," the woman said. "Do not fear them. Fear stops natural flow of what is healthy and right for personal growth. Your fate is good one. Do not let negativity get in way."

Lola managed to continue cutting, barely dealing with the turmoil she felt inside. Bewildered, she wondered how this woman knew these intimate details. Fighting back tears, Lola thought of the recent death of her beloved mother, a brain cancer victim who had died a long and painful death. Lola yearned for her mother's comfort and healing presence. Separating from Rick had scarred her heart, too. Her life was being pulled out from under her, and now she could lose her salon.

"Do not let resentment be heartbeat of troubles," the woman interrupted Lola's thoughts.

"I don't," Lola said, wiping her tears.

"You do."

"But... I'm only human."

"Don't make excuse that man is only human. Man is divine."

Regaining her composure, Lola continued cutting her hair.

"Cultivate inner calm. You must release your anger," the woman ordered, stiffening in her chair.

"I'm not angry," Lola blurted out. "I'm just hurt."

"Do not beguile yourself. Disease starts in mind. Catch it there before it manifests in body. Hurt goes into anger, anger goes into bitterness, bitterness to bile. Then sickness comes and hope is far off. That choice too... In your hands. You vital and strong; you will look old self soon."

It was difficult for Lola to comprehend what she was hearing. Who was this wise woman, Lola wondered? Could it be another April Fools' Day joke? Derrick was clever but surely not clever enough to pull off something like this.

Lola finished the haircut and brushed the cut bristles from the woman's neck with a soft goat-hair brush.

"You will understand dream before day is over," the woman continued to prophesy.

"What dream?" Lola asked. "Could you be more specific?"

"You will understand dream before day is over."

"Please, tell me more." Aghast, Lola held the woman's hand.

"When you relinquish control is when you will fly into the light." Patting Lola's hand, the woman smiled warmly. "Safety is in your destiny. Let love fill heart and mind, every cell in body will be filled with perfect life." Handing Lola a $50 bill, the lady nodded. "Be creative... Good way to practice concentration. Painting is your pleasure. Writing will be your therapy."

"But, I've never written."

"You will. Opportunities will open up. Keep feet on earth but lift face up to Heaven. Have courage... Many people depend on you, your thoughts, your attitude. People look to you and unconsciously recognize a strength in your spirit." The woman affectionately squeezed Lola's hand. "No matter what, remember that it is great privilege and honor to help mankind. Do not toss desires into wind."

The altruistic woman turned and exited as silently as she had entered.

This encounter made Lola realize that she still had pain to deal with from within. Baffled, she thought back to her nightmarish dream. Over and over again, she repeated, "run into the light."

Lola walked back into the supply room and stretched out on her familiar peach-colored satin chaise lounge, thickly cushioned with down, and took a minute to reflect on what had just happened. New insights and old feelings whirled in her mind. Perplexed, wishing the breeze from the open window would whisper secrets into her ear, she gazed into mid-air and wondered what destiny would bring next. Lola smiled, remembering Mimi's words of advice.

"When Lady Luck comes your way, take her hand and go with her because if you don't she will send her sister, Miss Fortune."

Chapter 3

The back door flew open. Jerked out of her dream state, Lola's heart raced.

Making a grand entrance, Raquel posed in the doorway for a long second, then slowly strolled in, graceful and self-assured, and knelt down to put her white leather purse on the shelf under the sink.

"Howdy, darlin'," Raquel said. "April fool. April fool."

Raquel had an exquisite face, picture perfect with soft-edged features and richness in complexion. She sprang up and tossed her hair, Clairol's Outrageous Cherry. Lola noticed how it looked like a bolt of red lightning.

"How come blonde jokes are so short?" Raquel asked.

"So redheads can tell them."

"Yeah... And if a blonde and a redhead jumped off of a tall buildin' at the same time, which one would land first?"

"The blonde, of course, because the redhead would have stopped and asked for directions."

"Very good, Lola. My, you're a fine filly in top form today. That's two points for you, and the day is still young."

"Yeah, I out-do myself sometimes. Hey, let's not keep score today. I've already counted as high as I want to go."

"What's wrong, honeychild? You look like you just had the holy sugar scared outta you."

"You could say that."

"I am sayin' it! Cissy, you've lost your tan. The bronze is gone. I mean gone!" Raquel patted Lola's shoulder. "Poor baby. Now, tell sister all about it. Rough night, or not rough enough?"

"This is serious. Don't you ever give up?"

"No... I'm alive and full of it, and I like it that way."

"I think you've been around Nattie too long."

"Long enough to know to go for the gusto and not take things too personally," Raquel said. "You know what's wrong with you? You think too much."

Lola proceeded to describe to Raquel the incident with the Oriental woman.

"She was something else. Her vibes were so powerful that her words hit me like a ton of bricks between the eyes, strong and hard. I'm knocked out just thinking about it."

"Heavy, heavy... Sounds like she's a walkin' fortune cookie."

"How could this have happened?" Lola questioned. "She knew so much about my life. How could she have said what she did?"

"Think about it. It's obvious. You needed to hear what she had to say, so the universe provided."

"Yeah, sure Raquel, and there is a civilization living inside the earth."

"Unreal... That woman sounds like a weirdo to me, probably's from another planet."

"Probably from another planetary system," Lola said, a shiver traveling down her spine.

"I met a guy like that in Hollywood once. Ooooooooooo, sugar. Freak City. Ugh!" Raquel shuttered. "Better you than me, darlin'."

"Thanks, I'll file that comment. It's not every day that I receive such compassion and empathy from a co-worker who really cares about my feelings."

"I'm sorry," Raquel pouted. "Well. You know I'd have frenzied out like I did with that Hollywood guy. Scared the holy tar out of me. Stuff like that gives me the heebie-jeebies."

"Believe me, this one has really thrown me for a loop. After all of the people I've had to deal with in this crazy business, this one tops it all. Every word she said had a profound meaning."

"You needed that," Raquel said, under her breath.

"Say what, girl?"

"Face it. You haven't been your old self lately."

"Oh? What's that supposed to mean?"

"Just lighten up, sugar. You know this is one business where you can't take anything for granted. The only thing that's for sure is that we haven't seen it all. But Nattie has, of course."

"Ha!"

"Besides, as sure as the sun will rise tomorrow in sunny California, you know something will top your spooky story. Sooner or later, it always does."

"I hope it's later, Raquel. With all I'm dealing with, I deserve a day of harmony."

"But she did tell you some good stuff, though, especially the part about findin' true love."

"I wonder who the mystery man is?" Lola asked.

"Probably someone in the neighborhood, someone right under your cute little turned-up nose."

"No way. Geeks are running rampant in this town. Plus, I never looked at another man while I dated Rick, so I really don't know who's out there."

"Oh, sure," Raquel said. "You're a creative person. Don't tell me you never checked out the fine art."

"Of course I did, but not in that way."

"Sure, I believe you. By the way, I have some cheap swamp land in Colorado for sale."

"No, seriously, Raquel, I can't think of one single guy I know that I would want to marry."

"Me either. Well, wait a minute. How about Larry?"

"Too boring and jealous, plus his house and car look like a pig's sty," Lola flinched.

"Well, how about Henry?"

"Blockhead, he doesn't know the difference between affection and sex. Plus, he loves the desert; I love the tropics... And he has a bad drug problem."

"There's hope after dope but he doesn't know it yet."

"I wish he would."

"Billy boy?" Raquel suggested. "He's cute."

"An egotistical controller, and too selfish and cheap. I hate having to order just salad at a nice restaurant."

"Steve?"

"He doesn't know how to communicate. He talks at me instead of to me. That would never work."

"Yeah... I want to be some man's partner, not his mother, maid, or nurse."

"That's what we're all wanting and waiting for, the real thing."

"My man is going to be so great. He will have been worth the wait. Not that I feel like an old maid at twenty-six or anything like that. Y'all know what I mean," Raquel explained.

"Maybe wanting love from a wonderful man is an illusive dream?"

"No... No it isn't. Now don't you go talkin' that way, sugar. The only thing illusive about it is that you'll never know which corner he's comin' from. When we finally meet our RPM, our lives will be changed forever."

"What's this RPM?"

"Right and Perfect Mate. What else?"

"I'll buy that."

Lola thought back to her relationship with Rick. It had deeply hurt that he had degraded her so much, especially about her being a "dumb, uneducated hairdresser." Knowing that she could never please him had left a frustrating feeling of inadequacy in her heart. Foolishly she had allowed her self-confidence to dwindle into a fraction of what it had been. In time, Lola came to realize that the problem was Rick's own feelings of unworthiness. She had tried to offer him her support if he would go for counseling. Willingly, she desired to love him through his behavioral problems but then saw that she could not. Lola knew that Rick had to seek the help for himself. It saddened Lola that because of Rick's macho ego, he would not allow anyone to help him through his growth process.

Nattie barged in the door, bringing Lola out of her deep thought.

"Hello, kiddies," Nattie said, smiling. "What are my sweet girls up to?"

"Ugh! A day in the life of a hairdresser." Raquel let out a big sigh and put her hands on her hips. "Don't you just love it?"

"I wouldn't have done it all these years if I hadn't." Nattie took a deep drag on her cigarette. "I'm taking a fast break from looking at Clardy. I needed to feast my eyes on your pretty faces. Love your outfit, Raquel. It's hot! That fifteen pounds you dropped really makes you look like a sheik runway model."

"Thanks. That makes me feel better, too."

"Balance... You can never have too much of it."

Nattie winked, showing Lola that she was offering her emotional support. Lola trusted Nattie, and she was grateful for her loyalty.

"Keep your chin up, babe. It can always be worse," Nattie said as she exited. "Love ya."

Reassured, Lola smiled, knowing that Nattie was rich in the accumulated treasures of age.

"We never know what'll happen next." Raquel took the make-up kit off of the top shelf.

"I know you won't get a lunch break at noon."

"What? How dare you book me like that. You slave driver, you know I get faint when I don't eat lunch."

"There's plenty of your favorite foods in the refrigerator. Anyway, I would have done his make-up myself if I had a few extra minutes."

"His?" Raquel's eyebrow went up. "Who is this *him*?" Raquel said with a sly grin.

"Trust me on this one."

"Dare I?"

"Of course, most definitely. He's a gorgeous young lawyer from Century City, a Frenchman with smooth speech, the kind that makes you melt," Lola smiled. "Ha! Knowing you, you'll probably have him for lunch."

"Ooo la la. Sounds too good to be true. Tell me more."

"That's all I know."

"No it isn't," Raquel coaxed. "You're holdin' out on me. You're just gettin' even with me because of the funny phone call this mornin'."

"Maybe I am."

"I knew it! He's probably a revoltin' creep slob with zits and everything. That's why you gave the slimy jerk to me. This is a cruel April Fools' Day joke Miss Lola Sharee Jamison."

"Cut the four-name stuff, Raquel, and quit bugging me. Believe me. Francois's a dreamboat."

"Francois?"

"You'll owe me one for this. If you can pull yourself away from his bedroom, or chandelier, or whatever. You can take me out to lunch to thank me sometime."

"Hmmm... That does it. Now I know you're lyin'."

"Suit yourself."

"You know I usually do."

"All kidding aside," Lola said, sitting erect, "I had a scary dream last night. It was a dream... I think."

"Oh, cissy, you poor girl. Tell me all about it. Did you dream in neon again?"

"Ugh! Just thinking about it makes me shake."

"This'll help calm you." Raquel got a Perrier out of the refrigerator and handed it to Lola. "Don't ya dare leave out one minute detail."

"I can still feel the heat of the violent red-orange flames that swept fiercely up this florescent golden staircase, nipping at the hem of my white silk gown." Lola shrugged her shoulders. "Horrified, I ran up the stairs, trembling with fear, not daring to look back. A voice from within kept repeatedly saying, 'run into the light.' There was no light, so I continued to climb, skipping every other step. 'Run into the light' kept echoing, making my ears want to burst. I looked up, and in the distance I saw a closed door at the top of the staircase. Smoke whirled all around me. I choked and gasped for air. I cried uncontrollably. My tears burned my skin. I knew I had to run to the top and take a chance that the door was open."

"Where's my lemonade?" Raquel fanned her face. "And?"

"Turning the doorknob brought more horror."

"Why?" Raquel gasped. "A bogeyman?"

"No! The door was locked."

"Ugh! I can't stand it. Ohhhhh..." Raquel leaned toward Lola. "What's next?"

"Coughing, my face burning from the heat, my skin feeling like it's melting, I pounded on the door with both fists. Nothing! I became faint. In a split second, my life flashed before me. Oh, I was so scared I quivered."

"That should be enough to wake anybody up," Raquel said, rubbing her arms.

"I fell to my knees, hysterical, pleading and screaming for some-one to help me."

"Who came? Superman? Rambo? Arnold?"

"No, silly."

"Well..."

"Just forget it." Lola pursed her lips.

"Wait a minute... Don't leave me hangin'. You have to finish before you have a stroke or something. You can't leave me danglin' like this."

"Yes I can. You're making fun of me. You don't give a hoot."

"Now Lola, please don't be that way. You're too sensitive for your own good."

"And you aren't?"

"Yes I am, now finish."

"Well... Mysteriously the door opened and a blinding shimmer-ing white light drew me in."

"You mean like it moved your body?"

"Yeah. I glided in mid-air." Lola relaxed back. "I felt exhilarated and free."

"Better than sex?" Raquel asked with a wink.

"It depends who the guy is." Lola rolled her eyes. "Anyway, a calming sensation enveloped me."

"Whew! I don't know what it all means, but it has a good endin', and that Oriental woman did say that you will understand your dream before the day is over."

"I hope so, but I'm not going to hold my breath."

"Oh, cissy, that just never works anyway."

"The nervous bride is up front," Nattie poked her head in the door, "waiting and drinking Scotch out of her half-empty flask. Get out your magic wand, Raquel. You're going to need it for this gal."

"I'm the miracle worker at this magic shop."

"Yeah you are."

Lola reminded Raquel to be sure and take before and after photographs of the bride for her portfolio.

"Ugh! What a way to start out the day. There's nothin' more vulgar than a woozy broad. I not only have to make the drunk look gorgeous, but I have to calm her, too."

Lola watched Raquel primp in the mirror. Even though her porcelain skin glowed, she applied more rouge to her chiseled cheekbones and more poppy-colored lipstick to her full, rounded lips.

"Lola, how about some blush?"

"No thanks." Lola pushed Raquel's hand away. "You wear more rouge than Miss Piggy. You always put my cheek color on too high and make me look like a goofy clown."

"Let me give you some bright new lips." Raquel whipped out her tube of lipstick.

"No thanks."

"Have it your way. I was just tryin' to help." Raquel looked into the mirror and blew herself a kiss. "You're a beautiful sugar baby, Southern-bred through and through."

"Do you always have to blow yourself kisses in every mirror you pass?"

"Yes, yes, yes. I love mirrors."

"Why is it that doesn't seem to surprise me?"

"I'm wonderful and happy, and I want the whole world to know it." Raquel continued in her breathy Southern drawl, "Did y'all hear from Ricky-Poo yet?"

"No, and I don't want to. He's not only history; he's an illusion."

"You should have gotten a new car out of the deal before you dumped that hunk." Raquel let out an aggravated sigh.

"I can see that Nattie's trained you well."

"Well, buyin' you a new car wouldn't have put a dent in his checkbook."

"No, but it would put a dent in my integrity."

"Miss Morals... I can count on you for that." Raquel assumed a model's stance, hands on narrow hips, long legs turned to the side, her right shoulder thrown forward. "How do you like the new skirt Winston sent me? Isn't it stunnin'? I just love pretty girlie things. And I look so sexy. It arrived wrapped around a bottle of champagne."

"Blatantly symbolic."

Lola glanced at the electric blue leather mini skirt, then at the low neckline of Raquel's sheer ivory-colored blouse. Her voluptuous breasts flowed over the top of her skimpy lace bra.

"I'm a prize package."

"I hope you're wearing panties today, Raquel. Because if you aren't, and you bend over at the shampoo bowl, you'll create another heat wave in the shop."

"Oh, that reminds me, Jimmy will be in this afternoon at one."

"Now, that guy is an April Fools' Day joke. If you married Mr. Peacock, you'd probably kill each other while fighting over who's turn it is to look in the mirror."

"No problem," Raquel teased. "We'd just mirror the walls of his entire house."

"How about the ceilings, hot shot?"

"They've already been done."

Lola told Raquel that Samson would be in at 5:30 that afternoon to play the prank on Derrick.

"Oh... I just can't wait to see the expression on his face." Raquel giggled in anticipation. "He'll just die, I know it. Such an awesome joke. We've really outdone ourselves this time."

"Yes... Hey, who else are you playing a joke on today?"

"*Moi?*"

"Yes, you. Don't play dumb, Raquel. I know the cheap thrill you get out of revenge."

"Revenge? Me?"

"Please..."

"Well, remember George, the one and only man who ever had the nerve to stand me up?"

"What did you expect from that conceited social climber? He got a wealthier date who had a fancier Jaguar who took him to a high class society event."

Lola listened closely while Raquel told her that she had bought George a bright lime-green fourteen inch dildo, wrapped it in gold foil and lace, sprayed a heavy musk perfume on the package, with no signature and no name.

"I sent the package to my cousin in Dallas with instructions for her to mail it to George's office in Marina Del Rey. Oh! I'd love to see that gorgeous mug of his when he sees it and reads the note."

"What's it say?"

"'Thinkin' of you,'" Raquel said. "Plain and simple, to the point. Just, 'thinkin' of you.' Don't you just love it? Can't you just see that egotistical playboy wonderin' which woman in his formidable stable sent it? Hopefully his ego will get the best of him on this one."

"I don't think so."

"What on earth are you talkin' about?"

"He's going to know it's you."

"No way! Never in a million years will he know that it was me who sent the present. One thing I really know extremely well is men. I was brought up with lots of them. I know how they think, how they act, and how they feel. I can easily read any man like a book."

"Don't be too sure," Lola laughed. "They have discrete ways of finding out things. Never underestimate a man. They have uncanny instincts."

"So do I. A man should never, never... I repeat, never underestimate me."

"Your words are big, Raquel. Talk is cheap."

"I don't think so. Look at my track record."

"I have."

"Oh, you..."

Lola told Raquel that she was glad her jokes were basically harmless this year, but by the mischievous look on Raquel's face, Lola knew something else was brewing.

"Well, out with it. You're not going to be satisfied until you tell me the rest."

"What on earth are you talkin' about, darlin'?"

"Spill the beans. Sooner or later, you'll tell me."

"No... No I won't."

"Yes you will. I know you better than you think. C'mon, I know your games. This is your last chance to divulge your hot stuff."

"I'll think about it."

"I'm not going to beg. It's for your good if you tell me. You know you don't work well when you're holding something in, especially gossip trash."

"OK, OK... You've made your point." Raquel straightened her posture like a mannequin and swished her long red hair around. "It's just an eensy-teensy little ol' joke."

"Raquel, nothing you have ever done is eensy-teensy. From your clothes to your men, you like everything grand and dynamic."

"Yeah. Hollywood style," Raquel smiled. "Well, remember that jealous bitch, Jezebel, the ugly poor-rich shrew who threw a drink in my face at Mark's party?"

"You mean Ms. Plastic Surgery, the one who didn't invite you to her big bash tonight at her Beverly Hills mansion?"

"Yeah, she's the hag." Raquel raised her arm and looked at her watch. With a cocky smile that spread from ear to ear, she said, "Well, just about now, a truckload of chicken shit is bein' delivered and spread on her front lawn, just in time for her big celebrity soiree tonight. And I know for a fact that she's at the gym, right now, workin' out that scrawny bag of bones. Why, a guy could get slivers screwin' her."

"Oh, Raquel, that's mean. How could you do such a cruel thing?"

"Cruel? Ha! That rich trash deserves it. Let's face it, this joke is a real classic. I'm just givin' to her what she lavishly dishes out to everyone else." Raquel polished her fingernails on her chest. "I've outdone myself this time."

"You'd better out-do yourself and make that homely bride look fabulous. Her fiancé is paying big bucks for this job."

"True glamour is something one is born with. Thank God I have it."

"Do I detect a trace of arrogance?"

"No. Just the truth." Raquel's hand swept long strands from her forehead. "Plotinus said that the soul can't behold beauty before it's become beautiful."

"Yeah. And Groucho Marx said, 'I never forget a face. But I'm willing to make an exception in your case.'"

"Case closed, Lola."

"At least for now," Lola teased.

Lola walked to the front of the salon, sat in the chair behind the reception desk, and began pricing the shipment of Paul Mitchell products that had just come in.

"Thanks for signing for this, Nattie."

"You sounded like you needed a breather. I want the scoop about that Oriental woman later. Fascinating..." Nattie said while dressing Mrs. Clardy's hair. She sang away between puffs on her cigarette. "I'm a steam roller, baby, and I'm going to roll all over you."

Raquel greeted the young bride-to-be, twirled her around in the styling chair, snapped a fast picture, and got started on her make-over.

"You're gonna be the most beautiful bride in the world. Trust me, hon, I'm gonna make you look sensational."

"Really? That would be a dream come true."

The phone rang. Lola picked it up.

"Contemporary Hair Design. May I help you?"

After listening a moment, Lola pressed the hold button.

"Nattie, can you fit in a fast haircut for a new client late this afternoon?"

"Dream on, Dearie. I haven't taken a new client in ten years. I'm waiting for the few clients I have left to drop dead so I can retire. Especially you, Clardy," Nattie threatened.

Lola explained to Nattie that it was Mr. Jenkins on the phone.

"Who's he?" Nattie wrapped a permanent-wave rod around the hair at Mrs. Clardy's nape. "Everywhere I go everybody seems to know me. I'm a celebrity."

"Nattie," Lola said, "he's Ethel's husband. You know, you did her hair for the last eight years before she died last month."

"Oh! That Mr. Jenkins. Whoaaa! Man oh man. Jake, the cake, with the cherry on top."

Nattie dropped the bottle of perm solution on top of her roll-about and beelined it to the front desk, pushing Raquel and Lola out of her way. The clanking of her high heels sounded like an emergency telegraph coming over a wire. Her mouth hung open. Her hazel eyes were fixed on the telephone receiver.

"Give me that phone," Nattie demanded. "Why didn't you say it was *the* Mr. Jenkins?"

"But..."

"Never mind, babe. Its cool."

Nattie hopped up, seated herself on the desk, crossed her gams, held the telephone receiver with her padded shoulder, and fluffed her lacquered hair with her hand. Within seconds, her stage created, Nattie pressed the hold button, took a deep breath, and spoke in a sugary tone.

"How may I be of service to you, Mr. Jenkins?" Nattie listened intently, then replied, "Squeeze you in for a haircut?" Nattie let out a coy giggle. "Honey, I'll squeeze anything you want me to." Nattie chuckled, took a deep breath, then said, "Darling Jake, if your hair-do isn't becoming to you, then you *should* be coming to me."

Nattie rolled her eyes and licked her lips while listening closely to Mr. Jenkins.

"I'm booked till 5:00, big guy. Why don't you come in then. I promise I'll give you the shampoo and haircut of your life. Then, maybe, we can go out for a little din-din afterwards. Bye, bye. I'll see you then, darling." Nattie breathed out a deep sigh. "And, yes... I'd love to go sailing after dinner. The sunset will be spectacular tonight, and so will I."

Nattie hung up the phone, jumped off the desk, and let out a howl.

"Yeooowwwww! We should have put a cold shower in the back of this shop a long time ago."

Kicking high like a can-can dancer all the way back to her work station, Nattie melodically sang in an operatic voice.

"Oooo baby, sha la la... Today is my lucky day. Dinner with a well-hung man in Marina Del Rey."

"How do you know what he's like?" Lola asked.

"Babe, don't play naive. After being in the business as long as you have, tell me you don't know how well-hung your ladies' men are."

Man-crazy Nattie never ceased to amaze Lola. She knew that Nattie was a resilient bird who always got up early enough to get more than her share.

Chapter 4

Time was moving too slowly to suit Lola. She still felt an unexplainable uneasiness in the air. Thinking about her stubborn landlady, Bertha, the salon, her dream, and the Oriental woman, she glanced around the room, watching Nattie and Raquel work. With grace in the movements of their hands, Raquel and Nattie created realities from their clients' illusions. Lola admired their creative ability and professionalism.

Meek-looking, a slight fragile damsel opened the door to the salon, poking her head in the crack. Her blousy shirt, covering her denim shorts, hung on stooped shoulders. Barely managing, she said, "Hi." Seeing a pained expression across her face, Lola immediately felt empathy for her.

"What can I do for you?" Lola asked in a sincere tone.

The young lady's chin almost touched her chest. Her eyes peeked over the dark rim of her glasses.

"I tried to cut my own bangs, and I've botched them up," she said. "I know it's last minute, but could you please, by any chance, straighten them out for me? I'm desperate."

"Sure. You're in luck. My next client won't be here for another fifteen minutes."

"Thank you, I really do appreciate this."

"No problem; you have great timing." Lola took a close look at her bangs. "Boy, you must have had a real heyday cutting these bangs."

"I know I shouldn't have, but..."

"It's all right. It was worth it if it made you feel good. Anyway, fixing it up is part of my job. Everything can be solved."

"Everything?"

"Yes, there's no such thing as a permanent problem." Lola noticed the girl was uneasy and on the verge of tears. "There are just situations that have to be dealt with."

The girl followed Lola to her work station while discussing the weather. When she sat down, she started pulling on a loose thread on her shirt, and freely poured out her life's problems to Lola.

"I just don't know what to do. I feel like there's a volatile storm inside of me," she said, a nervous twitch in her face. "Sometimes I get so frustrated that my mind turns to taffy, and I want to scream."

Lola could see that this girl was ready to blow off steam and desperately needed someone to listen.

"Be still and peaceful, and the answers will come," Lola assured her. "Let the natural process happen."

It never ceased to amaze Lola how quickly some people opened up to a hairdresser, sharing intimate details of their personal lives.

After saying what bothered her, the girl became silent. Tears welled up in her big blue eyes. She began to weep.

"C'mon... Why is a sweet girl like you crying?"

The pent-up tears rolled down the young lady's face.

"Let it all out, babe." Nattie brought the girl a glass of water. "We've all been there."

"Thank you, ma'am."

"'Ma'am'? Honey, you just call me Auntie Nattie."

Lola watched the timid girl smile. Her face relaxed, she sat more comfortably in the chair.

"Nothing can be that bad," Lola said. "Listen, you're a newlywed. This should be the happiest time in your life."

"I know, but my aunt and my mother-in-law have been making life absolutely miserable for us. They demand so much of our time, and if we don't give it, they make us feel guilty. Our privacy is out the door. They pop in constantly, never phoning first. My nosey aunt had the nerve to get on her hands and knees and check for dust under our bed. They ruin everything they borrow from us. They're trying to control our marriage and tell us every move to make, including what style of furniture to buy. Nothing we do pleases them."

"Why don't you just try to please yourselves?"

"I wish we could."

"If they really love you unconditionally like they say they do, they'll accept your choices. Their type of so-called love isn't benefiting you. True love should build, not destroy. Unfortunately, people throw the term 'I love you' around too freely. Words are cheap. Look for a person's actions; then act accordingly."

"What do you mean?" the young girl asked, a serious look on her face.

"Use your discretion. Choose the people you want in your personal life wisely. Your time is valuable. It's your choice how you spend it."

"You make it sound so simple," she whimpered.

"And you make it hard. Look, do you love your husband? Are you happy with him?"

"Oh, yes... Very much so." She was quick to respond. "He's the best thing that's ever happened to me in my whole life."

Lola handed her a tissue and told her to hold her head still so she could finish the cut.

"You, your husband, and your home are number one," Lola insisted. "Remember that."

"I know. But I wish they'd never come over."

"Don't allow it."

"But they're relatives."

"So what!"

"Blood is supposed to be thicker than water."

"Your true family are the people you are in harmony with. Mutual respect and trust is so important. Your relatives aren't honoring or respecting you and, they're a pain in the neck."

"They sure are."

"Are your aunt and mother-in-law happy, loving people?"

"My aunt is a bitter old maid, and my mother-in-law is a controller who picks on everyone and everything." The girl sighed in disgust. "She figures if she beats people down enough, she can maintain her feeling of superiority towards everyone."

While she listened, Lola thought of Rick who had been a manipulating controller that she was glad to be free of. His cruel, dominating words of destruction had left their mark on her pierced heart. Already healing, Lola felt a freedom from knowing her relationship with him was behind her forever.

"Unfortunately, we all run across people like that in our lives," Lola said with compassion in her voice. "I can see you're a sincere, sensitive person." Lola put her hand on the young girl's shoulder. "I'm going to tell you something my grandfather told me years ago. And listen good because it works. If you want to be happy, be with clean-hearted, happy people, and if you want to be successful, be with honest, successful people. Unhappy, negative people will bring you down. You will never bring them up. They have to want to do that for themselves."

"Is it really that easy?" She sat up straight and dried her tears.

"I sure hope so," Lola answered.

"But you sounded so self-reliant, sure of yourself."

"I'm trying to do it, too. Unfortunately, we don't get good at it overnight. Sometimes I think I'm so focused and balanced, and then... Pow! Back to line one. We have no control of how others behave, but we can choose to associate with people we feel in tune with. Discernment..." Lola said. "It's one of those little big words."

"Anyway," Nattie butted in, "who in the world has the right to make you miserable?"

"Yeah..." The young woman straightened her backbone, her voice strong. "I'm a person, too, you know."

Lola saw a new strength emerge in this young woman because she knew someone listened and cared about her feelings, and it gave her added courage. Lola listened, giving the girl freedom to speak what was in her heart. The girl spoke freely, answering her own questions. The determined look on the young woman's face showed Lola that she was ready to make some changes in her life and start sticking up for herself. After finishing the haircut, Lola asked her if she was going out that evening.

"Yes, my husband's office party is tonight. I dread going because I'm so shy, and I never have anything to share."

"Honey, chill out." Nattie reached for the *Globe*. "Take this home, read it from cover to cover, go to the party and chit-chat all night. I guarantee you will be the most colorful character there."

Lola spritzed and fixed her bangs and within two minutes, styled a French braid in her mousy, sun bleached hair. The girl handed Lola a twenty-dollar bill.

"Thank you for everything, especially for taking the time to let me get things off my chest."

"Put that money back in your purse. It's on the house today. Go be happy and enjoy inventing the real you."

"Keep us posted," Nattie said. "Love ya, babe."

Lola and the young woman embraced warmly. Saying goodbye, she walked out with a vibrant self-confident power in her stride. Lola remembered fondly the people in her life who had given her the same advice years earlier, especially her Aunt Beth, not only a relative but a cherished friend.

"Sweet kid," Nattie said. "She'll make it."

"Yes, but why do shy people think they need permission to speak up for themselves?"

"She won't some day. Trust me on that. I can see that she's just about reached her limit. Once she gets her self-confidence and claims her power, added to her sincerity and humility, she'll grow into a strong woman and will bring a lot of good into this world."

"Like you, Nattie?"

"Yeah, you've got that right, babe."

Life is a never-ending learning process, Lola thought, and was amazed at how perfect strangers could relate from the heart and find comfort.

Chapter 5

Lola was ready for some light-hearted fun when she watched Judge John Garrett through the bay window, approaching the salon. He was a tall, marvelously distinguished elderly gentleman with an elegant stride. Fire danced out of the regal-looking aristocrat's icy blue eyes when he swung open the door.

"How's my darling Lola?" he said, handing her a leather-bound book embossed in gold, his voice full of the richness that money buys. "I know how you love Emerson."

"Thank you. It's a beautiful antique," Lola said. "This is a treasure."

"Yes, nothing like Emerson. He's classic."

With extended arms, he wrapped his strength around Lola and gave her a bear hug that lasted too long to suit her.

"Watch it there, buster."

"Oh, baby," he said. "Every time I squeeze you, you ooze out love."

Lola broke the embrace, then lovingly snapped him on the chest with the back of her fingers, and delivered him his favorite Mae West line.

"Honey, is that a pistol in your pocket, or are you just glad to see me?"

"Oh, honey," he growled like a tiger. "Just thinking of you turns me on, let alone being this close to you. You notice that I wore pants with pleats in them today?"

"Yes, and believe me, I appreciate it; you disgusting old fart. Actually, I'm surprised you can still get it up."

"I can do more than that."

"Promises! Promises!" Lola teased. "That's what they all claim."

"Talk is cheap, honeybunch," he said, pointing to his chest. "My act is the fact."

"Yeah, sure, we'll see about that, big fella."

Early in her career Lola had learned that each client was an individual with their own type of communication and expression. She knew if she expected to please anyone, she must quickly zero in on their true nature and produce what that person needed, whether it was receiving a new hair-do, wanting to be listened to, or sharing a hug. Accepting that this was all a part of her occupation, Lola set boundaries of what she would and would not tolerate. Hand-picking her clients wisely, she was gratified and honored to have built an intriguing clientele of very special people from many interesting walks of life.

Lola first met Judge Garrett in her salon through a referral of another judge. Immediately, she noticed his flirtatious nature and insisted up front that their relationship would be professional and platonic or nothing at all. She had put the ball in his court. He had agreed to behave and keep his hands to himself, but not his words, which flowed as smooth as maple syrup. Lola accepted the fact that his type of flirting was common with rambunctious older men like the judge. Understanding and accepting this typical behavior, Lola knew it was his way to communicate and still feel like a sexual being.

"Slap my face, Lola." Judge Garrett pointed towards his cheek. "Go ahead, baby. Slap my face."

"Why on earth should I slap you?"

"Because if you knew what I was thinking, you'd slap my face."

"Now, are you a dirty old man because you think it's expected of you, and it's the 'in' thing to do, or have you always been nasty?"

"Truthfully, the doctor's got me on a new heart medicine and it's made me horny as hell," he answered with a wink and sparkle in his eye.

"Don't think you're going to take it out on me. Look, I have several clients who are high-class hookers. Do you want their numbers?"

"Are they clean?"

"Please!"

Judge Garrett followed Lola to the shampoo area, pinching her derriere along the way. Lola twirled around and shook her fist in his face.

"Watch it there, Judge, or me and my five brothers will knock you for a loop."

"I can hardly wait." He grabbed her clenched fist and kissed it. "Coming from you, I know it's going to hurt good."

"Nope, this one's just going to hurt."

Lola respected and trusted Judge Garrett. She took delight in sharing his friendship and was grateful that he had always been supportive, encouraging her to go for her dreams.

"I'm ready, dear." He relaxed in the shampoo chair and closed his eyes. "I may fall asleep on you."

"You won't be the first."

"It's been quite a morning."

"You, too, huh?"

"Yes, I wish common sense would come back into style. Ahhh... Wake me when it's over."

Lola knew not to raise his feet up on the foot rest because he had told her several years earlier that he was a man who liked to have his feet planted firmly on the ground.

Lola studied his face while the water warmed up. Long strands of silver poked out of his bushy eyebrows, overshadowing his eyelids, a symbol to Lola of reticent wisdom. Threaded spider veins were embedded in the sides of his prominent nose. His large ear lobes flopped onto his ruddy skin, soft white fur grew inside of his ears, and his handlebar mustache covered the moistness of his curved-up lips. Lola pictured Judge Garrett to be vibrant and virile in his youth. She wished she could have known him in his prime. Lola hoped the man she married someday would have his fine qualities.

"You have such beautiful, wavy hair." Lola ran her fingers through his curls.

"Yeah, a few of the stubborn ones usually stand up and wave at each other."

"You're such a card," Lola said, warming to his teasing.

"I know, and I love you."

"You just love to say that."

"Yes I do, because you're my girl."

Lola sprayed warm water on his head, massaged his scalp, working the shampoo into a luxuriant lather. Her fingers rubbed the top of his head, then methodically moved down behind his ears and to the back of his head, gently manipulating each muscle.

"You know just what to press to take the tension out of my neck." He moaned softly, like a love-starved puppy.

"Lucky for you."

"I'm a lucky guy in more ways than one."

Lola knew he enjoyed being stroked and caressed, so she took a few extra minutes to give him a tender shampoo.

"Dear, you have the touch of an angel."

"How do you know what an angel feels like?"

"I'm eighty, darling. I've experienced Heaven and Hell."

The admiration Lola had for Judge Garrett warmed her heart. Grateful to be a part of his life, Lola knew he appreciated the fact that she did not fawn over him like so many other people did. Her love for him was genuine, and she knew he knew it. It saddened her that a powerful, noble man's man like the judge stayed with a wife who was cold and selfish. Even though his wife refused to fill his life with romantic love, his emptiness never kept him from giving generously to humanity with his time and money. The hospice he had helped to create was the one that had helped her mother. Lola marveled over how he chose to use his wisdom, knowledge, and money in such a constructive way.

"Time to get up, Judge." Lola patted him on the shoulder.

"Kiss me to wake me up." Eyes closed, he puckered his curvaceous lips.

"You're dreaming." Lola bent down and gave him a fast peck on his lips.

"I'd need ten of those to make one big one." He stood and eyed Lola up and down. "Great pants, baby."

"Why thanks. I always knew you could recognize great style."

"I do have an eye for the finer things in life." He curled his handlebars.

"I don't doubt that for a second," Lola purred back, running her fingers over the silky gold fiber of her harem pants.

"You want to be my Scheherazade?" he asked.

"I've already been your Scheherazade once a month for five years now, and I'm not dead yet."

"That's because you tell a good story."

"Indeed *you* do."

Judge Garrett lit his pipe and took a few puffs, inhaled the smoke slowly and tranquilly, then sat down in the leather styling chair.

"I love this new blend," he said.

"Rum and Maple?" Lola asked, cutting his hair and breathing in the aromatic tobacco smoke.

"How did you know?"

"It was my grandfather's favorite."

"Was he a good storyteller like you?"

48

"Yes," Lola replied, dreamy eyed. "As a little girl, I'd sit on his lap. Rocking back and forth in his rocking chair between puffs, he'd act out and sing and tell me all kinds of his fascinating adventures."

"You're fortunate to have been well loved."

"I know. The older I get the more I see and the more I appreciate my upbringing." While cutting his hair, Lola sat on her styling stool and wheeled around.

"You are the only hairdresser I've ever seen who sits and rolls around while she works."

"You know how I love a front row seat. Plus, this way I never miss a trick. I can cut into anyone's hair growth pattern in their neckline and get the hair to move just right."

"Finishing touches."

"It's the cherry on the cake. Plus I can whisper sweet nothings in the right man's ear." Lola quickly kissed his cheek. "So, tell me, who was the angel in your life?"

"My mother, God rest her soul," he reflected, speaking softly.

Judge Garrett became silent while tears filled his eyes. A long minute passed, and Lola questioned whether to continue so he would have an opening to divulge the feelings deep in his heart.

"You must have been close to your mother," she said, sensing he had something to release.

"I was, but I didn't realize it until she was gone; then it was too late." He took a deep breath and continued. "I was a selfish sonofabitchin' moron to have taken for granted the purest love I ever knew. Looking back, I can see that my mother had the finest qualities of any woman I've ever known."

Lola kept her silence. This was not the first client she had had who was not at peace with his mother's passing. Lola knew he needed to set free the guilt he had held on to for years. She put her hands on his shoulders, tenderly kissed his cheek in a nurturing way, then continued to cut his hair.

"I was an arrogant, snot-nosed punk," Judge Garrett confessed, crouching in his seat and wiping the tears from his eyes. "We had lost everything during the depression. Papa had died in a train wreck. Times were hard. To make sure I never did without anything, Mama cleaned people's houses and took in ironing. I loved parties, gambling, and booze. I hate myself for taking advantage of Mama's goodness. I did more for the whores I dated than I did for my own mother. I violated my mother's purity with my destructive ways. I used her just like my father did." He sighed deeply, then continued. "Mama never said a word, never complained once. After the war, I went to Stanford for my law degree. I seldom wrote or called my mother. I'd take my wife and son and go home for a short visit once a year, usually around the holidays. How could I have been so unaware? So stupid?"

Lola had always felt he had a certain heaviness in his heart but she never could pin point why. Now she knew. Judge Garrett carried the same burden that millions of people throughout the ages have carried.

"We all do the best we can at the level we are at."

"Like a damn fool, I let my big ego blind me. I didn't realize I was so selfish. Thought I was the almighty, indestructible superman golden-boy. The sun rose and set on me."

"But that was a long time ago." Lola spoke in a soft tone, rubbing his shoulders. "You can chalk it up to youth."

"I can't. I've experienced too much. The realities of life have been thrown in my face," he said, staring hard at Lola through the mirror. "I'm not in denial anymore."

"I know you're not, Judge," Lola spoke in a gentle whisper, "but you have made up for your past by helping humanity. Whether it's for cancer or AIDS, your name is on the Board of Trustees. The science building at the university has your name on it in big, bold letters. Your name and reputation has drawn help and money for thousands of people." Lola stopped cutting his hair and tenderly put her hand on his shoulder. "Your mother would have been so proud of you."

"The greatest thing my mother taught me through her actions was the art and benefit of giving selflessly. I have contributed to society in my own way, and I am honored to give, but it's not enough to make up for what I should have done for my mother. She sacrificed so much for me, and I never ever showed my appreciation. The really sad thing is that it took so little to please her, but I never took the time," he said through tears. "I'm a multi-millionaire. I could buy her anything now, but it's too late. I can't even give her my time, my love, or anything."

Lola handed him a tissue. He wiped the corners of his eyes with the back of his hand, then blew his nose.

"The greatest gift you can give someone you love is your time. Unfortunately, I learned that lesson too late in life. Promise me Lola, to always take time for the people you love because they won't be around forever."

"I promise," Lola soothed.

"Using one's mind and thinking things through are very important, but living from one's heart is the key to happiness."

"Yes…"

Lola's thoughts flashed back to some of her loved ones who had died. Her precious, sweet Grandma Rose had taught her her love and reverence for nature. Uncle Zeke, the fine artist, set the seed and desire in her heart to paint and create beauty. Her caring Godfather gifted her with her first Shetland pony and taught her to carefully care for the things she loved and valued. Her neighbor's cook, Pearl, taught her how to cook special Cajun recipes and sculpt fancy ice carvings. Missing them terribly, she cherished the priceless memories of their special times together. Later, she had become at peace with their passing because she knew that the love they shared was one that would fill her up for all of her life and beyond. Many times, with comfort and smiles, they visited her in her dreams.

"Judge, please don't be so hard on yourself. Your presence alone gives people strength and joy."

"I hope so. Thank you for saying that. I just wish I could erase the blame and torment I feel."

"They say the wall between heaven and earth is a two-way mirror. Our loved ones can see us, but we can't see them. I'm sure your mother's in Heaven right now feeling sorry that you're still carrying this burden. It's the most natural thing in the world for a mother to forgive her child. She's forgiven you."

"Thank you, Lola. You're my precious lamb," Judge Garrett said, his eyes still wet with tears. "The deep guilt hurts worse when you know you've been bad to a good person."

"Let me love you through it. Right now, let the pain go. Please…"

Nodding his head and sighing deeply showed Lola that he felt a release. It was heartbreaking for Lola to watch a bigger-than-life man hurt, a man she held so dear. This was one more instance where Lola realized that mightiness, prominence, and money did not make a person immune to feelings, flaws, or tears.

Lola thought back to the loving relationship she had had with her mother. Like with her father, their intimate times together were filled with respect, trust, loyalty, and much laughter. Lola felt honored to have had such a fine person for a mother. Because she did not want to end up a statistic like the judge, she had purposely taken extra time with her mother to make memories, to make sure her mother knew her sentiments. Lola had peace within because she knew that their mutual love for each other bonded them together forever.

Lola was used to people pouring out their deepest secrets to her. In all of her years of hairdressing, she had learned that one of the greatest heartaches people from all walks of life carry with them is that they had harbored ill feelings toward their parents when they died. Lola felt empathy for these people. Seeing their pain made her even more grateful for the richness she and her parents had shared.

Judge Garrett brushed his tears, sat up straight, and framed a match with his hand to light his pipe.

"Here's to you and your buddy, Jack Daniels," Lola said, handing him a jigger of whiskey.

"Thank you, sweetheart. I think I'll have the next shot in a cup of coffee."

"Coming right up."

"I had my secretary type up this lease for you." Judge Garrett pulled a folded paper from his suit pocket and handed it to Lola. "Have Bertha sign it today and you'll be set."

"Oh, I don't think it's going to be that easy."

"I had a visit with her on the phone yesterday. Don't worry, she'll sign it."

"But she won't even speak to me," Lola said, biting her lip.

"She's a tough old tyrant from way back."

"Yeah, I remember how mean and abusive she was to her husband. That poor skinny guy didn't have a chance," Lola shivered. "She'd backhand him, and he'd fly across the room."

"Bertha's father was one of the meanest men I've met in my life. They nicknamed the old fisherman 'Shark' because he'd bite people in bar room brawls." He patted Lola's arm. "There's still a little softness in Bertha's heart."

"Must be way down deep."

Lola laid the paper on her work station and thanked Judge Garrett. His kindness had surprised her again. Several times throughout their relationship, the judge had generously offered Lola free legal advice, and his help this time meant more than she could say.

"Thank you. You've always been there for me, and I appreciate it."

"It's my pleasure, dear. You know you can call me anytime, for anything. I've told you before, you're my girl."

"I did like you told me, just in case Bertha wouldn't sign. Carey down the street will rent me a booth in her salon. I've already told my clients."

"They'll find you even if you go to the moon."

"Yeah, they like being spoiled. More than that, they love getting compliments on their hair and make-up. They think they can't survive without me, but I know I'm replaceable."

"You? Replaceable? You're one in ten million, babycakes."

"I'm just a pebble on the beach."

"Yeah! But what a pebble." He puffed on his pipe. "What will the others do if Bertha doesn't sign the lease?"

"Nattie won't admit it, but I think she'll welcome retirement. Derrick's freelance photography is turning into more of a full-time traveling job. He's only here four days a week now, and half of that time he spends fooling around in the facial room with his married clients."

"How about Raquel?"

"Well, I taught her how to do special techniques for applying make-up for film and got her a part-time job at the movie studio doing make-up for a television series. It's one day a week and good money; plus she'll work at Carey's part-time."

"Why didn't you take the studio job?"

"No way. They film every Monday and that would get in the way of my oil painting class," Lola said, thinking about the pleasure she took in her hobby. "My teacher is ninety years old now and only teaches on Mondays. Even though he sleeps half the time, his class is the highlight of my week."

"Smart decision. Your teacher is one of the finest around. He's taught accomplished painters for over sixty-five years."

"Yes, I'm fortunate I was able to get into his class. You know, he has the knowledge of fifty teachers. I videotape his demonstrations and lectures, then play them over and over until it all sinks in."

"That's my girl. You've created the best of both worlds. Too many people go for the bucks and miss out on the finer treasures in life. You're one person who's been focused and committed while going for your dreams."

"I may not be the wealthiest person in the world, but I try to be true to myself. I have a fun life, and one of these days, I will study art in Paris."

"I see terrific progress in your paintings. Paris will be waiting for you."

"That's a lovely thought."

Lola smiled, her mind wandered to the busy streets of Paris. She pictured herself standing in front of an easel, paint brush in hand, capturing the colorful people and architecture of the city streets on her linen canvas.

"I marvel over your landscape in my study. Looking at it takes me to the soft green English countryside."

"Thanks, I'm glad you're enjoying it. I only wish I had been in England when it was painted."

Lola thought about how much she loved to travel. She hoped it would not be long before she boarded an airplane to somewhere fun and exciting.

"You will some day. Your desires are strong and of great variety. By the way, my friend Matthew told me to tell you that when you get a collection together, he'll hang your work in his gallery."

"Really? I'm flattered," Lola beamed. "Matthew has one of the finest galleries in Beverly Hills."

"He loves your use of rich hues and the way you use complementary colors to create vitality in your paintings."

"That's great. Tell him I'll be ready pretty soon. Now you be still. I'm almost finished."

"My time with you is too short." Judge Garrett quickly reached over and slid his hand between Lola's thighs. His devilish grin stretched across his entire face.

Lola jumped back, then grabbed his ear and pulled it straight out. With her scissors, she pretended she was going to cut his ear off.

"You'd better shape up, buster, or I'm going to cut this baby off and make a Vincent van Gogh out of you."

"You're uptight," he laughed. "You need a good screw."

"Bullshit, fool." Lola hit his arm. "Quit harassing me! And since when do you know what I need? You men are all the same. You think a good screw will solve everything. If I slept with every guy that wanted me, I'd be on my back all day long!"

"And I'd be first in line."

"I ought to slap you silly."

"Oh, you're my feisty one. I love to rile you up."

"You're lucky I know how to overlook things," Lola said as she ruffled his hair.

Lola finished his haircut and brushed the hair from his neck with a goat-hair brush. She ignored his advances because she knew from past experience that when a man expressed intimate emotions and exposed his vulnerabilities, as the judge had just done, he usually struck out with some sort of sexual gesture towards the person who had witnessed his weakness. Lola figured that this was a way they regained their sense of control.

"You're all done, Judge. You're ready for the world."

Judge Garrett gave Lola a bear hug, kissed her on the cheek, then handed her a $100 bill.

"*Joie de vivre*, darling. Keep having fun, and keep painting. My wife and I want your latest floral for our dining room."

"You've got it, just give me a few weeks. It's still drying."

Lola wished that just once Rick would have encouraged her to pursue her art. Instead he ridiculed her work and told her that she would never make it into an art gallery. Matthew was one of Rick's clients, and Lola knew that some day soon Rick would surely see her paintings hanging in his Rodeo Drive gallery.

While Lola walked Judge Garrett to the front door, she noticed he began to perspire heavily. Seeming short of breath, he loosened his tie with fumbling fingers.

"Are you all right?" Lola asked, her body tense with uneasiness.

"Yes, dear. Not to worry."

"You don't look OK. Please, come and sit down."

"I'm fine," he assured her. "A little fresh air will do me good."

"No, please, listen to me. Come... Sit down and relax."

Suddenly, grabbing his chest, Judge Garrett fell to the floor. Alarmed, Lola watched him fall.

"Ugh! Help me!" Eyes enlarged, he screamed out in excruciating pain.

Trembling, feeling helpless and devastated, Lola frantically reached toward him, scooping him into her arms.

"Judge Garrett!" Lola shook his limp body. He did not move. "Wake up!" He lay still, his eyes closed. "Nattie, call emergency! Quick!"

Nattie dialed 911.

"Butch, send the boys on down, pronto, and I mean pronto. Judge Garrett's having a heart attack." Nattie listened a moment, then bellowed out, "What the hell do you mean whose client was it this time? Just send the damn ambulance. He's out cold and his lips are turning blue. Too many unnecessary questions waste valuable time." Nattie scowled, then slammed down the phone. "What the hell does he mean whose client was it this time? Damn fool. They're not always mine."

Lola had started mouth-to-mouth resuscitation on Judge Garrett. Terrified, her heart pounded so hard that her ears throbbed. She knew she must try her best to save him so she put her fear behind her and pounded on his chest.

With fright on their faces, clients sat like mannequins. A silent heaviness clouded the salon.

"I just feel so bad." Raquel rushed over and knelt down. "Tell me what to do to help."

"Feel his pulse!" Lola said, between breaths.

Shocked beyond words, Lola watched Raquel unzip the zipper of Judge Garrett's trousers, then adeptly slide her hand inside his boxer shorts, caressing him with a gentle motion.

"What are you doing?" Lola shouted. "I said his pulse! Not his penis!"

Raquel cocked her head back, turned toward Lola and leered.

"Penis. Pulse. Pulse. Penis. It's all the same thing," Raquel said in her breathy drawl. "Trust me, sugarplum. They don't call me magic fingers for nothin'."

"You're disgusting. It hurts me that you're treating him like an object, a cheap piece of meat!"

"Grow up, Lola. You've seen plenty in this business. Y'all should've learned detachment by now."

"But not with him! This is Judge Garrett. I love him."

"Oh sugar sugar, glory be... Call me disgustin', but I have definite proof that he ain't dead yet."

"Hot damn, I learn something new every day." Nattie leaned in close. "What kind of goods has he got in there, Raquel?"

"Give me another minute and I'll tell you for sure. Sometimes it takes me a while to raise the dead."

"How dare you!" Lola blurted out. "Where's your reverence for this dear, sweet man? You two aren't helping matters."

"Oh, yes we are," Raquel winked.

Lola ran her hand over Judge Garrett's forehead. His skin felt cool and clammy to her touch. He was pale and still unconscious, and Lola feared he might die. Beginning to cry, she tenderly hugged him in the shelter of her arms.

"I just spoke to Mrs. Garrett," Nattie said. "She's on her way to Mercy Hospital."

Hearing the siren, knowing that help was near, Lola calmed down a little.

"Nattie, have the door open and ready for them."

"I'm a step ahead of you, kiddo."

Within minutes the paramedics carried a gurney into the salon and administered to Judge Garrett.

"He'll be OK," Nattie said, rubbing the small of Lola's back to comfort her. "Just say a prayer. God listens to everyone."

"Nattie, look." Lola watched the judge slowly open his eyes. Overwhelmed with relief, she reached out, held and kissed his hand. "Oh, Judge, you're going to be all right. I just know it," she said as they rolled him out to the ambulance.

Lola comprehended the gratitude expressed in his eyes.

"Shhh. Save your energy, Judge." Lola lightly touched his lips to stop him from speaking. "Don't try to say anything now." She gently stroked his face, then held his hand. "We'll have plenty of time to talk later."

Lola watched the mischievous glint return to his eyes. A smile broke his parched lips. While walking next to him to the ambulance, she felt him squeeze her hand. A sign of hope, she was relieved to feel his life force. Seeing that he was trying to speak, Lola leaned her face towards his.

Looking into her eyes, Judge Garrett spoke in a groggy tone.

"I didn't want to wake up so soon. I was having the most wonderful dream. Ahhh... I wanted it to go on for a long, long time."

"North and South brains are both in good shape." Lola kissed his cheek. "I'll be in to see you soon."

Lola watched the paramedics put Judge Garrett into the ambulance, close the doors, and drive away. With a heavy heart, trembling, Lola turned to go back into the salon. Reverently, she prayed that he would be fine.

Chapter 6

Lola watched the bride-to-be take a swig of scotch from her flask. Without even asking, Lola grabbed it and took a big gulp, then sat down at her desk. She laid her head down and meditated, allowing her mind to drift, her thoughts to wander. The warmth of the sun's rays through the window caressed her back and helped to neutralize the stress she felt from the trauma of Judge Garrett's heart attack.

The bride was stunning in spite of her hiccups. Raquel's deft hands had sculpted a Grace Kelly French roll with soft wisps framing her face. She added a sprig of baby's breath to the side of the roll. Lola marveled over the exquisite artistry of Raquel's work. The bride's transformation, a sophisticated hair-do and glamorous make-up application, turned her into a beautiful woman, one fit to be on the cover of any fashion magazine.

"Just one more shot of hair spray," Raquel said. "Oh hon, you look just so pretty."

With a joyous expression, the bride continually stared at herself in the mirror. Lola smiled, seeing how pleased the bride was, then saw the look of satisfaction on Raquel's face. Lola knew that feeling well, too. It was second nature for Lola to give of herself, but there was an extra special feeling for her when, with her creative ability, she gifted a woman with a sensational look of glamorous beauty.

"Thank you so much, Raquel," the bride said, beaming, embracing Raquel. "I never thought I could look so beautiful. I had always dreamed of looking like a model. I just never thought I could."

"It's all the tricks of illusion," Raquel said. "Make an appointment sometime. I'll give you a make-up lesson."

"I will. You've made me so happy. I *am* a beautiful bride."

"Of course you are, darlin'. I told you so. You do look fabulous, even if I have to say so myself."

"My fiancé will be so pleased. This day is so special to us, and you've made it even more wonderful. Thank you so much."

"You're very welcome. This was fun for me, too. I always loved doin' before and afters, especially for brides."

Lola handed Raquel a camera.

"You look terrific," Lola smiled. "Congratulations on your wedding."

"Thank you," the bride blushed.

"Now pose pretty," Nattie said.

"Head up and to the side."

Raquel snapped a picture, sent the bride on her way, and started a bleach-foil weave on her next client at her work station near the front door. Neurotic Mrs. Clardy pushed up her cuff and looked at her watch while uncrossing and re-crossing her legs. Lola wished Nattie and Mrs. Clardy would relax and converse in a normal manner.

"Nattie, I hate the obnoxious odor of this permanent solution."

"I hope the smell of it slaps your brain."

"I just may slap you. Now... You'd better rinse this perm off of me immediately, or I'll end up a burnt fuzz ball."

"You won't be cooked for another five minutes, so just relax and keep your big trap shut," Nattie said. "You'd better keep your chin up. I don't want that alkaline solution to run down your forehead and get into your eyes. You're already blind as a bat from all of those books you read."

"One can never read enough."

"It's ruined your eyesight."

"It would have done you well to read more books in your lifetime."

"Why? And end up with a cluttered brain like yours? No thanks!"

"It's important to read. It keeps a person from getting Alzheimer's."

"Oh? Really?" Nattie snapped back. "Hmmm... For your information, I do read a lot."

"Devouring five tabloids a week does not exactly make you a literary genius. As the saying goes, 'If you think education is expensive, try ignorance.' You are an embarrassment to yourself, and you don't even know it. A little more knowledge about literature, manners, and the finer things in life would give you a little substance to camouflage your shortcomings."

"You of all people should know that I don't give a damn what anyone thinks." Nattie took a stiff stance, growling while pointing at Mrs. Clardy. "Don't you raise that eyebrow higher than the other. It makes you look like a snob."

"I'm not a snob."

"Yes you are."

"No I'm not."

"You're a damn liar, Clardy. There's nothing more disgusting than for a rich bitch like you trying to prove how humble you think you are. Behind your safe wall of money and power, you pretend you live, and you fool yourself into thinking you are a compassionate human being."

"I like my lifestyle. It's what I chose to build."

"And you're the chicken who has lived her life for, and through, everyone else. And what did you get for it? Wrinkles! That's what. That's why you're face looks like a plateful of worms. You're a miserable, empty bag. You bury your face in those books ten hours a day. You're hung-up... Don't even know how to have fun. Why, the only place you've worn those lacy crotch-less panties I gave you is to the gynecologist. You must have come to earth to be a spectator because you sure as hell aren't living life."

"How dare you judge me and speak to me like that with your unruly tongue. Why... You're nothing but cheap trash!"

"Just remember, I'm the one holding the scissors," Nattie said. "Cheap trash is cheap trash, whether it's rich or poor."

"Your life is nothing to brag about, nine marriages and all. You and your young pizza man are the talk of the town. Shameful! A woman of your age. Then you have the audacity to think you are the cat's meow."

"I'm the one! I'm the one! I may not be as well read as you, you so-called high society ugly blueblood, but I hear what I need to hear. I'm a talented artist. And you are my living proof that I can make a silk purse out of a sow's ear." Nattie picked up a styling comb and held it in Mrs. Clardy's face. "See this? For you... I have to turn it into a magic wand."

"If you had to do it over again, Nattie, would you still fall in love with yourself?"

"You betcha I would, only I wouldn't have waited until I was fifteen years old."

Lola found Nattie's and Mrs. Clardy's dialogue disturbing, especially on a day like today. She raised her head, shaking it from side to side.

"Nattie, please... Let's go for a little harmony in the shop today."

"Sure, babe." Nattie began to whistle "Amazing Grace."

Mrs. Clardy picked a fuzz ball off of her sleeve.

"Maybe I should get a new hair-do, Nattie. What do you think?"

"Clardy, what you really need is a new face. You're cursed with that mug, probably to teach you lessons on vanity and humility. I hope at least your mother loved you."

"At least I had a mother to love me."

"You're a cruel biddy, Clardy. You went to hell to get that line. Don't rub glass in the wound."

"You deserved that. I won't apologize."

"They don't call you 'Mouth' for nothing."

"Don't push my buttons, Nattie. You'll be sorry."

"Ladies... Please!" Lola said. "You two have been friends for years. Show the positive side of your friendship."

"I don't need to put up with a persnickety poop like her," Nattie said. "I've given her just about all the time I'm going to."

"Nattie," Lola said. "Please..."

"Clardy," Nattie said, pointing her finger. "I ought to kick your shriveled ass right out of my chair."

"You wouldn't dare, especially in the middle of a perm."

"You won't be the first one I've done it to."

"I'd cry."

"Good. A salty tear would add moisture to your dried up prune face."

"People can't help what they look like."

"It's your critical, negative thinking all these years that's made your face so ugly. Shakespeare said that there's no art to find the mind's construction in the face."

"I'm earning my wings by putting up with you, Ms. Nattie Smith." Mrs. Clardy pursed her lips in mock disapproval. "I'm earning my wings."

"Dream on, dearie. What makes you think they're going to let you into heaven? You'll be lucky if you make it to the gate. Bribe St. Peter with your charm. That ought to get you a good seat in the balcony."

"Gold is always tested in the fire."

"In your case, it's fool's gold."

Lola closed her eyes tightly and tuned out Nattie's and Mrs. Clardy's odd conversation. It never ceased to amaze Lola how the two ladies could come up with new insults week after week, year after year. Lola surmised, from observation, that some people derived pleasure from arguing. She knew to not question their spiteful communication, remembering her grandmother's words of wisdom:

"Keep life simple, and be careful what you question or wonder because to really find out something, you have to live through it."

Lola's thoughts were interrupted when a gush of wind came in with the delivery boy.

"Flowers for Lola Jamison."

"Thank you," Lola said, reaching out to receive the colorful bouquet of tulips, daffodils, baby's breath, and lush fern. She handed the delivery boy a tip.

"Well... Who could these be from? Oh, they're so beautiful."

"Now hurry and open the card," Raquel said. "Maybe they're from Rick."

"I hope not. One thing I hate is to get flowers from a man who is history. It makes it hard for me to enjoy them," Lola said. "Whoever sent it, though, knows that tulips are my favorite flower."

"You can put the flowers on my work station," Nattie said. "I love flowers and I don't care what creep sent them."

"Hmmm..." Lola read the card and smirked, handing it to Raquel. "Read it aloud."

"'Thinkin of you'," Raquel said with the expression of a cat who had just swallowed her first mouse. "George thinks it's you, dearie darlin'." She squirmed in delight, trying to contain her excitement. "I love it. He will never, never, never in a million years figure out that it was *moi* who sent him that pretty lime-green dildo. It was wrapped so pretty and all, sprayed with the most delightful perfume."

"I treat him like the slimeball that he is." Lola shuddered in disgust at George's arrogance. "How could he possibly think it was me that sent that damnable thing?"

"How does George know you love tulips?" Raquel said, standing rigid with a sly grin on her face.

"Perish the thought. Give me a little credit, won't you? It was a lucky break on his part," Lola said. "And stop being a jealous twit. It's bad enough you went out with the scumbag. If you would think with your brain first, you wouldn't end up in such messes all the time." Lola watched Raquel strut to her work station and set the bouquet on the marble vanity.

"You know I thrive on messes," Raquel said. "It's my way of livin' on the edge. Plus, I know nice people like you will always be there to bail me out."

Lola questioned whether she helped or hindered Raquel by helping her so much of the time.

"Wake up, Clardy, your timer went off," Nattie said, putting her cigarette out.

"I know, I know. Just because my eyes are closed doesn't mean I don't know what's going on. I heard the bell. My hearing is perfect. We all know that is quite remarkable for a woman of my age."

"Yeah, sure... Nothing ever gets by you."

"That is correct."

"Since when have you ever had a clue?" Nattie slunk back to the shampoo bowl. "Grab that cane and follow me, and if you raise it higher than two feet, I'll give you a fast judo chop."

"Did you learn that from your pizza boy?"

"No, the sailors on the docks during WWII taught me self defense. Too bad they didn't prepare me for you."

Mrs. Clardy trailed behind, leaned her cane against the wall, and lay back in the shampoo chair.

"Close your eyes," Nattie said. "Trust me."

"Yeowwww!" Mrs. Clardy howled in agony, startling everyone. "Damn you, Nattie! That hurt! What in the hell did you do to me this time?"

"Got it!" Nattie held up a one inch coarse hair and waived it in the air. "I've been wanting to pull this long sucker out of your chin for the last two weeks."

"You're revolting, Nattie. Pretty comical, huh? Hair removal is painful. You could have at least given me some kind of proper warning."

"Why? So you could whimper like a sickly dog?"

"Even a dog deserves civil treatment."

"My poodle lives like a queen."

"You treat your Mitzi better than you treat people." Mrs. Clardy straightened her diamond-studded watch.

"Shut your big fat mouth. You're lucky I take such good care of you," Nattie said, beginning to rinse out the permanent solution.

"Those permanent-wave rods are hurting the back of my neck. Do something about it. Ugh... That repugnant odor."

"Bitch! Bitch! Bitch!" Nattie said while putting a folded towel under Mrs. Clardy's neck. "I can't take them out until I rinse and neutralize your hair. You're the only client I have who doesn't fit in this shampoo bowl. I ought to stretch that short neck of yours."

"Just try it, girlie, and you'll be sorry. And prop my feet up. Having them hang down puts a strain on my lower back."

"If you'd put out some hard cash to a young buck and get laid once in a while, your back wouldn't be so damn stiff like an ironing board."

"How dare you talk to me that way, you vulgar hussy. Your mind is always in the gutter."

"I'd rather it be in the gutter than in a stagnant mud puddle like yours," Nattie said, adjusting the towel under Mrs. Clardy's neck.

"Why does that water temperature keep changing from hot to cold? You know I hate that. It irritates my nerves."

"You're nothing but a crabapple. You should know by now that's what happens when Bertha flushes the toilet upstairs. That's plumbing in these old buildings. Relax if you can. Pretend you're lying in a coffin. It will be good practice for you."

"At the rate you're going, you'll end up in the morgue a lot sooner than me."

"Oh yeah?"

"Yeah!" Mrs. Clardy snapped. "And quit tempting me to help you along."

"You can't even help yourself. How would you help anyone else?" Nattie sprayed tepid water onto Mrs. Clardy's scalp. "Why, you couldn't even find your way out of a brown paper bag. If it wasn't for your butler and maids, you'd be a real basket case."

"You two should go on stage. Preferably the first one out of town," Lola said.

Lola tried to tune out the banter between Nattie and Mrs. Clardy. It was how they chose to communicate. Like an earthquake, it was something Lola knew she could not stop.

"You keep talking like that and I'll have a number put out on you," Mrs. Clardy threatened, following Nattie to her styling chair.

"I already have a number," Nattie said, tap dancing. "I'm a ten, baby, and don't you forget it."

"Maybe on a scale from one to a hundred."

"You'd better watch it there. Just remember, I'm the one with scissors in my hand."

"Yes, and you're the one who named her first shop Scissorhappy's. I know I'm in a vulnerable position. Just don't you go getting scissors-happy again this time. I had to hide for two weeks after my last haircut."

"Just two weeks, huh?" Nattie's brow of revenge surfaced. "Hmmmmmmmm... I must be losing my touch."

Lola entered her own space and watered a basket of philodendron. She felt the silky texture of its leaves, then with a soft cloth she tenderly dusted the velvet green, finding peace and solace in caring for her plants.

Chapter 7

The strain of the day had already gotten to Lola, and it was only 10:45. Lola, too exhausted to wiggle, flopped onto the love seat and laid her head back.

"I need for this day to be over. Poor Judge Garrett. I can't believe that stubborn Bertha; the suspense is getting to me."

"Don't make a big deal out of it, babe," Nattie said. "Where's all that faith you talk about?"

"I walk my talk. I always do what I say I will do."

"Now listen good," Nattie said. "You only have control of what you eat and the way you wear your hair. You've got to know that, no matter what, things will turn out for the best. You're young and beautiful. You've got your whole life ahead of you. Lighten up."

"Get real, Lola. Get over the fear," Raquel said. "What's the worst that can happen? Either Bertha signs or you start over again."

"Easy for you to say. I've worked so hard."

"Hard work never goes to waste." Nattie pulled hair out of a hairbrush. "Once you've made it, you can make it again."

"I look at new beginnings as a real challenge. I'm open to goodness," Raquel said. "Now, remember what that Oriental woman said this morning."

"How can I forget?"

"You never know what's around the corner."

"If you're lucky you don't," Nattie said. "Makes life more interesting that way. Keeps you on your toes and doesn't leave much time for a planned reaction, that way your true feelings emerge."

"I'm too numb to think about true feelings." Lola closed her eyes and tuned out the world. Feeling helpless, she sat in silence while waiting for her next client to show up.

The front door opened. Wind gushed in and brought Lola out of her dream state. She noticed Raquel's elevator eyes feasting on Craig, the body builder who stood six three. White short shorts and a tank top accented his hard, distinct brawn; his locks of blonde hair, the color of wheat, draped his neck. His well-muscled broad shoulders, softly furred with golden hairs, glistened in the light. Wavy eyebrows framed his hazel eyes, fierce with provocative sensuality.

"Hi, doll," he said, affectionately pinching Raquel's cheek.

Lola watched, and as always, Craig's arresting good looks totally captivated Raquel. The magnitude of his smile left Raquel speechless. Mouth watering, she dropped her comb.

Walking towards Lola, Craig carried himself with vigor and assurance. Lola laughed to herself when Nattie threw a towel at Raquel and told her to wipe her drool.

"Well... He's just so cute he makes me nervous."

"Attention, Earth, one, two, three." Raquel's client giggled, then tugged on Raquel's sleeve, bringing her back down to earth.

"He's such a dream," Raquel sighed. "I just can't help myself. Truthfully, I don't want to help myself."

Craig approached Lola with a dazzling smile and outstretched arms, speaking with deep-throated ease.

"What's wrong, baby? You look like you need a hug."

"I do."

Craig sat next to Lola, relaxed into the pillows, and gently rubbed the back of her neck.

"I'm here for you."

Craig put his well-toned, buffed arm around her shoulder.

Feeling comfort from him, she proceeded to tell him about Judge Garrett's heart attack and the lease. "I'm glad you came in today," Lola said, patting his arm. "Somehow I always feel better when you're around."

"That's nice." He pulled her closer to him. "I'm glad you feel that way."

"Your friendship has always meant a lot to me," Lola answered with a hug. "You're a loving teddy bear."

"It makes me happy to hear that."

"Your common sense approach to living seems to make life more simple."

"I don't believe in stress. I do what I can to avoid it."

"Looks like whatever you are doing, it's working."

Lola liked his profile, his strong chin and mouth. Craig had a remarkable strength in his face. Lola smiled, admiring his sweet expressions. The sound of his tranquil voice soothed her soul.

"I live in a healthy environment," he said, "and I associate with trustworthy people who are committed to a sensible lifestyle."

"I know what you mean. I feel blessed that I've always had good friends."

"Me, too." Craig tenderly kissed Lola's lips. "Now that Rick is out of the picture, I want for us to enjoy more than a friendship."

Lola was startled. Confused, she stared into Craig's eyes. Memories of Rick flooded her mind, like a hidden current.

"How did you know about me and Rick?"

Feeling his hand squeeze hers gently, Lola knew he sensed her uneasiness. Lola knew she was looking at a man she could trust, a nurturing man who knew how to extend loyalty, fidelity. Confused, not knowing how to respond gracefully, she said nothing.

"Men know certain things." Craig whispered into her ear. "I'm going to be honest and up front with you. I've waited a long time for this moment. Now that you're free, I don't want anything to interfere with us being together."

"What are you talking about?" Lola said, astonished.

"I fell in love with you when I first saw you at the gym a year ago. But you were with Rick, so I kept my distance. I respected what was between you two, but it wasn't easy."

"You're a good actor," Lola said, staring at her hands, twirling her diamond ring. "I had no idea."

"I've never stopped loving you, thinking about you."

"Wait a minute. Where have I been all this time?"

Craig's words startled Lola. She never in her wildest dreams ever thought that he would have such deep feelings of love for her.

"You were blinded by a guy who never deserved your company," Craig said, holding Lola's chin in his hand.

"How do you know so much?" Lola looked deep into Craig's eyes.

"Remember that black eye Rick had last September?"

"Boy! That was a real shiner. He said he had an accident at the gym."

"Well, I was the accident."

"What are you talking about?" In a haze, Lola looked hard at Craig. "I don't understand."

"I caught Rick in the sauna with a sleazy bimbo. I went nuts when I thought of him two-timing you. You deserve better. I cherish you, Lola. Give me a chance to prove it."

It hurt Lola to hear another confirmation of Rick's infidelity, but at the same time it made it easier for her to detach from Rick.

"What about Lisa? I thought you two were engaged?"

"She ran off to Europe with a multi-millionaire."

"I'm sorry to hear that. You two seemed so devoted to each other."

"I guess the ring I got her wasn't big enough."

"Are you OK with what's happened?"

"I am now. I had known for a while that it wouldn't have ever worked out between us. I only own three health clubs and that didn't provide enough money for Lisa. She's just another pretty face who wanted to play for awhile." With long fingers, Craig brushed the curls from his forehead. "I can see now that she did me a favor."

Lola stood up and elegantly tossed her hair. She thought that Lisa may have done her a favor when she remembered what the Oriental woman had said earlier that morning.

Excitement tingled within her heart, her eyes twinkled, and she began to see Craig in a new light.

"C'mon, give me one of your famous hugs before we get started," Lola said, feeling more at ease with the new romantic possibilities in front of her.

"My pleasure."

Craig clasped his hands behind Lola's waist and picked her up as easily as if he were lifting a feather. Her gold slippers fell to the floor. Her arms lay over his shoulders. Lola giggled because the curly hair on his chest tickled her nose.

"Relax," he said.

"I am relaxed."

"No you're not. I can't start to press the pressure points around your spine until you're loosened up."

"OK, OK."

Lola took a deep breath, closed her eyes, and went limp like a rag doll while he still held her in mid-air. She felt Craig's hands pull firmly into the lumbar area of her spine, hold the pressure for three seconds, release, and move up to the next vertebra and repeat the same procedure.

Tranquilized, Lola entered a state of timelessness. The sound of his heavy breathing seemed as far away as a bird in flight. Continuing to massage her spine, he progressed to her shoulder blade area. Softly nibbling her neck, he let her down.

"How's that?" he asked. "Feel better?"

"Yes. Thank you. What a great gift."

"I'm eating my heart out, big guy," Nattie said. "Let me know when it's my turn."

"Next time you come into the gym," he replied.

"The works?"

"Yeah. Anything for you, Nattie."

Craig assured Lola that Samson would be in the salon to play the prank on Derrick.

"He'll be here at 5:30."

"Great! This will be the best joke yet. Maybe Derrick will think twice about dating married women after this stunt."

Lola noticed Craig's powerful stride as they walked back to the shampoo area. She could tell that he was confident and comfortable with who he was.

"Now it's my turn," Craig said while relaxing into the shampoo chair.

"You're in for a treat."

Lola put a towel around his neck, then fastened the plastic cape to secure it.

"I know. Your touch sends me sailing."

"You have lots of cowlicks and a sexy nape." Lola smoothed the towel over his shoulders.

"That sounds scientifically kinky." Craig laughed aloud. "I think I'll take it as a compliment."

"Good."

"Really. What does it mean?"

"The hair growth patterns on your head and neckline grow in circular undulating movements."

"Undulating? Hmmmm... And?"

"Well, as the old saying goes, the more cowlicks a person has on their head, the more action they will have in their life."

"Oh, really?" Craig smiled. "How many do you have?"

"Enough to take me into old age."

Feathering his neck with her long, dexterous fingers, Lola asked him to scoot down a little in the chair. "It will be more comfortable for you."

"I can't get more comfortable than this."

"Oh yes you can."

She liked him for the humor that glinted behind his eyes and for the sincerity in his nature.

After turning on the water, she weaved her fingers through his thick head of hair while waiting for the water to get hot. Lola noticed his fiery eyes squint with amusement while he looked up at her lips and full breasts.

Because he was tall and his chest was so big, she knew she would have to stretch her body a little extra to get in a balanced position to shampoo him which would make her chest even closer to his face. This embarrassed her even though she had washed his hair countless times before, so she ran her thumb and forefinger over his eyelids.

"Close your eyes, Craig, I don't want to get water or soap in them."

While the steam rose, she leaned over and applied warm water to his curls while running her fingertips over his scalp. Without breaking contact with his skin, her hands moved in a methodical rhythm.

"Listen to the sea," she said, cupping her warm hand over his ear.

"Yes," he smiled, "we will together, tonight."

Lola slid her hand behind his head, rotating his cervical vertebrae with nimble fingers. Purring like a lion, Craig took Lola by surprise by quickly raising his head and kissing her breast.

"Gotcha." Craig laughed with delight.

"I can see I have a live wire on my hands," she said, grabbing his nose and shaking it.

"I must admit, I've fantasized about doing that for a long time."

Lola shut off the water and looked at him in amazement. Delighted, she had never seen this playful, fun side of him before.

"I'm warning you, buster," Lola said, making a fist. "You'd better behave like a gentleman or you'll end up with a knuckle sandwich for lunch."

"Let me taste it." Craig held his mouth open, daring her by running his tongue over his lips.

"Delectable," Lola said, putting her finger in his mouth and lightly touching the tip of his tongue. "This is just an appetizer."

"Oh... My body is tingling. Being around you excites me."

"You're on your own, baby," Lola teased.

"You turn me on. I can't help myself."

"You'd better help yourself, or this luxury shampoo will have an early demise."

The lather became luxurious mounds of suds. Lola massaged the pressure points on the top of his head. Her hands moved with dexterity behind his ears and on to the top of his cranium.

"What a woman." With a slight moan, he said, "I've got a huge erection, babe, and you're responsible."

Lola glanced down at the plastic cape.

"You pitch a helluva tent, honey. You must be great on a camp-out."

"What are you going to do about it?"

Lola leaned over and eagerly kissed his wanting powerful lips, thrusting her tongue into his open mouth.

"I'm going to make it bigger and harder than ever!" she whispered in a provocative tone, their lips touching.

While rinsing the lather out of his hair, she noticed beads of perspiration on his forehead.

"Did the oven get a little too hot?" She ran her wet fingers over his skin to soothe him.

"There's only one way to cool me off, Lola."

"That's right, sugar. You've asked for it, and you're going to get it."

"This must be what Heaven is like."

"Well, where you're going, it won't be hot." Lola turned the hot water off and sprayed his face with cold water. "Cool and icy, huh? This should do the trick."

Craig jumped up, choking, then turned and looked towards Lola. She saw a mixture of joy and mischief surge from his facial expression.

"You've just declared war."

"You're on," Lola joked, her heart pounding like a conga drum.

Bolts of lightening shot from his eyes into hers. Lola could feel the electricity explode between them.

"I'm ready," Craig announced.

"Not as ready as I am."

Lola's attraction for him heightened while adrenaline flowed in the marrow of her bones. Lola sprang back when he yanked his plastic cape off and lunged towards her.

"You really have had it now," he said.

"Who's had it?" Taking him by surprise, Lola sprayed cold water at his crotch.

"You have!" Whooping aloud, Craig leaped in the air. "Ugh! That's it. You've had it now."

"You're quite a dancer, Craig," Lola laughed, continuing to shoot water at him. "That's some pretty fancy foot work. Can't wait to go out dancing with you."

"Dancing? You'll love my style." Cornering her, Craig swept her into his arms. "You haven't seen anything yet."

"Put me down!" Lola hit his chest. Her long hair flew furiously in the air. "I mean it. Put me down." Lola bit his ear, then sucked on his earlobe. "I have to cut your hair right now. Mama Corelli will be here at 11:30."

"You can cut my hair another time." Craig took long strides towards the door of the facial room, kissing Lola between her screams. "We have something more important to deal with now."

The door closed. Lola's uninhibited laughter softened as the click of the lock on the door echoed in the air.

Facing him, Lola stood in silence. Feeling his body radiate heat, she wondered what his next move would be.

Craig held her golden locks between his fingers and smelled her strands of hair as if they were a prize rose. Lola saw a tenderness and sensitivity in the way he moved his fingers.

"The highlights in your hair sparkle like the ringlets of a cherubim angel."

"It's just the chandelier."

"You're my angel." He took her hands into his, kissing her palms, then her wrists. "You're holding my destiny in your hands."

She held his face, stroking it gently. Her eyes searched his in desire. His want of her was overwhelming, leaving her knees weak. Lola yearned to release her fiery passion, but did not know if she should just yet. It was too soon. With mixed feelings she pushed him away.

"Come here," he pleaded, arms extended, a serious expression covering his face.

"No. Not yet. I feel like you're sweeping me away."

"I want to. Please? I've waited long enough."

Yielding to his seduction, Lola cast herself into his arms, pressing her cheek against his firm skin, feeling their warmth flow into each other.

"I love you." Craig held her tightly, embracing her passionately.

She glanced up into his contented-looking face and saw that his eyes were closed. Secure like a butterfly in a cocoon, she felt his body curve around hers.

"It's too soon to say that." Lola held back.

"But it's what I feel. Each time I say it, I will feel closer to you."

"Can't get much closer than this," Lola said, trying to lighten the mood.

"Yes we can." Craig moved closer.

With their arms intertwined, she felt his palpitating chest beating into hers, strong and powerful, their hearts throbbing together as one. His warmth enveloped her, making her feel the way Rick never could.

"I'm sorry, Craig." Lola pushed away again. "This is moving too quickly for me."

"Darling, you can't ignore your feelings."

"I'm not, it's just that I..."

"Shhh..." Craig put his finger to her lips. "Don't deny the special feelings we have for each other."

"But..."

"You are so beautiful, and you have my heart in the palm of your hand." Craig quieted her with a gentle kiss.

"Tell me again."

"You are so beautiful. It's a pleasure to tell you. I'll tell you millions of times for the rest of your life... If you'll let me."

Lola had always wanted to hear those words from Rick. It hurt her that he would not say them, yet he did tell her girlfriends that they were beautiful and sexy. Rick seemed to enjoy fawning over other women in front of Lola.

"Why the tear?" Craig brushed her cheek.

"Just because." Lola turned her head.

"Look at me. I'm sincere. I want us to be a part of each other's lives for a long, long time."

Lola felt secure in his arms but needed to feel secure with his words as well.

"Your words flow too smoothly," Lola said.

"They're real. You must know that. Lola, I want and need your friendship, your time. And your love."

Overwhelmed with desire, she slid her hands behind his head. To gratify her passion, she pulled his mouth to hers, zealously welcoming him. She felt his warm hands tenderly cradle her breasts. Shivers ran up Lola's spine as his hands glided over her body.

"I've dreamed of caressing you for so long, touching you like this." Firmly, he pulled her closer to him. "Be the angel in my life. Lola, love me."

"But Craig..."

"Please don't make me wait any longer." He sighed deeply. "I will if I have to but I want to make love to you now. Don't look at this as just a fast fling. For me it's the beginning of the most beautiful event in my life."

Lola felt his body tremble with passion. Knowing he was an ethical man with a remarkable reputation, she felt he was sincere. Lola listened to her instincts and trusted him. Unable to help herself, she melted into his fire.

The power exuded from his kisses overwhelmed Lola, taking her breath away. She pulled back. Not knowing what to do, she looked away. Even though she pined for more, she wanted to wait until later. Nervously excited, her eyes fluttered, telling him what her mouth would not say. Delirious at the thought of being in his arms, and not thinking, a 'yes' escaped her lips. Too late to stop what was happening, Lola surrendered to her fevered senses.

"I love you, darling." Whisking Lola up in his arms, Craig laid her on the facial bed. "Dreams do come true. You have just proven that to me."

In rapturous delight, Lola flowed with the power that only true love could bring.

"Lola, my sweet Lola." Craig tenderly kissed her breasts, his tongue glided to the softness of her stomach.

"Dream girl?" Lola welcomed his heated hand that slid between her quivering thighs.

"Yes, dream girl," Craig said in a provocative, soothing tone. "Let's fly high."

From the mirror above, Lola watched the firm muscles of his naked torso ripple with every movement, making her desire him even more. Torrid passion exploded like a blast of dynamite in textured granite. Fog misted the ceiling mirror, making their bodies look like floating light in a sea of purple passion.

"Lola?"

"Yes?"

"Say yes."

Lola's eyes, dilated with sensation, gazed into his.

"Yes, my darling, let's love each other... Now."

Experiencing the joy of the unity in their lovemaking, Lola knew this would be the beginning of the most beautiful event in her life, too.

Chapter 8

Leaving the salon, Craig held the door open for Mama Corelli, the lovable, portly cherub. He nodded, accepting the peppermint candy she pulled out of her brocade vest pocket.

"Thanks, Mama." Craig hugged Mama, then turned towards Lola. Smiling, he stated, "Dinner at six."

"You're on."

Lola knew her eyes told him more than her words did. Beaming, she watched Craig walk briskly away, his face to the sky, until he was out of sight.

"I'm jealous," Raquel whimpered. "I'm eatin' my heart out. He's such a great guy... That body! Ugh! What a *man!*"

"Don't be jealous," Lola said. "Everybody gets their turn, sooner or later."

"I hope it's sooner than later."

"Hot damn!" Nattie whistled. "I've taught you well, Lola. That was quite a water fight. Reminds me of my good old days."

"Shame on you, Nattie!" Mrs. Clardy had a sour look on her face. "You've been a bad influence on this dear, sweet, innocent girl."

"Oh! Shut up!" Nattie spouted. "This is life. It's alive. That's more than I can say for you."

"Don't tell me to shut up. You're always the one who has diarrhea of the mouth."

"Oh?" Nattie pulled extra hard on a swatch of Mrs. Clardy's hair. "I ought to rip your hair out by the roots."

"Ouch... Hey! Watch it there."

"Surely," Nattie sneered. "I aim to please, being professional, and all."

"You have too much hair in that pin curl."

"Yeah! Yeah! I've got eighty-nine hairs in it instead of ninety. I'd hoped after all these years that you'd quit telling me how many hairs to put in each curl."

"I have to keep an eye on you. I don't want to even think about what would happen to me if I didn't."

"I just may shave your head like a clown. Then people wouldn't have to wonder what you are."

"Oh, hush. You're the one who belongs in a circus."

"Are you still having the Congressman and his wife over for dinner tonight?"

"Yes. And I'm cooking my specialty," Mrs. Clardy said with pride. "It's a fabulous dish. Everybody comments on it."

"How can they not!" Nattie said. "My lands... Tell me you're not going to serve that menu. Please, Clardy... That's a dinner from hell! Anyone deserves better than that."

"Boston butt drizzled in duck lard is a mouth watering entree, fit for any king. They'll love it."

"Yeah, they'll love it because you put so much money into his campaign."

Nattie finished setting Mrs. Clardy's hair, then put her under a bubble hair dryer.

Lola noticed that Mama Corelli was quick to sum up Lola's situation with Craig. Her eyes dancing with delight, Mama Corelli swung her arm to slap her chubby hip, then stomped her foot.

"That's it!" Mama said. "You've had enough fun! It's time to get married and join the rest of us in our misery."

"Why enjoy one man when I can enjoy them all?" Lola laughed, hugging Mama Corelli.

"Love is a sweet addiction." Mama shook her finger towards Lola. "The look you two lovebirds gave each other wasn't a frivolous one. That sparkle in your eye means only one thing. I detect passion if not true love."

"You've got that right, Mama," Nattie blurted out. "I love it when romance is in the air, especially when it's one of our own girls."

"You're just like my mom." Lola held Mama Corelli's hand. "I never could hide anything from her or you."

"That's right, and you never will." Mama Corelli kissed Lola's cheek. "He's a good boy, I've known he was a very special person from the first moment I laid eyes on him. I'll give you an engagement party at our restaurant. It'll be Roberto's and my present to you. Hey, I redid the banquet room just in time, brought in renaissance paintings from Italy, and everything. Lola, set the date and let me know."

"Is that how it's done in Rome?"

"Precious *cara*, that's how it's done all over the world. Ah... Young love, I remember it well." Mama Corelli handed Lola a white paper bag.

"Mama, I don't even have to ask you what's in it. I can smell them. Thank you."

"We can all smell them, Mama," Raquel said. "You make the best raviolis in the world. My Daddy's still talkin' about them."

"You make everything good," Lola said. "What's the key to your success."

"Just like anything else, you have to take extra time to learn and practice finishing touches. My old aunties in Italy taught me how to cook when I was four years old. But the real key to being a great cook is to bless the food and always pray that the angels cook through you. I've been surprised myself at how delicious some of the dinners I've prepared were. Oh... I would cook for the world if I could." Mama Corelli pointed to the bouquet of tulips. "Beautiful flowers. My Maria got some just like it earlier today. She's going nuts now because the card only said 'thinking of you.' Men play funny games."

"Yeah, Mama, they sure do, just like little boys." Lola, trying to keep from laughing, winked at Raquel. "Sometimes I wonder if they'll ever grow up."

"No, they don't, so don't expect it." Raquel winked back at Lola and took a more self assured stance. "I'm the expert on men. Trust me... Men never grow up."

"Let's talk about food," Mama Corelli laughed. "All children, including me, love raviolis."

"You're too cute, Mama." Lola put her arm through Mama Corelli's. "C'mon, let's get your shampoo going."

Lola remembered how she had walked arm in arm with her great Auntie Helen, the special woman who had introduced her to reading classic literature. She knew that her aunt and Mama Corelli, both filled with unconditional love for all of mankind, would have been good friends had they ever met.

"I hate it under this contraption," Mrs. Clardy shouted from under the hair dryer. "I can't hear a thing. Keep it on low. You know how I hate the heat."

"Just calm down and accept it," Nattie said. "Beauty is no pain."

"Says who?"

"The ones who are born with it."

Lola focused on Mama Corelli and tuned out the goings on in the salon, especially the distorted, bothersome conversation between Nattie and Mrs. Clardy.

"Mama, what's kept your marriage happy all of these years?" Lola asked.

"Time sweetened our love." Mama smiled, nodding her head. "Living by the Golden Rule set the foundation for trust and respect."

"'Do unto others as you would have them do unto you.' I buy that, but what added the spice to carry you through fifty-five years of marriage?"

"Simple things like tender moments in prayer, love for our children, family, and friends. And intimate, frivolous jokes. A gentle kiss on my hands in appreciation for all I do. A warm bath together. Roberto looking through my eyes to my heart and understanding my true feelings, no matter what I'd say. And good, healthy food, and best of all Roberto holding me in his arms every night and falling asleep after I do. Ha! Lucky for him I fall asleep fast."

Lola thought back to her nights in bed with Rick's back to her. Loneliness thrown in her face, it had hurt. Her heart an empty cave, she felt she would have been better off sleeping alone. Lola looked forward to the day her future husband would hold her in his arms until she fell asleep. She thought back to the loving feelings she enjoyed in Craig's embrace and remembered what her great aunt had told her when she was a teenager.

"If you can sleep the night in a man's arms and wake up rested, then he's the man for you."

"Mama, was it love at first sight with you and Roberto?"

"After one look at him, my mother's words of wisdom, God rest her soul, became clear in my mind. 'Communication of the mind and communion of the heart.'"

"And?"

"I married Roberto because I was in love with him, and I still am. Lots of my friends married for other reasons. Then when life's heartaches set in and they do, they didn't have the pure love to carry them through. Joy left their lives, and little by little, their spirits died before they did." Mama Corelli affectionately patted Lola's arm. "I love you too much. Promise me you will marry for love."

"I promise. I've been true to myself so far."

Lola had had many chances to marry, but she chose to wait for the man who she felt would be her true partner in life, a man with her same passions, dreams, and goals. Even though she deeply loved Rick, she knew it would never work out because they desired different things.

Mrs. Clardy slid on her glasses, ruining the pin curls over her ears. "Come and fix these, right now before they dry wrong. Hurry up...I don't have all day!"

"You're going to burn in hell for that, Clardy." Nattie cussed as she redid the pin curls, then turned the hair dryer up to hot, saying under her breath, "After all these years, you'd think she'd learn how to put her glasses on without messing up the clippies and pin curls."

Mrs. Clardy sat erect, her long legs tight together like novels on a shelf. Her book held up, even with her thick glasses, she read aloud. "Then the ocean waves..."

"I hate it when she reads out loud. It's so annoyin'," Raquel said, "especially when it's Faulkner. Do da, do da... He's such a borin' writer, page-long paragraphs and all. For once, I wish she'd read Jackie Collins or Judith Krantz."

"Trust me," Nattie said. "She couldn't handle the excitement. An enema and a yearly bird watch are Clardy's speed." Nattie sang, "I'm gonna wash that man right out of my hair" while she mopped up the watery mess Lola and Craig had made.

"Thanks, Nattie, for cleaning up for me."

"Don't mention it. Anything for love. I love that Craig, always knew he was husband material." Nattie reached for Mrs. Clardy's coffee cup. "Let me refresh that for you."

"Hmmm... And you thought you could fool me by putting three cubes of sugar into my coffee. Did your memory fly out the window?" Mrs. Clardy asked. "I want two and a half cubes, and that's all there is to it. No more, no less. Now, don't be lazy. I demand you do it right to please me. I pay you plenty. Now earn your money!"

"You pay the money for my experience and talent," Nattie said. "You're not only paying for my professional services, but you're paying me to not ruin your hair."

"Give her the sunflower seeds, Nattie," Raquel said. "It's time. I've just about had it with Miss Personality today."

"Me too," Lola said. "I'm ready for a good laugh. I think we all are." Lola told Mama Corelli to sit back and watch the show. "I've got to get the camcorder."

"This shop has always been like an amusement park. I love it." Mama Corelli folded her hands in her lap, in anticipation of action. "And you guys even do good work. How about that?"

Lola directed the camera towards Nattie and Mrs. Clardy. "Rolling, Nattie."

Nattie sauntered towards Mrs. Clardy and offered her the bowlful of sunflower seeds.

"Here you are."

"Are they fresh?" Mrs. Clardy demanded, unaware of what was going on.

"Yeah! Yeah!" Nattie dramatically spoke out, "Just the way you like them."

Lola filmed as Mrs. Clardy grabbed a handful. Several seeds dropped onto the floor.

"Pick those up, Nattie! Right now." Mrs. Clardy ordered, "I don't want to slip and fall on them when I get up. If you would have held the bowl the right way, they wouldn't have spilled. You must like to clean up messes because you sure make enough of them."

"One of these days, Clardy," Nattie said shaking her fist, "I'm going to send you to the moon."

"Don't get so damn theatrical. Now, where's my napkins?"

"Here you are." Nattie handed her three napkins; one to hold the seeds, one to hold the shells, and one to wipe her lips. "Just like you like, and they're pink this time. I remembered."

"Well, good for you." Mrs. Clardy held a seed, her little finger in the air, and proceeded to crack it with her protruding buck teeth. "These *are* fresh."

"Bucky, bucky," Raquel giggled. "If she only knew how stupid she looks, wrinkled nose and all, like a lizard's back. I'm glad Lola's gettin' this on film. I've tried explainin' this scenario to people. Somehow I can't come up with enough descriptive words to tell the story effectively."

"She eats them just like a starving chipmunk," Nattie laughed, "cracking those seeds louder than anyone I've ever heard, and to top it off, she mutilates half of them and gets the shell mixed up with the seed. You know she's got to be lame to not be able to crack a seed."

"But she's high-class. Her money makes it so," Raquel said. "Can't you see her little finger in the air? We ought to snap a picture of her eatin' her seeds and mail it to her hoity-toity bridge club."

"I should call my friend, the executive editor at the *Herald*. Have him run it, front page."

"Good idea, Nattie."

"Her face must hurt," Nattie said, adjusting her bra strap.

"Why do you say that?"

"Anything that's that ugly has got to hurt."

"That's cruel, Nattie," Lola said.

"It's obvious her mother gave birth in a barn."

"That's even more cruel."

"Yeah, I know. Ha, ha... It's a shame that this woman has brought so much misery to people. Lola, be sure to get this on film."

Nattie walked over to Mrs. Clardy, bent towards her and said in a sugary tone, "If assholes could fly, you'd be a jet."

"What did you say?" Mrs. Clardy poked her ear out of the hair dryer. "Speak up. Use proper enunciation. I could hardly hear a thing you said."

"I said that a jet just flew overhead," Nattie hollered.

"So? Big deal. What else is new? Don't bother me with silly pea-brain conversation. Trivia never interested me. You should know that after all these years."

"Oh! Sweet revenge." Nattie popped her bubble gum. "How I love it."

"Mama, shall we mail that to *Funny Home Videos*?" Lola put the camcorder down.

"Most definitely. She eats funny in our restaurant, too. Licks her fingers and sucks on them till all the sauce is gone."

While folding under the linen collar of Mama Corelli's print linen dress, Lola noticed, on Mama's neck, a two inch cut with eight stitches.

"My lands," Lola exclaimed. "What on earth happened to your neck?"

"Roberto did it, and believe me, he's sorry. He's stayed in a drunken stupor since it happened because he realizes he almost killed me."

"Wait a minute. What happened to wedded bliss?" Lola asked, shocked. "And don't leave out one detail."

Lola continued the shampoo and blow-dry while Mama Corelli told her story, talking with wide sweeps of her arms.

"I went to the dentist late Wednesday afternoon to have a root canal done on my back molar. Everything seemed to be doing OK until later that night when I got real dizzy. So I took pain pills, then went to bed. I rolled around, tossed and turned, but I couldn't fall asleep. I took two aspirins, then tied a wool scarf around my neck, thinking the warmth would make my jaw feel better and help me sleep."

"Did it?"

"No, I was as sick as a poor little lamb. I've since found out that that damned dentist, who's supposed to be a specialist, did the wrong thing."

"Mama, this is terrible! But why the cut in your neck?"

"Well, the heat the scarf created made matters worse. I felt suffocated and had a hard time breathing. I pulled on the scarf and made the knot too tight to untie by myself. Being real dizzy and all didn't help matters too much. It was 3:00 a.m., *cara*. The middle of the night. I nudged Roberto. He didn't wake up, so I pinched his rear, and he mumbled 'later.' Can you imagine? Here I'm sick, and he's thinking of that! Oh, that man, I love him so, but, ugh... I hit him in the head and pleaded, 'Help me, Roberto. Help me. Help me. Get this scarf off. I can't untie it. I'm dying! I can't breathe.'"

"Poor Roberto. He must have been terrified."

"He was. He panicked. His overreactions are always so dramatic. He comes from a long line of actors, you know, but he's also a typical warrior. Poor guy; he was ready, willing, and able, but his fingers don't work too good. You know... arthritis."

"And?" Lola worked double time as her curiosity grew.

"Before long, I was yelling, 'No, Roberto! No! No!'"

"What'd he do?"

"You know my Roberto, he's slow when he should be fast, and fast when he should be slow. It's a miracle we got six children. Anyway, instead of getting a scissors and cutting the scarf off, he ran to the kitchen and fetched a serrated knife." Mama Corelli shook her head in disgust. "Scared the hell out of me, almost had a heart attack, but I had no choice. Terrible to be in a vulnerable position. I asked him later, after this mess was over with, why he didn't use a scissors. He said the only thing he could think of at the time was a butcher knife. My luck he can't think of a scissors; he thinks of a knife! A big dangerous one."

"You mean to tell me he sawed the scarf off with a serrated butcher knife?"

"Yes, that's what I said. I can't believe it either." With pursed lips, Mama Corelli rotated her head from side to side. "I screamed out but I couldn't break his concentration. For once in his life, he concentrated. He was intent on completing his mission, his way, as usual. My eyes bugged out as I watched that twelve inch blade go back and forth, back and forth. Made me more dizzy. He stood with one foot on the floor and his bent knee on the mattress. As he hovered over me and continued sawing that damn scarf, he just kept saying, 'Don't worry, Mama, I'll help you. I'll get this sonofabitch off'." She threw her hands in the air. "And he did."

"Oh my God! This is unreal," Lola said. "Where was Maria all this time?"

"Oh, my poor girl." Mama Corelli shook her head. "My *cara* Maria had dashed into our bedroom, half asleep. I think her horrified expression mirrored the traumatized look on my face. Her eyes grew as big as saucers. My Maria went into hysterics."

"I'm so sorry."

"My Maria, she always did hate the sight of blood. She's no good in an emergency, not like Nattie."

"What an awful thing for you to have to live through; so scary."

"Yeah. I feel like I flew over hell and my wings got burned. Poor Roberto, though. I told him not to feel guilty for almost killing me, but he's still in shock over what's happened. Every time he looks at the stitches in my neck he cries. Men should cry too, but this takes the cake. He and Randy have been boozing it up at the restaurant for three days now. Randy's slept there for the past two nights."

"Debbie's husband?"

"Yes, he's a real bastard, no good. I love everyone, but he's so selfish and mean, no character. It's hard to be around people like that."

"So that's where Randy's been."

"If he doesn't shape up by tomorrow, I'm going to call the cops on him. He hasn't showered for three days, and you know that's not very good for business."

"Randy and Roberto must be a real pair." Lola grabbed the curling iron.

It had been one month since Lola had cut Randy's hair. She knew Randy to be a drunk, just like his mother and father. Randy had used his family's riches to throw around, act like a big-shot, and buy everyone off, but now with Debbie in the hospital, faced with tragedy, he chose to drink and stay in his state of denial.

"Burying his troubles in whiskey won't make things any better at all. Randy's too emotionally weak to handle what's happened to Debbie, with the fire and her sickness and all," Lola said. "He won't accept that her face is burned and that her beauty may be gone."

"Damn ego. He always prided himself on having a glamorous wife. Her heart is so beautiful. Debbie's a good girl; she deserves better than Randy."

"I agree, but she's hopelessly in love with him." Lola rolled her eyes. "It's so sad. I went to see Debbie at the hospital last night on my way home from work. Several of my clients are nurses on the burn ward, so they let me in to see her. About thirty percent of her body is burned. She needs to know that Randy's there for her now. Debbie said he hasn't been to visit since the paramedics brought her in three days ago."

"Sonofabitch, I've tried encouraging him to go. He just cries, and drinks, and cries some more," Mama Corelli said. "Life would be so much easier if people were more emotionally developed."

"Some day, Mama. Hopefully some day soon. Till then, I'd like to give Randy a piece of my mind."

Lola knew from experience the importance of being there for a person in their time of sickness, and it angered her that Randy was too self-centered and self-absorbed in his own pity to go see and comfort his wife, Debbie.

"Nattie, I need your help," Raquel said. "My client's hair is takin' just forever to bleach up light enough. I don't know what else to do."

"Did you use 60-volume peroxide like I told you?"

"No, thirty. I was afraid sixty would damage her hair."

"Look, with a teaspoon of EXT conditioner in the bleach, I guarantee nothing will burn. Sixty would have pulled her up in four minutes flat."

Nattie walked over to Raquel's client, checked the strands of hair poking out of the foam frosting cap, then turned the dryer up to high. "This will make the bleach take more rapidly."

"Great! Our Nattie to the rescue again."

"It's coming up OK. Rinse it in five minutes. I'll mix a Wella toner to cut the gold. It'll turn out fine."

"Thanks, Nattie. You're always there for me in a jam. Is there ever an end to learnin' about hair color?"

"All in a day's work, babe. Besides putting up with people's crap, hair color is the most difficult thing we do. If you put the same hair coloring formula on fifty women, each would turn out differently. No one's expected to learn it all in one day."

Watching Raquel and Nattie discuss tricks of the trade, Lola knew Nattie had a special place in her heart for Raquel because Raquel reminded her of herself in her youth. Lola felt that they, not having family close by, found joy and companionship in their friendship.

Lola heard the back door creak open and the refrigerator door slam. Bertha, munching on three pieces of pepperoni pizza folded into one, entered like a slow-moving mountain. Her tattered, knee-length muumuu was ripped under the arm, exposing her hairy armpit.

"Nattie, are you ready for me?" Bertha moaned.

"Am I ready? I was born ready. Go ahead and sit on the shampoo chair," Nattie said. "I'll be right there after I take another swig of wine. Hopefully it will deaden my sense of smell."

The footrest on the chair was not sturdy enough to hold up Bertha's fat legs so Nattie pushed a wooden stool toward her and placed Bertha's legs up on it, one at a time.

"This gout's given you piano legs," Nattie told her. "All that red meat you eat is giving you too much uric acid."

"I love my meat," Bertha grunted.

"It's been two months since your last haircut," Nattie said, starting to wet Bertha's greasy, dirty hair.

"Yeah. It stayed in real good."

"You've got that right. My haircuts are the best. That's why they grow out so well."

"No," Bertha said, "I meant the roller set."

"Am I understanding you correctly? Are you telling me that you haven't washed your hair in two months?"

"Why should I wash it when it still looked good?"

"Get rid of the blinders. You need new glasses, babe. Can't you smell your stinky head? God knows how many varmints are running around on your scalp. Ugh!" Nattie put rubber gloves on. "Forget the shampoo for now. You can soak in disinfectant first. Then I'll give your scalp a good scrub with an SOS pad."

While Nattie set Bertha's hair in rollers, Lola saw her hand Bertha the lease agreement Judge Garrett had brought in.

"Check this out," Nattie ordered.

Bertha read it, grunted, and passed more gas.

"Hmmm..."

"You want to sign it now?" Nattie asked as she flipped the fan on, tiptoeing a few inches higher, hoping the air would be fresher smelling a little higher up.

"Nope."

"Well, then, you can sign it later."

"Maybe... End of discussion," Bertha burped.

"I told you to quit eating those smelly pickled pig's feet!"

Bertha belched again.

"As if your digestion isn't bad enough."

Lola began to walk over to Nattie and Bertha, to talk to Bertha about the lease. Nattie darted her a 'later, babe' look. Lola knew to not question Nattie's motives, knowing Nattie had her best interest at heart, so she continued styling Mama Corelli's hair.

Nattie finished setting Bertha's hair, then put her under the hair dryer next to Mrs. Clardy.

"This will give you thirty minutes to think about the lease," Nattie said. "I've got the pen ready when you are."

Lola noticed that immediately Mrs. Clardy's nose began to twitch. Soon, in disgust, she put her book down and fanned herself with both hands. Gasping, her face turned the color of cheap lipstick, her eyes begged for help.

"Do something, Nattie," Mrs. Clardy demanded. "Her body odor is awful."

"Her what?" Nattie pretended to not hear.

"Don't make me repeat it. You know darn good and well what I'm talking about. The woman's a *hog*."

"I'm not about to give that stinkpot a bath. It's bad enough I had to wash her head."

"But, Nattie, it's not just one thunder."

"Thunder? Who have you been baby-sitting for? Why don't you just say it. Bertha's passing gas!"

"Nattie, you have no class," Mrs. Clardy stated. "Now, take care of this matter. I'll beg if I have to."

"It's human nature," Nattie shot back. "Keep on reading."

"How do you expect me to concentrate? Why... Bertha's an animal," Mrs. Clardy screeched. "If there was another hair dryer, I'd move. I demand you do something... Immediately."

"Say please," Nattie laughed.

"This is no time for your stupid, silly games," Mrs. Clardy said in disgust.

"Oh, yes it is."

"I'll just suffer in silence. Have it your way."

"I usually do."

"OK, OK." Mrs. Clardy shook her fist. "Please."

"Excuse me?" Nattie cleared her throat.

"Pretty please? Now do it before I die."

"Did you say die? Like in the hair dryer? That would be a first for me."

"You passed firsts a long time ago. Now, that's all you're getting out of me."

"April Fools' Day, Clardy."

"You're the April Fool."

Grabbing the can of air freshener, Nattie sprayed generously, and hollered, "Hey Clardy, did you know elevators smell funny to midgets?"

"Ugh! I don't know who's worse, you or Bertha!"

"Bertha is." Nattie finished spraying. "This should do it. You owe me one for this."

"I owe you no such thing. What you are doing is common courtesy."

"Geezzzz... Bertha's snorin'," Raquel said. "We all know what's next. Get the Lysol out again."

"The deeper sleep she falls into, the louder her snoring becomes, the farther her legs drift apart, and the more gas she'll pass," Nattie explained to Raquel's client. "Damn those pig's feet anyway."

"Like an old dog easin' it on out," Raquel said. "Back in Texas we had an old cocker spaniel like that. And..."

"Nattie! Raquel! Please!" Lola exclaimed. "We're lucky Bertha only comes in once in a while."

"Am I dry yet, Nattie?" Mrs. Clardy gagged.

"Not yet. Five more minutes."

"I don't know if I can last that long. Bertha smells worse than the permanent-wave solution. In fact, worse than anything I've ever smelled. She belongs in the elephant's cage at the zoo."

"Either that or out on the range."

Nattie threw an oversized towel over Bertha's lap and popped her on her thigh to awaken her. "Keep your legs together. You're stinking like a mackerel and killing us off."

"Where's the chocolates?" Bertha asked.

Nattie offered her the crystal bowl filled with truffles. "Watch her polish these off, girls."

"Bertha eats more chocolates in one day than I eat in one year," Raquel sighed.

"You'd better go easy on the chocolates," Nattie warned Bertha. "They'll add to your diarrhea."

"But I love chocolates."

"Ugh," Raquel said. "The woman knows nothin' about discipline or nutrition."

"Some day," Nattie said. "She'll learn the hard way, everyone will eventually."

Lola knew that Bertha was a slob, mean and cantankerous, but because of her own convictions, she chose to treat Bertha like a human being. Lola spoke kindly to Bertha, ran errands for her, and drove her to the doctor when she needed a ride. Lola hoped that some day Bertha would soften her hardened exterior and allow goodness to come into her life.

At her work station, Nattie fluffed and finger waved Mrs. Clardy's hair, then grabbed a can of Aqua Net hair spray and sprayed her ringlets for two minutes.

"That should hold you for a day or so."

"Just spray a little more, Nattie. Don't be so cheap and skimpy with the hair spray."

"But I just sprayed for two minutes."

"It wasn't enough."

"You want hair spray? You've got it..."

Nattie sprayed Mrs. Clardy's hair for another two minutes.

"That's fine now." The spray covered Mrs. Clardy's hair with a wet film of lacquer. "I want to make sure I get my money's worth."

"Now, Clardy, listen good. Sit on your hands and keep them out of your fine hair till the spray dries. I don't want to see one of your hand prints in your new fancy hair-do." Nattie put the clippies away, then lit a cigarette. "I mean it. I'm in no mood to re-do anything."

Lola noticed that, while Nattie's back was turned, Mrs. Clardy had put her hand on her wet hair sprayed hair. She knew Nattie would tear into Mrs. Clardy for ruining her creation.

"Damn you anyway, Clardy," Nattie said, outraged. "Look what you've gone and done now. You've put a damn hand print on the side of your hair. It looks like a kindergartner outlined the fingers."

"No I didn't."

"Well if you didn't, who did? You big baby; you never could keep your hands out of your hair. I don't know why the hell *you* don't fix it every week!"

"There's no hand print in my hair!" Mrs. Clardy stomped her feet.

"Fine! Have it your way. There's no hand print. Just don't tell anyone who's fixed your hair. I have a reputation to keep up, you know."

"We all know that. Thanks for a pleasant morning, Nattie."

"Pleasant? For who?"

"For you, of course. I'll see you same time next week."

"Maybe, maybe not," Nattie said.

"You always have to have the last word."

"Yeah, I like it that way."

"Happy Birthday, Nattie," Mrs. Clardy opened her purse and reached in for a neatly wrapped brown box. "You know I could never forget your birthday, even if I wanted to."

"Thanks, Clardy," Nattie said after she opened the box and saw a gold heart shaped locket. "Just what I needed."

"I know. You can put your pizza man's picture in it."

"Consider it done. I love that guy."

"Love?"

"Yeah, you know me. I've always had this love/hate thing with men. I love the ones who are good in bed, and I hate the ones that aren't."

"Nattie! Your mouth is filthy."

"More women should be so honest. Hey Clardy, what's the extra skin called on a penis?"

"I beg your pardon?"

"No, it's called a *man!*"

"You're repulsing me! I'm ashamed to even know you!"

"Admit it, Clardy. I'm the highlight of your life."

"Hardly. Now, be good, Nattie."

"You be good, or be good at it."

"You're revolting!"

"Don't leave mad. Just leave."

Lola watched Mrs. Clardy walk out the front door, blow her whistle, and wave her cane at her limousine driver. Obediently, he opened her door. She got in. He closed it. Like a rigid soldier, he walked to the driver's side of the car, got in, sat behind the wheel, and drove away the misery.

Chapter 9

Lola checked her watch. It was almost noon. Pointing her finger towards Raquel, she said, "I'm glad we canceled the prank on Derrick. It was fun to joke about but too ruthless."

Lola noticed Raquel's sly smile. "You did cancel the flowers, didn't you?"

"What makes you think otherwise?" Raquel asked.

"With that look on your face, you've given me reason to wonder."

"You girls are asking for it on this one if you go through with it," Nattie said. "Derrick's motto isn't just an 'eye for an eye and a tooth for a tooth.' It's a 'head for an eye and a hand for a tooth.' And you know how he despises it when people think he's gay. It drives him nuts. I mean bonkers! That macho guy is liable to do anything. I mean it, Raquel. You're really playing with fire this time."

"But you said you canceled the flowers."

"Oh Lola, this trick is just too darn good to pass up," Raquel said. "Anyway, it's April Fools' Day. It's all in light-hearted fun."

"With anyone else? Yes. With Derrick? No!" Nattie shook her finger in warning. "Just remember... You play, you pay, especially with Derrick. When everything explodes, be assured I will say I told you so."

"Oh, Nattie, you've got it all wrong." Raquel adjusted her tight skirt. "He'll think it's just hysterically funny. Trust me, I know him. He'll love it."

"Love? No way... Your brain's not working to well today. How long's it been since you've been laid?" Nattie rubbed cream on her hands. "I can already smell the smoke."

"Raquel, I thought we agreed to not pull this scam." Lola hung her head in dismay. "Derrick's not going to like this one bit. He'll flip!"

Lola knew that Derrick had a wild streak and that he prided himself on being a street-smart Romeo. Even though Derrick would not admit it, Lola felt that he still carried the childhood hurt and anger of being left at an orphanage by his mother. Lola had questioned clients who were psychologists, and their theory was that Derrick could have extreme difficulty in committing to an intimate relationship. Lola had encouraged him to get professional counseling, but he had refused. She hoped one day he would change his mind and say yes and do what he had to do to attain freedom from his bondage.

Lola heard the back door slam. Derrick entered the salon with Kiki, the blonde bombshell, his latest married conquest.

"Hi, babes. What's happening?" Derrick, sleek and medium-framed, with dark, tousled hair, blew everyone a kiss, then passionately French-kissed Kiki. "Any phone calls for me this morning?"

"Jason at Paramount wants you to call him tomorrow morning," Lola replied.

"Great! That job will take me to Sweden for a week."

"Your photo career is really taking off," Lola said. "I'm so happy for you."

"We all are." Nattie blew Derrick a kiss. "I'm as proud as proud can be. Living like a jet-setter is a snazzy way to go."

"Thanks, your encouragement and support's meant a lot."

Derrick put his comb in the back pocket of his tight black leather pants. "Hey, Lola, I took Bertha to breakfast yesterday. Boy! That woman eats as much as a dinosaur. Whew! Watching her devour food is a sight to be seen, like a cow chewing cud. Man, it was so revolting! First she dropped a big wad of gum into her ice water, then ordered enough food for an army. She'd sweat and eat... Eat and sweat... Then she'd dab that damn hanky on her chubby cheeks and wipe the drips. At one point, she put her mouth to the plate and just shoveled it in. I'd never seen anything like it, except for Dorothy, of course."

"What did y'all offer Bertha to get her to sign the lease?" Raquel asked. "Let me guess, darlin'... One of your famous, fiery photo sessions, bear skin rugs and all? Or a whiff of your exotic toxic cologne?"

"Raquel, is that any way to talk to a loved one?"

"Loved one?"

"Yes. Anyway, the lease is in the bag. We'll all be together for a while."

"I hope so." Lola sighed deeply. "But from the way Bertha's acting, I'm not holding my breath."

"I'll say one thing," Nattie said. "Bertha's gotten extra attention and a lot of great meals out of the deal."

"Miracles happen every day." Derrick snapped his fingers. "Hey. Yo! Beautiful tulips, Raquel. Nannette down at the bakery got a bouquet just like yours. For some funny reason, she thought I'd sent them. Ha! The worn-out broad's dreaming. You women... I'll never understand your thinking."

"You're a walkin' erogenous zone from another planet," Raquel said. "We don't expect you to have the vaguest idea of what we women are all about."

"At least we men try to understand. We're taught that on our planet, you know, compassion and all that good stuff."

Derrick walked into the facial room with Kiki clinging to him like a cheap shirt.

"C'mon, babe," he said. "Let's take five in the pleasure palace."

They emerged within a short period of time, Kiki's lipstick smeared across her face. Derrick winked at Lola, made a fist, and put his thumb in the air. Lola thought that a twenty-eight year old man like Derrick should be more mature. Disgusted with his behavior, Lola knew Derrick's routine with women. His scam, obvious to Lola, started at the shampoo bowl with him singing sensual love songs that complimented his flirtatiousness. Derrick was fun and sometimes entertaining, but it never ceased to amaze Lola how women fell for his fake line of love. Lola continued her book work and hoped for the best when the flowers arrived. She wished Derrick would keep his irrational temper under control.

"Relax and enjoy, baby." Derrick laid Kiki back in the shampoo bowl and whispered in her ear while licking it.

"Oooo... You don't have to tell me twice."

"You say you are a pleasure seeker, my sweet passion queen?"

"You know I am, you hot-skinned animal." Kiki sensuously licked her upper lip and cooed, "Ooooo..."

"Well, woman, you've found the right man. I'm going to give you the most erotic shampoo of your life, and that's just for starters."

"I'm wanting all the good stuff you've got." Kiki giggled and wiggled her body in anticipation.

"I may just wear you out."

"I hope you do."

With the temperature just right, Derrick sprayed water on her head.

"Warm enough?" he asked. "Can you handle the heat?"

"If it was as hot as you, loverboy, I'd scream."

"We can manage the screams later."

"Yeahhhhh...." Kiki breathed, sighing deeply. "Let's film it again next time."

With his long, flexible fingers, Derrick manipulated her scalp with slow, smooth strokes. He mingled the shampooing with soft kisses to her dreamy blue eyes, clouded with hazy sexuality.

"Derrick darling, the way you look at me turns me on." Kiki reached up and brushed her fingers across the dark curling hair on his chest. "The raw fire of your skin burns through my fingers all the way to my pulsating heart."

"Your heart, huh?" Kissing her, Derrick buried his face in the softness of her big breasts. "It's mutual, love."

"I know, and I'm glad." Kiki puckered her lips, then blew a kiss. "The magic of your mouth drives me into a wild frenzy."

Shampooing, with hands moving at a snail's pace, Derrick bent down and, lips touching hers, softly sang an Italian love song.

"Mona Lisa... Mona Lisa...." His tongue ran around the rim of her full open mouth. "You taste like sugar."

"But you said I was sweeter than sugar."

"You are, Kiki. You are as sweet as the nectar of life."

"It's a real turn-on that you're such a fine poet."

"Oh, babydoll, you've got a set of lips, a set of everything." Derrick caressed her with his alluring brown eyes, then sucked on her bottom lip. "Ohhhh... Where have you been all of my life?"

"Waiting just for you, snookums."

Mounds of thick lather grew. Derrick swayed back and forth like a willowy tree in the wind while brushing the hardness behind his zipper against Kiki's arm.

"What are you thinking, my sensual Kiki?" Derrick asked in a low, sexy voice.

"What do you think I'm thinking?" Kiki said, stroking him between the legs. Arching her hips, the plastic cape covering Kiki undulated with the rhythm of sex beating in her body.

"I hope you're fantasizing about what I'm going to do to you later."

"You're a mind reader," Kiki said, her tongue met the smooth wetness of her teeth.

"That's because we're so in tune with each other, lover."

"You're sending wild fire through every nerve of my body." Kiki gasped, a moan of passion escaped her lips. "It's hard for me to control myself."

"You know I love to make you tingle." Derrick's palm, warmed from the water, caressed the curves of her face. "You're skin's so silky." He shuddered, his leg rubbed against her arm again. "I love a soft woman."

"And I love a hard man."

"And?"

"I love your new cologne."

"Ah... A woman who knows quality."

Lola observed the deadlock of passion growing between Derrick and Kiki. His pat routine of seduction was nothing new to Lola. It was just another part of his multiple personality.

Raquel walked over to Lola and whispered, "The sleezebag makes me sick. He's gotten worse with age. Don't ya just wanna gag?"

"Yeah, you'd think that after all these years, he'd come up with a few new phrases. And that cologne... Ugh! Smells like ant poison."

"Probably has pig sweat in it. Somethin' in it is supposed to drive women wild."

"Kiki must have cardboard for brains. Why, he used those same lines when we were in beauty school."

"Don't remind me."

"Raquel," Lola asked in a teasing tone, "did you ever feel his pulse through his tight leather pants?"

"Oh, gag city. Hush up now. Cissy, you've got a memory like an elephant."

Lola glanced around the salon, reveling in the quiet. It felt mellow and warm; soft rock music filled the air. She wished it could be like that for the rest of the day while she tried to deny her gut feeling that said it would not.

Looking through the etched windows on the door, Lola noticed a young man bringing in a large bouquet of two dozen yellow roses mixed with baby's breath, china bells, and maidenhair fern. The timing of the delivery could not have been more perfect although she still wished Raquel had not gone through with the joke.

"Pssst." Lola pointed with her chin and gave Raquel an angry look.

A smirk come over Raquel's face, she gloated and raised her hand and with her fingers gave the OK sign to Lola, perturbing her more.

"You'll be sorry." Nattie shook her head. "You didn't listen to me on this one. You should have. All hell's going to break loose."

"I tried to tell her," Lola said. "Lot of good it did me."

"Don't be a party pooper," Raquel whispered while the delivery boy walked in. "This here arrangement's magnificent, Billy."

"Flowers for Mr. Derrick Maxwell," Billy said.

Lola could feel trouble. Raquel rushed over to receive the beautiful bouquet.

"Y'all outdid yourselves again. Thank you, hon, but there's got to be a big mistake here. This splendid bouquet has just got to be for little ol' me. Everyone knows how I just love flowers, especially roses. Why, I always get the prettiest, grandest bouquets that come in here."

"Maybe they *are* for you," Lola said, hoping to deter Raquel's behavior.

"Actually," Raquel said, "Derrick's name *is* on the card."

"What's all the commotion?" Derrick looked up, his curiosity piqued. "What's the big deal? We get flowers in here all the time."

"Derrick," Raquel held up the bouquet. "These beauties are for you this time."

"Really?" Derrick said, grinning from ear to ear.

"No way," Lola said. "It can't be."

Lola snatched the card out of Raquel's hand. Raquel quickly grabbed it back.

"He's never gotten flowers before," Lola said, giving Raquel the eye.

"Bottles of wine and candy, yes. Trips to Catalina and Tahiti, yes. But never flowers. Never, never, darlin'," Raquel said. "You little fox you. What did y'all have to do to get somethin' so gorgeous? Somebody spent a pretty penny here. Mmmm... mmm... mmm..."

"Raquel!" Derrick demanded. "Enough is enough. Bring that card over here, and read it to me. My hands are filled with suds."

"Suds? Is that what you call it?"

"Raquel! Don't be that way."

"You can wait," Raquel answered in a haughty voice, teasing him.

"No I can't," Derrick replied. "Bring it here. It's not every day a man gets flowers. Kiki, did you send these to me?"

"No... But I wish I had."

Raquel, knowing Derrick's curiosity had been aroused, kept smelling the roses. Lola knew that Raquel dared not look at her for fear of laughing out loud.

"If Derrick wants me to read the card, then I'll read it," Raquel said.

"Then read the damn thing," Nattie said. "Get it over with."

Raquel, taking tiny steps, briskly strutted over to Derrick and Kiki at the shampoo bowl, opened the card, and began to read it aloud in her breathy Southern accent.

"My dearest, darling, Derrick. You are the sensuous flame of my life, my essence."

"Well... Go on." Smiling, chest inflated, Derrick gloated.

"It is with such pleasure that I send you this exquisite bouquet of flowers in appreciation for the sheer ecstasy you have brought into my life." Raquel cleared her throat. "The excitement and joy you've created in me are still glowin' brightly, burnin' in my soul. Thinkin' of the powerful throbbin' of your lips makes me quiver all over. Our rapturous encounter was the most wonderful highlight of my life. Please, unleash your hunger again; take me past naked desire to fulfillment. Call me and let me thank you for your passionate love again, and again, and again."

Lola knew that it would not be long until Derrick would be in for a rude awakening. She could see Kiki's anger and jealously growing.

"Whoa! That's hot." Derrick puffed up like a proud parrot, beaming with pride. "Who's it from?"

"If you smile any harder, your face will break," Nattie said.

"Well, who wrote the note?" Derrick asked.

"Note? You call that a note?" Kiki's doe eyes turned into angry slits. Her smile became a nasty scowl. She lay rigid, glaring at Derrick. "What's this all about?"

"That note's got to be from Tammy or Karen," Raquel said.

"I asked you in a nice way who sent the flowers?" Ignoring Kiki, Derrick demanded to know.

"Who is this Tammy and Karen?" Kiki blurted out.

"Raquel? I'm waiting? Don't try my patience," Derrick said, glaring. "Now, read the rest of it like a good little girl."

"Don't you patronize me with that silly voice!"

"Raquel!"

"OK, OK, you've made your point." Raquel continued reading. "I'm yours forever, precious gem. With all my love and kisses... Bruce."

Derrick stood like a wax figure, speechless. It was the first time Lola had ever seen him without words.

"Who's Bruce?" Kiki demanded to know.

"No one, Kiki." Derrick gazed in shock. "Trust me on that one."

"I want to trust you." Kiki sat up. Furious beyond words, her eyes shot daggers to his heart. "Excuse me? Bruce?"

"Kiki, don't be that way. You're the one I love."

"Which Bruce is it?" Raquel asked. "There's just so many guys around named Bruce."

"That's what I'd like to know," Kiki said.

"That's a damn lie, Raquel, and you know it. Now, cut the crap," Derrick threatened. "Who really signed the card?"

"Bruce... Or do you call him Brucie?"

Raquel handed the card to Derrick. Lola watched his eyes grow large with contempt. The rage within him turned his face a frightening red.

"Who wrote this shit?" he asked, perplexed.

"You liked it before you knew it was from Bruce," Nattie said.

Lola managed to keep a straight face. Never before had she seen Derrick caught so off guard. Even though she did not approve of what Raquel had done, she was curious to see what would happen.

"I don't even know a Bruce." Derrick ripped the card into shreds, then threw his hands in the air.

"Well... Obviously Brucie knows you!" Kiki jumped up, grabbed the plastic drape from around her neck and threw it to the floor. "You lying sonofabitch, Derrick! Who *is* this Bruce? You told me you were straight! Like a fool, I believed you. Huh! Karen and Tammy? I should have known there was something wrong with you when you told me you were raised on a fruit farm in Fresno."

Kiki stomped her feet, hit him with her purse, then kicked him in the groin. Trying to catch his breath, Derrick doubled over in pain.

"I'll fix you! How dare you lie to me!"

"Ugh! Kiki... How can you turn on me like this? I love you."

"Love? Shit... Obviously love and sex are the same thing to you, just like my husband." Kiki whopped his chest with her fist. "How could you do this to me? Things like this are supposed to happen to other people, not me!"

"Kiki, please darling," Derrick said, defending himself. "I swear I'm not gay."

"Yeah! You're probably tri-sexual because you'd try anything!" Kiki looked toward Raquel and asked in a demanding voice, "Is Derrick bi-sexual?"

Raquel threw her arms up, shrugged her shoulders, and rolled her big green eyes.

"Tri-sexual sounds just about right."

"Can't you see, honey?" Derrick pleaded. "Kiki... Now listen to me. Can't you see this is a prank?"

"All I see is red. Blood red."

"Kiki, you've got to hear me out. Please... Trust me, baby. I've been set up. It's just a stupid April Fools' Day joke."

Tufts of shampoo from Kiki's long hair fell to the floor as the long-legged creature ran out of the salon screaming obscenities.

"I despise you, Derrick!" Kiki cried. "You lied to me! I hate your guts. I forgave you for other things. I put up with your whips and chains, and the hooks in your nipples, but I'll never, never forgive you for this one. I repeat... Never!"

"Thanks a lot. Thanks for nothing!" Seething, Derrick turned towards Raquel. "How could you *do* this to me?"

"Real easy." Raquel puckered her lips and blew Derrick a kiss. "April Fools' Day, darlin. Shall I sing 'Mona Lisa' to you? How about a sensual massage at the shampoo bowl? Or would you rather I tickle your crotch and twirl from your nipples?"

Derrick, angered and outraged, threw his arms in the air and roared like a lion, "Yaa-ahhh-aaaahhahahhhaaa!!!"

"Living in the jungles must be tougher than I thought. Maybe, he's part ape?" Nattie put her finger into her ear, and shook. "You've got to wonder about someone who eats four bananas a day."

"This is the lowest you have ever stooped!" Derrick pointed his finger at Raquel. "Trust me... You're going to live to regret it."

"C'mon, Derrick, lighten up," Lola said, trying to soften the mood. "It was done in fun. It's just a silly joke, and a good one at that. You've got to admit it was a real classic."

"It was. The birdbrain outdid herself this time. I'm so mad I could chew nails. The heat from my anger could melt steel."

"Chill out."

"Cool off? You must be kidding? Are you out of your mind?" Derrick opened the door to the broom closet and repeatedly banged on the leather punching bag that hung from its ceiling.

"I'm putting your face on this, Raquel. Only you could have written that trash, you and your damn romance novels."

"I love those, Derrick. I read at least two a week."

"That figures." Swinging madly, violently, he continued to vent his steam towards the punching bag. "Ugh! Kiki of all people. It took me three months to get her."

"Oh, uh huh... The mighty conqueror."

"Remember," Derrick shook his fist at Raquel, "the day's not over yet."

"Talk is cheap, Derrick," Raquel said.

"Not as cheap as you're going to be. Chopped liver doesn't go for much."

"I'm really scared, Derrick, you lightweight wimp. You and your stupid ol' lines. This should teach you to leave married women alone."

"That's none of your damn business."

"Yes it is. When you violate one woman, you violate us all."

"Don't instigate, Raquel." Nattie put her two cents worth in. "You're playing with fire. I told you so. Now, cool it. Be civil and respect each other. We have work to do. This is a professional salon, you're prominent hairdressers, trend setters. Just look at yourselves. Now maintain... Focus."

"Time will tell, you can be assured of that," Derrick threatened, glaring at Raquel. "I'll get you for this one, and rest assured it'll be where it hurts the most. Don't be a crybaby when the volcano blows."

Frustrated, Lola felt the tension in the room and she wished the episode had never occurred. She knew that Raquel, sometimes like a flighty child, got over things easily and merrily went on her way. Knowing that Derrick thrived on getting even, and especially after this incident that marred his manhood, Lola wondered how Derrick would repay Raquel.

Chapter 10

Lola breathed a deep sigh of relief. Surviving past noon, and Derrick's flowers, she felt things would finally start to settle down... Except for Raquel.

"Somethin's in the air. I know my instincts, they're developed like an animal in the wilderness," Raquel said. "My stomach's flutterin' in a funny way."

"Too much champagne on the moonlight cruise last night," Nattie said.

"No, this is a different kind of tingle," Raquel said. "It's just that I can't quite put my finger on it, but I do know that somethin' new and excitin' is about to happen. I feel it in my spirit. I didn't have a dream or nothin' like you, Lola, but this feelin' that's surroundin' me now is givin' me the quivers."

"Good quivers?"

"Yeah, sugar, the best."

Lola watched Raquel stare out of the bay window in deep thought. Her bright green eyes, lit with anticipation, stared off into the wispy white clouds.

"Lola..." Raquel said. "Girl, now tell me straight out. Are you sure this Francois guy is good lookin', or are you just tryin' to pawn some goofus off on me?"

"All you deserve is a goofus," Derrick said, still seething, cutting his client's hair. "If that..."

"I know it's April Fools' Day, Raquel, but you have to believe me when I say Francois is an eligible bachelor hunk supreme," Lola assured her. "Honest."

"But he *is* a lawyer, and you know how I hate lawyers. They're so dogmatic. The arrogance of their thinkin' makes me sick. And they actually have the audacity to think that it's a man's world."

"It *is* a man's world," Nattie said.

"Ha!" Raquel said, "No way. Where have you been?"

"I've been dreaming, girlie," Nattie said with a wink. "Look here now... Any woman who says it's not a man's world ought to take her sunglasses off and get her cataracts removed. Maybe in fifty years the majority of men will finally admit that we're equal partners in life."

"But I've really never felt that we aren't equal."

"You're young, babe," Nattie said. "You have your health, beauty, and your family's money and social standing behind you. You've earned respect with your talent, plus you work in a female environment. Even chauvinistic, abusive men turn into teddy bears when they come through that door. We see it all the time," Nattie continued, while brushing Bertha's hair. "Look, men and women need each other, but until men lighten up their control and quest for false power, a smart woman, especially a sharp cookie like me who loves her freedom, should learn how to play the game."

"Oh, I don't know about that." Raquel sprayed perfume behind her neck.

"You will, babe," Nattie said. "Everything comes to the surface when the time is right."

Lola knew that Raquel was wise for her years but she also knew that more sound judgment and clarity would come to her with experience and time. Throughout Lola's association with Nattie, Nattie had sown seeds of wisdom and faith into Lola's fertile mind, and with life's trials Lola was able to understand more clearly what Nattie had meant. Nattie, like Lola's father, taught valuable lessons by setting examples with actions.

"Lola, tell me more about this young lawyer guy." Raquel applied more lipstick to her puckered lips. "Francois... His name even sounds dreamy."

"Look, let's not blow this out of proportion," Lola said. "It's a simple job for a thirty second television commercial. Now get with the program. You're just doing the guy's make-up. Don't make a big production out of it. It's only a half hour out of your life. You'll have forgotten about him by the time Jimmy gets here at one o'clock."

"OK... OK," Raquel answered. "You've made your point."

Lola rolled her eyes, teasing Raquel. Tickled, she knew that Raquel had bit the bait. Francois was a dynamic man and Lola knew that fireworks between him and Raquel would probably ignite soon.

"But..." Lola said, posing like Marilyn Monroe, "he *is* a romantic-looking, debonair Frenchman."

"Ooo la la! A European," Raquel said. "Is he as handsome as Craig?"

"Oh, yes, but in a different way. Let me put it like this, dear, sweet girl... Your hands will be more than full, might have to gasp for air to keep up with this Adonis."

"I doubt that. I've yet to meet a guy that I can't handle."

"April Fool, then, babycakes. You're about to meet your match."

"Now I know you're lyin', Lola." Raquel put her hands on her hips. "We all know I've yet to meet a man who's strong enough to tame me."

"You'd better hope she's not lying," Nattie said. "A real powerhouse of a man who knows how to pack a hot pistol will bring a lasting smile to your face, a smile that you'll wear till the day you die."

"Raquel, what the hell do you think you really have to offer a man?" Derrick asked, still angered.

"Poor Derrick," Raquel snapped back. "You're still mad that you lost your hard-on over a bouquet of flowers. It serves you right for dating married women. Just remember, what goes around comes around."

"Smart ass. Holier-than-thou bitch. Worry about your own back yard and your own back porch," Derrick threatened. "And don't think you've heard the end of this. You either, Lola. I'll bet you were in on that crazy gag."

"Derrick darlin', your words are as harmless as you are," Raquel said.

Lola, while concentrating on her ledger sheet, thought about how Raquel and Derrick acted like children on a playground. It comforted her to know that behind their bickering, their relationship and respect for one another was genuine.

Lola's mind wandered back to some of her favorite boyfriends who had been Frenchmen. She smiled, knowing that their reputations as romantics had been well earned.

"My curiosity about Francois has gotten the best of me," Raquel said. "Now, Lola, exactly just what part of France is he from?"

"Paris, the City of Love."

"Any man in his right mind should know to not give you a second glance, let alone get involved."

"Shut up, Derrick," Raquel sneered. "Jealously doesn't look good on anyone."

"Cut it out, kids," Nattie interrupted. "Let's get on with our day. It's been a doozy so far. God knows what's next," she added, putting finishing touches on Bertha's hair-do and collecting her money.

Lola approached Bertha with lease in hand. She wanted to take this opportunity to try again to persuade Bertha to sign the lease.

"May I have a minute of your time?"

"Don't bother me now," Bertha muttered, glaring at Lola. "Just get out of my way. I'm finished here. I'm hungry. I have to eat."

Bertha left, sliding her feet, dragging the weight she could not lift. Frustrated and feeling vulnerable, Lola felt a heavy hopelessness in her heart.

"Be patient," Raquel said. "She's just a controller, likes everything to happen accordin' to her own timin'. She'll sign it later. She will, sugar... I just know it."

Lola was aware that the future of all of them was in Bertha's hands. She could only hope for the best. Unlike Raquel, though, Lola was afraid to start over again. New beginnings had been difficult for her. Raquel's father, a Marine, had been transferred often when she was young. Lola wished that she could be more adaptable like Raquel had learned to be.

Lola was about to thank Raquel for her optimistic support when she noticed Raquel's face light up like a Christmas tree while watching the strikingly good looking young gentleman walk up to the salon door. Strong and powerful, each of his long strides seemed to shake the ground beneath his feet.

"My kind of man," Raquel mouthed to Lola while smoothing her mini skirt. "Intoxicatin' kinda guy."

Lola knew that the largeness of his presence would immediately attract Raquel's attention. Laughing to herself as he swung open the door, Lola watched Raquel thunderstruck, standing like a mime frozen in space.

Francois' shifting eyes quickly swept across the salon. He was even more exquisite than Lola remembered him to be.

Feeling his magnetism spark her skin like electricity, Lola watched Nattie raise an eyebrow and position herself in a spot so as not to miss one single movement of the scenario. Lola admired

Francois' strength as he stood mightily with the confidence of a man who knew he was well hung.

"Hello," Francois said in an alluring baritone, his eyes piercing into Raquel's. "Are you Lola?"

Lola noticed that Raquel was taken aback by his compelling good looks. Raquel, eyes opened wide, stood awestruck.

Lola could see that her breath had vanished at the sight of his extraordinary appearance, and she knew that the magnitude Francois exuded was the kind Raquel loved to conquer, needed to conquer, wanted to conquer.

Flustered, Raquel acted like she was overwhelmed and dizzy. Having trouble speaking, she blurted out, "I'm Lola."

Lola was shocked at her behavior, but she remained silent. Never had she seen Raquel so shook, so caught off guard.

"I'm pleased to meet you," Francois said, standing upright and tall.

Dressed in classic pleated pants, a polo shirt draped over his rippling muscles, and brown loafers the size of battleships, Lola knew he resembled a model in *GQ* magazine. His straight ebony hair was brushed to one side. Bronzed skin covered the finely-chiseled bone structure of his face. Prominent eyebrows framed intense sapphire eyes, looking to Lola like precious gems in a bed of white snow.

Assured of himself, he extended his hand to Raquel. "How do you do, Lola."

"I'm sorry," Raquel said, fumbling and leaning against the chair for support. "That's Lola over there."

"Hello to you all," Francois said in a confused tone. He turned and offered his hand to Lola. "It's nice to meet you. How do you do?"

"Fine, thank you. I see you found us OK," Lola said, trying to cover Raquel's embarrassment.

"Yes, Sam gave me perfect directions." Francois paused a moment while studying Lola's face. "I remember you now... From the Chamber of Commerce party. I never forget an attractive woman with a sweet dimple."

"Yeah, " Lola blushed. "That was a fun night."

"Yes it was, only it went by too fast. I want to thank you for getting me in at the last minute like this. I appreciate it. Sam recommended you highly."

"Oh, I always tease Sam about being my agent. You have a very talented man doing your television commercial," Lola said. "His writing is very effective, and his creative eye is trained to look for the most minute details. That's why he wins so many awards for his commercials. I've sure learned a lot from Sam."

"I'm confident I'm in good hands with both you and Sam."

"Thank you. Actually, because I don't have the extra time, Raquel will be doing your make-up today. She's very talented."

Lola noticed Raquel's rose-blushed face as Francois fixed his gaze on her. Lola knew from past experience with mighty, charismatic men that Raquel must surely feel the effects of his crystal clear eyes, enough to make her knees weak.

"Trust me," Lola said. "Raquel will take good care of you."

"How do you do?" Raquel said in a sensual voice, putting her hand out to shake his. Gleaming, her eyes moved into his.

Francois looked into the depths of Raquel's green eyes. Lola could tell that Francois was fully aware of his rugged, masculine appeal and that he knew he could get just about anything he wanted and anyone he desired. Yes, Lola thought, Raquel had finally met her match. While Raquel studied him silently, Lola wondered if Raquel would gain her composure enough to take care of business. Knowing that Raquel had never had such an exhilarating response to any man, Lola took delight in watching a love story in the making.

"It's a pleasure to meet you, Raquel," he said with his saucy, provocative French accent, his words breaking the intent look they shared.

To Lola's relief, his words seemed to interrupt Raquel's uneasy state of being.

"I'm sure it is." Raquel's delicate hand was almost crushed by his strong handshake. "Be gentle with the merchandise, honey. These hands are gonna bring you good luck today," Raquel said, her strong confidence back.

"Luck?" he said, surprised.

"Yes, luck," Raquel said, her eyes piercing his. "Lucky people bring good luck to others."

"What makes you so lucky?"

"Let's just say I was born lucky."

"Then I'm a lucky guy to know you." His steely blue eyes shot Raquel a covetous glance.

"You've got that one right. Now, what's you name, big fella?"

"Francois Devereaux."

"The third?"

"Yes... How did you know?"

"You look like a third."

Lola could tell Francois was the playful type. Her instincts told her that Raquel was in for a ride, what kind exactly, she did not know. Time would tell. It usually did, especially with Raquel. Amazed, Lola watched Raquel's eyes hungrily slide slowly over his every curve. It was obvious to Lola that Francois did not get his magnificent body from baling hay.

"So, you're the make-up artist." Francois let his eyes roam over Raquel's figure.

"And you must pump iron." Raquel stood back and caressed him with her eyes.

Lola looked at this Hercules as he stood strong in his delight. Francois eyed Raquel up and down with the finesse of a fox. Raquel posed like a runway model and let him enjoy his feast.

"I see you like fine art," he said with a smirk.

"I think we both do," Raquel answered with a wink.

"I do," he said, admiring her voluptuous bosom through her sheer blouse.

Lola watched Raquel take another pose and felt that Francois milked the situation. Watching his sensuous face, direct and challenging, Lola pegged him as an aggressive young lawyer with an ego bigger than his dreams.

Raquel strutted towards the facial and make-up room, emphasizing the sway of her hips like a hula dancer. Lola laughed, knowing that Raquel, like Nattie, enjoyed using the salon as her theatrical stage.

"If you lose me, honey, just follow the scent," Raquel said, tossing her long red hair.

Francois marveled with approval at the oscillation of Raquel's hips under her electric-blue mini skirt. Lola saw his face beam with joy as she enjoyed the show, which got better as the day wore on.

"Ahhhh..." Francois said. "That skirt is so tight that if you had a dime in your pocket, I could read the date."

"Francois," Raquel said in rebuttal, "is it true that every lawyer has a pimp for an older brother?"

"Why, yes, *mon chérie*," he said with a devilish grin, "so they always have someone to look up to."

Within seconds, Francois was at Raquel's heels. Lola was glad that he looked at her with something deeper than mere lustful male interest. She felt that their attraction for each other had the possibilities to turn into a meaningful friendship.

"What's the game plan, sweetheart?" Francois asked in a tantalizing tone.

Lola watched Raquel execute her sleek moves as she opened the door to the facial room. After Francois entered, Raquel darted a provocative glance towards Lola, wiggled her eyebrows, and waved her hand like Miss America. Raquel leaned against the wall, accidentally pushing in the button to the salon's intercom system. Surprised, Lola wanted to tell Raquel what she had just done, but before she could say anything, Raquel had shut the door. From the look on Raquel's face, Lola knew that, curtains or no curtains, live theater was about to take place.

"Nattie, did you see what Raquel just did?"

"Yep," Nattie smiled. "Oh, young love."

"How could she not feel the button in her back?" Lola asked.

"That's the last thing on her mind," Derrick said.

"Yeah," Nattie said, shampooing her client. "Derrick, get the tape recorder. We don't want her to try to deny anything."

"This is going to be *hot*. After all, we know who showed her the ropes," Derrick boasted.

"Please... Spare me!" Lola said. "That intercom is about the only thing in this old building that works well."

"Shhh..." Nattie said. "The show's started. The anticipation reminds me of the good old days of radio when I was a child. I love to be entertained. Amos and Andy was my favorite. They were so funny."

Embarrassed for Raquel, Lola shook her head. It *was* April Fools' Day. Pranks happened, one way or another. Willingly, she went with the flow and hoped for the best.

"Here?" Francois asked, his voice appeared loud and clear over the intercom.

"Just follow the fingertip, honey, and hop on up," Raquel said, her voice echoing throughout the salon.

Lola knew that Raquel had her clients sit on the facial bed instead of the chair.

"But of course," Francois said. "This looks more comfortable."

"It is," Raquel said. "I'm so tall, darlin', that it's difficult for me to apply make-up when someone sits low in a chair. I don't want to end up a hunchback, you know."

"You'd still be beautiful. If there were a million-dollar bill, your picture would be on it."

"Francois, your words are music to my ears. Oh! How I love a well-bred charmer. You're definitely a man with good taste. I can tell you and I will get along just fine."

"Shhh..." Lola said, trying to quiet Derrick's snickering.

"She's so full of it," Derrick said. "Brought the buffalo chips all the way from their ranch in Texas."

Lola saw Derrick's jealousy surface and it disgusted her. Then Francois' full-bodied voice floated through the air again.

"I don't doubt for a second that we will be good friends."

"We'll see," Raquel said. "Just slide onto the table, honey... Boy, that was fast."

"I'm ready," Francois said.

"I'm sure you were born ready."

"Fourth of July, to be exact. 4 a.m."

"Do you always wake women up that early?" Raquel asked in an intriguing tone.

"Real women, yes!"

"Real women?" Derrick exclaimed. "Raquel's not even human! What does he think he's got in there?"

"Something you couldn't handle," Nattie laughed, rolling her client's hair. "Raquel's won blue ribbons and a lot of money for riding Brahman bulls. The rodeo circuit is still waiting for her return. Takes a real he-man to tangle with that."

From past experience Lola knew that Francois' type of man would get sexually aroused while having his make-up applied. Lola knew that Raquel could handle the situation. Lola had always joked with Raquel about having to put a large plastic drape around a man's neck because at least if his erection went into full bloom, it would be covered and she would not have to deal with it. "Unless, of course, I decide I want to," was Raquel's usual response.

"Let me fasten this drape around your neck, darlin'," Raquel said. "I wouldn't want to ruin your clothes with make-up."

"That isn't necessary, *mon chérie*. I'll just take my shirt off and make life easier for both of us."

"No, that won't be necessary.... Hmmm... You're quick. Go ahead, have it your way."

"Lola, the guy is slick," Nattie said, pouring herself a glass of wine. "Hot Dog! He's already half naked."

Lola laughed out loud because she knew that Raquel thrived on having a real live-wire on her hands, a playmate to flirt with.

"After your puffed up chest goes down," Raquel said, "you can throw your shirt on the chair."

"I'm ready now, gorgeous."

"I'll bet you are."

"Let's get this show on the road."

"Are you always this considerate?"

"No," Francois said. "Only for you."

"Feels like a heat wave," Raquel said. "You sure breathe hard."

"Hopefully the heat won't melt the silicone."

"Excuse me? Silicone? I ought to slap you for that comment," Raquel said. "Wrong woman, dearie."

"Thank God. I like my women to be natural."

"Natural at what?"

"At what comes natural," Francois said, laughingly. "But of course."

Lola felt that Raquel was playing with fire and thought that maybe it was a good thing that the intercom was on.

"Cute titties, Francois," Raquel said. "What's with that one single hair growin' out of the middle of your chest? Must have taken all your hormones to grow that crop. Good thing you're a lawyer instead of a farmer."

"That's all that grew. What can I say?"

Lola knew that Raquel talked to him like that to intimidate him and calm him down. It was all part of the territory.

It warmed Lola's heart to hear the vulnerable sweetness of a little boy come out in Francois' voice at that moment. Lola knew that Raquel had figured that statement would give her an edge over the situation and hoped his embarrassment would dampen his predator instincts. Sam was a stickler for promptness, and Lola hoped that Raquel kept her focus on getting Francois ready in time for the commercial.

"I need some popcorn. How about it, Suzy?" Derrick asked. "A little popcorn for the pretty lady while I finish your hair?"

"This isn't the movies."

"Lola, a show is a show," Derrick said. "Anyway, this is better than the movies."

Lola wondered if Derrick would ever grow up. She wished he would go for counseling. She knew professional help would help him get beyond his hang-ups.

"What are you doing?" Francois asked.

"I've laid out the products and brushes I need to begin the application. This light moisturizer will prepare your skin for the foundation."

"With her supple fingers," Derrick mimicked, "she massaged the lotion onto his face and neck, then feathered her hands over his shoulders."

"Eat your heart out," Lola said. "My, you're quite an actor."

"You sound like one of those romance novels you hate so much," Nattie said. "We don't pick on you men for having your magazines."

Lola's mind flashed through the day's happenings. Never in her wildest thoughts had she ever dreamed she would have had to live through what she had over the past six years. Sometimes she wondered if she had known what was involved, if she would have chosen cosmetology as her profession.

"That warm lotion feels so good on my skin," Francois said in a sexy tone. "Your tender touch relaxes me. Your fingers move to every muscle on my face and neck."

"It's all in the job," Raquel said. "Lucky for you, I'm good at what I do."

"This is heavenly," he said. "I feel that a glorious angel is touching me."

"That's because I'm from heaven," Raquel teased.

"Do you have proof?"

"Just watch me adjust my halo," Raquel said. "Tell me what color you see?"

"Candy-apple red. I thought angels had white halos?"

"Only the borin' ones, sugarplum."

"Something tells me you're not boring at all."

"That somethin' is right," Raquel said with confidence.

Lola knew that small talk would get Raquel through this predicament, just as it had many times before. Within minutes, like so many other male clients had done, Francois would relax and go with the flow.

"You do your job with such expertise," Francois stated. "I'm impressed."

"This latex sponge for blendin' helps make my work look good," Raquel said. "Is this your first commercial?"

"Yes. I thought it would be a good way to advertise my new firm."

"Congratulations on your new law office."

"Thank you. I'd love to show it to you sometime soon."

"That'll be nice," Raquel said. "I'd like that. Did y'all decorate it yourself?"

"Yes. I had a great time designing the interior."

"Tell me about it," Raquel said.

"No mirrors on the ceiling like in here, but there is a jungle of plants, statues of tigers and eagles, rich cherry woods, cloisonné lamps and fixtures from China, Impressionistic paintings from France, a marble bust of myself, and lots of brass from Italy. I've envisioned this office since I studied at Harvard."

"Louis XIV furniture?"

"Why, yes. How did you know?"

"Just a feelin'. It's my favorite, too," Raquel said. "Dreams do come true, don't they, darlin'?"

"I'm living proof of it," Francois said. "That's one of the wonderful things about life. My parents were right. They always told me to plant my seeds in fertile soil, focus, and commit to my goals. And I did. I've worked long and hard to get to this point in my life. It is an honor to be able to work. Every ounce of effort has been worth it all."

"I'm happy for you. Many people in this world wish they could say what you just said. But the wannabees aren't disciplined enough to go for their dreams and follow through with what it takes to get the job done."

"Are you?"

"Yes. I'm happy with my accomplishments so far."

"How long have you been in the beauty business?"

"Darlin'... I've been fixin' hair since Barbie."

"What do you consider your greatest achievement in life?"

"Playing the piano. You see, as a hairdresser, I make one person at a time happy. As a concert pianist, I make hundreds of people happy all at the same time."

"Now I know why you're so good with your hands. You sound like a responsible person."

"I like responsibility, but I like it with enjoyment. Daddy taught us to play as hard as we worked."

"Likes responsibility? Ha..." Lola exclaimed. "Six years... I'm still waiting for her to show it."

"Your definitions of responsibility are different," Nattie said. "You girls are both angels, but you're from different clouds."

Knowing that human beings are individuals, Lola knew Nattie was right and that she should rid herself of pre-conceived ideas.

"You can practice your lines on me if you'd like," Raquel said.

"Isn't that what I have been doing?" Francois teased.

"The commercial, silly."

"Thank you, but I've practiced them all last night, and I have them down pat. It's funny, Raquel, you excite me, but you make me peaceful, too."

"You just like a woman's touch."

"Yes... A gentle woman like you."

From the sound of their conversation, Lola felt that Raquel and Francois were earning each other's trust and she knew that was the foundation of any solid, lasting relationship.

"You have an incredible face," Raquel said. "Just look at these curly thick lashes, long and luxuriant, gorgeous almond-shaped eyes... Your cheekbones and nose are those of a nobleman."

"Why, thank you."

"Does your beauty go all the way to your heart?" Raquel asked.

"What do you think?" Francois asked.

"I hope it does."

From that statement, Lola knew that Raquel liked how she felt with Francois, but because she cared about Raquel, she hoped this blooming relationship would have a good future. Nattie's words of wisdom, "true love makes you strong," echoed in Lola's mind. Like she had done many times herself while applying make-up to an attractive man, Lola knew that Raquel would let herself fantasize about getting romantically involved with Francois. Lola's reflection was interrupted by the intercom.

"When our eyes meet like this," Raquel said, "I feel like you're lookin' into my heart like it's an open book or somethin'."

"What's that supposed to mean?"

"You know... You're delvin' into my private space, and that's not nice."

"Yes it is. You're doing the same to me and you're touching my heart."

Lola knew that Raquel had never believed in love at first sight, and wondered if Raquel was changing her mind. From their conversation and intonations over the intercom, Lola knew that Raquel and Francois seemed to be in the process of discovering each other.

"I hate to admit it," Francois said, "but, I haven't been looking forward to this."

"It's not so bad. Actually, people love havin' their make-up done. I guarantee you'll live through it. I haven't lost a client yet."

"You won't lose me," Francois smiled. "Why do I need make-up?"

"The light colors bring areas of the face forward, and the darker colors push them back," Raquel explained. "I'm usin' highlights and shadows to make planes of depth on your face."

"Like a portrait artist?"

"Yes. The camera would film your face flat if I didn't create this illusion. Plus, I have to even the tone of your skin with foundation and powder it well with French milled powder so the cameras won't pick up shiny spots on your face," Raquel said. "There are better ways to shine, darlin'."

"How did you get to be so smart?"

"Oh... I listen to people when they talk and I've taken the time to cultivate what I was born with." Raquel continued to work. "Now don't you go and try to break my concentration with that piercin' stare. I'm not gonna flinch just because you're scrutinizin' every square inch of my face. Sam demands promptness. He trusts me, and I want to keep it like that."

"I've never seen such incredible skin."

"Thank you. It's as soft as it looks," Raquel said. "Hey, you! Ah, ah, ah, big boy... Put that hand down."

"Your skin must feel like fine silk."

"It does. Hands off the goods, sugar. You've got to take my word for it on this one. Now cool it. You're perspirin' and radiatin' heat like a furnace."

"Is it always this warm in here?" he asked.

"No."

"You are so pretty. I love looking at your face."

"My face, huh? You'll have to raise your eyes a tad bit higher. Here's a Kleenex... Your mouth is waterin', and your hormones are actin' up."

"What's this for?" he asked.

"To catch your drool. You'd better shape up or I'll powder this puff and smack you in the face. Now relax. I have a job to get done here. I'll put the fan on a little higher."

"That breeze feels better," Francois said. "It got a bit stuffy in this small room."

"Chill out, darlin. It won't be long till show time. Just relax, bubba baby, I've got the fan on high and it's not doin' much good. You're perspirin' too much. The foundation is runnin' and makin' a mess. You're makin' my job hard for me."

"It's hard for me, too," Francois said.

"Please, don't remind me, and quit smilin' like a Cheshire cat," Raquel said. "I'm gonna blot your face with this tissue and re-apply the foundation."

"Oh... The music, your touch, that perfume, I just can't help myself," he said.

"You'd better help yourself, or I'll give you a knuckle sandwich you'll remember for a long time."

"Coming from you, the pain will be pleasure."

Lola surmised that Francois was the type of man who thrived on fiery verbal exchange, and that he enjoyed this type of flirtatious warfare.

"You don't give up, do ya?" Raquel said. "Now, calm down, buster."

"I'm relentless. Darling, I..."

"Put that nasty hand down," Raquel said. "Don't you darlin' me. And grabbin' at my breasts like that... Shame on you. And I thought you were well-mannered. I'm gonna bop you upside your head. This is one mission you won't complete. You just keep your hands to yourself."

Lola could hear Raquel tease Francois in her coquettish manner. From the sound of Raquel's voice, Lola knew that she was loving every second of her rendezvous with Francois.

"I knew it was coming," Derrick said, grabbing his curling iron. "Love them jugs. I knew he'd go for her boobs before long. He's definitely a boob man."

"We know that's what you'd do," Nattie said.

"Is it?" Suzy asked.

"No, Sweetie... Everyone knows that I'm a true gentleman."

"Sure, Derrick," Lola said. "Don't make me gag."

Lola could tell, from the sounds of things, that Francois was in hot pursuit of Raquel, and Raquel, in turn, was giving him a run for his money. Like a well-bred aristocrat who wore his money well, Francois' style was smooth and sophisticated. Lola knew that if any man could tame Raquel, it would be Francois. Lola felt that Francois was the kind of man who would embrace life like a mountain climber would tackle a ten-thousand foot cliff.

"You are a work of exquisite art, Raquel, and I am a true Frenchman."

"And 100% man," Raquel said.

"Oh, I love a redhead who flares easily."

"Shape up, now. I mean it," Raquel said. "I'm gonna powder you for the third and last time."

"You're pretty quick with your hands, little lady."

"Men like you leave me no choice."

"I'm in love."

"You're not in love, Francois. You're in heat."

"Yes, I deny nothing."

Lola knew Raquel could handle his advances because she had dealt with a lot more than he had dished out. Besides, Lola liked his lovable character and playfulness. He ranked high on her list for his sexy lips alone. Lola felt that Raquel and Francois' attraction for each other was mutual, and she was pleased. She loved Raquel like a sister, and she wanted the best for her.

"Now, hold still," Raquel said. "Just a dash of lip tint and we'll be done. Now rub your lips together. Uh huh, side to side."

When Lola heard Raquel laugh out loud, she knew it was because Francois was rubbing his lips together with the grace of a baboon. As a make-up artist, Lola had told Raquel that most men made a big production out of rubbing their lips together. They looked like adorable little boys. Lola laughed as she thought if only the men knew how cute they looked.

"Now, blot your lips, and you'll be ready to roll," Raquel said.

"How's that?" Francois asked.

"I've yet to meet a man who didn't know how to blot his lips. Why is that?"

"As young boys we watched our mothers and aunts. As young men, we watch the ladies."

"Great. We're finished."

"Thanks, Raquel."

"The pleasure's been all yours, darlin'."

"It sure has. So how about dinner tonight?"

"Only if you promise to behave."

"Me?" Francois teased. "Behave?"

"Yes."

"OK, I promise... Your place or mine?"

"Mama Corelli's down the street will be just fine. Come back to the salon around six. I'll be finished workin' by then."

"Fantastic... Sounds like a deal. I will be counting the minutes."

"Listen!" Lola said, putting her thumb in the air. "I knew he'd ask Raquel out. He sees what he likes and he's going for it."

"He'd be a damn fool if he didn't," Derrick said.

"Those two have something good going on," Nattie said. "This was all meant to be. It feels right. He'll be a nice addition to our family."

Lola hoped Francois would be Raquel's Mr. Right, and instinctively felt that Raquel was closer to her dreams than she thought.

"What's that look in your eyes, Francois? It's so sincere," Raquel said. "We're finished. Time to go to work and film your award-winnin' commercial."

"No... On the contrary," Francois confirmed, "we're just beginning right here."

"Oh?"

"I love the way you moisten your lips with that sensual tongue," Francois said. "It drives me wild."

Lola knew that Raquel welcomed his words and would ignore the strong voice of reason within her that said a firm 'no' for now. From the cracking in Raquel's voice, Lola could tell that Raquel was excited and her heart was pounding wildly.

"My darling, you're eyes are lovely and you've captured my heart," Francois spoke softly. "I not only think you are a remarkable, beautiful woman, but I have a profound sense of your inner beauty."

Lola heard Raquel purr like a baby cheetah and knew that Raquel must be loving the jungle magic between Francois and herself.

"Words are too powerful to be thrown around loosely," Raquel warned.

"There is nothing loose about me, especially my words that express my deepest feelings for you, my sweet."

"But, Francois... You hardly know me."

"I know all I need to know. My father knew at first glance that he would marry my mother. Darling, my words are not frivolous. Know that. I want for us to get to know each other very well, and I look forward to sharing intimate moments with you. Ah... Making memories with you will be so wonderful."

"Yes, they will."

"Boy, will you just listen to that smooth romantic!" Nattie said. "Damn he's good. So poetic. Sends me sailing."

"Take notes, Derrick, file the good stuff," Lola insisted. "You could add some fresh material to the lines you've been using to con your women."

"You two just can it," Derrick said, shaking his finger. "I've had enough of all of you for one day."

Lola laughed, knowing Derrick had already memorized every one of Francois' lovely words.

"You are the spectacular woman I have seen in my dreams," Francois said. "So beautiful, every ounce of you is pure love."

"Déjà vu?" Raquel said. "I love the way you ripple kisses down my neck. I wanna believe you."

"Déjà vu, yes. From another time and space, we were one. Believe me, it's so natural for me to embrace you, to be so close, smell your fragrance..."

"Oh, Francois..." Raquel purred. "Your reckless passion is doin' things to me."

"Look out!" Lola said. "It's getting hot and hairy in there."

"Tremors of pure desire bolted through her body," Nattie spoke, acting dramatically. "Breathless, heart vibrating, she yielded to him, answering his kisses with her mouth opened fully. Wanting the kisses to go on, she clung to his rugged body, feeling distinctly his heated skin and hardened muscles beneath her hands."

"Put a lid on it, Nattie," Derrick said. "You sound like one of those stupid romance books."

"The magnetic pull of his masculinity drew her in closer to him," Nattie continued in an authoritative stage voice. "Uncontrollable sounds of passion escaped her lips. Gently, he brushed back her crimson hair with his hand and put his full lips to her ear and blew gently."

"Don't tell me you read that trash?" Derrick asked.

"Never had the time." Nattie popped a big bubble. "I was too busy living it."

"Nattie, you're too much," Lola said. "You should have been an actress."

"I have a captive audience right here," Nattie laughed. "My client's got tint on her head. She ain't goin' nowhere."

Lola watched how Nattie made light of the situation. Lola was uncomfortable listening to the intimacy between Raquel and Francois. His melodic moans expressed his desire for Raquel. She knew it was an intense moment, and she did not want to interrupt it even if they did not know she was listening.

"Speak to me, *mon chérie*," Francois said, full of want. "Raquel... I love you. Tell me you love me, too. Tell me you're feeling what I am feeling. I need to know."

"But..."

"Don't make this difficult for me. I've never been so honest with a woman in my life. So many times I've wanted to tell a woman what I just told you, but I couldn't. Finally, I know what the poets have been writing about for centuries. Darling, tell me you're feeling the same as I am cherishing," Francois pleaded.

"Look me in my eyes and tell me the truth," Raquel sincerely said. "Are you still practicin' with the pretty ladies or do you really want the real thing?"

"Believe me when I say this. I've wanted a commitment for a long time, it's just that I never found a woman who made me feel so alive."

"What I'm feelin' is beyond anything I've ever felt," Raquel said. "My chest is burstin' with a power that makes me feel so good that I want to cry tears of joy."

"Let me hold you close. Tell me more."

"I've never felt like this before, Francois. Don't toy with me." Raquel's voice cracked with emotion. "I won't allow that. I'm not into games. Either you're the greatest con artist, or you're a sensational romantic."

"My intentions are honorable. I will prove it to you."

Lola wondered how he would prove it.

"Just watch... He'll give her money," Derrick said. "He knows that money talks to a woman like Raquel."

"Your ruby ring is so beautiful," Raquel said, sighing, "and it looks so good on my finger, but does this means I'm supposed to trust you and let you sweep me off of my feet?"

"Yes... But of course," Francois said. "In our society money makes a difference. Here's my wallet. There's $9,000 in my checking account. The credit cards have a combined $100,000.00. You've got all afternoon to spend it. Please, be my guest. This is the start of something very special for the two of us."

Lola was amazed at his generosity. Never had she personally experienced anything like it from the men she had dated, men who claimed they loved her, but she had always known it was possible because her father naturally gave freely to her mother. Warm thoughts of Craig enveloped her. His phone call earlier confirmed her feelings and their relationship. Lola felt secure in her growing love for him.

"How about that gorgeous gold cross and chain?" Raquel teased. "It would look just splendid around my pretty little ol' neck."

"Yes it would, but this was a gift to my great-grandfather from the Pope. I have not taken it off since my twenty-first birthday."

"OK, I'll let you pass on that one. Oh, Francois... How I love sayin' your name. I have such feelin's in my heart."

"A throbbing ache for him grew between her thighs," Nattie giggled. "She wrapped her legs tightly around his waist, their mouths still ravenously desiring each other's. Trembling against his virile nearness, his naked chest melded to hers. She felt the thundering of his heart pounding against her breasts. Her surrender to him was shameless, instant, and total."

"Nattie," Lola exclaimed. "Cut it out. This is embarrassing. We should have told Raquel that the intercom was on."

"What? And miss out on the entertainment? Lighten up, babe."

"I wouldn't trade this for nothing," Derrick laughed. "And to think that I have it all on tape. Oh, I'm going to have fun with this.

I'll get her back for that idiotic flower stunt. Damn her anyway... I'll never get Kiki back after that stunt!"

Lola knew Derrick well enough to know that he would get his revenge. She just hoped it would not hurt Raquel.

"I do love you, Francois," Raquel said. "Until now, I never believed in love at first sight."

"I love you, too, darling. I *always* believed in love at first sight. You are truly the woman of my dreams. I've vaguely seen you many times. I've gambled, but I've waited," Francois said. "I got so tired of waiting."

"Me too."

"Having you in my arms like this, feeling your spirit and warmth, assures me that it was worth the wait."

"For years I had illusions of sharin' passion with a powerful, sensual man; a free-spirited guy who knew no boundaries. Now my dream's becomin' a reality. I feel like I'm in a daze."

"For me, too, my sweet darling."

Lola noticed that the facial room became quiet.

"I'm glad that's over!" Lola said. "We've invaded their privacy enough."

"He's dimming the lights from the chandelier," Derrick joked. "Now he's smothering her body with tender kisses while unbuttoning her blouse. Not knowing exactly what to expect, Raquel lets go and trusts him. She watches his hands burn a path from her bare breasts to her curvaceous hips. His mouth demands full surrender. Breathless, his fierce heat against her, Raquel willingly allows him take her to heights unknown."

"Hey, Derrick," Nattie said. "You learn fast. That was a spicy dissertation."

"Derrick, you must have read a few romance novels yourself to be able to whip out lines like that."

"No way! I'm a suave guy with style. Open your eyes and take a good look, baby. I wouldn't be caught dead reading lewd trash like that."

Lola knew he had. She had remembered those same lines from one of the romance novels Raquel had recently loaned her.

Chapter 11

"My God! Will you listen to those carnal sounds coming from those two lovebirds! Just listen to Raquel!" Lola said, rolling her bugged out eyes towards Nattie. "Do you believe this?"

"You can bet Raquel isn't checking out the cracks in the ceiling," Derrick laughed. "In more ways than one, that sex kitten is a wild woman."

"Her lungs are as big as Texas. The entire neighborhood can't help but hear that howl. I hope the vibrations don't crack these old windows." Nattie lit another cigarette and took a deep drag. "Ah... Love is in the air. One look at Francois and I knew that he was the one to do the trick for Raquel. Every woman needs a Francois in her life, at least once."

"Unbelievable! How could such a big noise come out of a girl her size?" Embarrassed, Lola shook her head. "I never knew Raquel was a screamer."

"Screamer? You call that a screamer? Why, there's not a word in the English language to describe *that* sound. Calling her a screamer is an understatement." Nattie shook her head. "Hot damn! I thought that sexy cowboy made her sing out loud. That was a murmur compared to what this Frenchman's bringing out of her. Boy, she's got a set of lungs."

"She's got a set of everything," Derrick laughed. "She used to be a mezzo-soprano. Evidently he's found the right technique to make a soprano out of her."

"Something you couldn't do," Lola laughingly said.

"Yeah! But I had a helluva good time trying."

"Yeah, all three minutes of it," Lola taunted. "Encounters like that aren't worth messing up the sheets."

Lola giggled and listened to everyone laugh. She knew that romantic interludes in the facial room had always been common practice, but Raquel's hollering was too much for her to fathom.

"Just listen to her. My oh my, the girl has no shame. I've never heard anything like this in my life," Lola said. "My neighbor, Joe, whose bedroom wall is next to mine, has made a few women wail out in ecstasy, but never anything like this!"

"I always knew she was part wildcat," Derrick said, putting another tape in the recorder. "This is Class-A evidence. It'll be a long time before I let her live this one down."

"Gathering ammunition?" Nattie asked.

"Yep... I sure am. She'll do anything to get this tape and this is just the beginning. I'm going to get her good for what she did to me this morning."

"Derrick, don't be that way. Revenge is disastrous. Come on out and just admit that she got you this time. Laugh and shrug it off."

"No way, Lola."

"Don't hold a grudge," Nattie said. "It will only make you sick."

"Boy, from the sound of it, I guess Raquel finally met her match," Lola exclaimed.

"To say the least. Can't wait to get the details." Nattie popped three bubble gums into her mouth and chomped on them like a ravenous dog with a biscuit. "I remember singing like that one time, one of the many highlights of my colorful life."

"Colorful is a soft-pedal. Tainted would be a better choice of words," Lola said. "I've worked with you for six years and I've never heard you tell the same story twice."

"And you won't, either. Why, I've got multitudes of tales to tell, enough stories to fill up a shelf in the library. Maybe I'll write a book some day and give Joan Collins a run for her money."

"Spare me, Nattie," Derrick said. "You've been saying that for years. Talk, talk, talk. Everyone wants to be a writer. Everybody has a story, but few write them. Put a pen to the parchment and show a little integrity. Write the damn book. Get a ghost writer if you have to. Pay to have it edited. Make your fortune on the trash, laugh all the way to the bank, and retire all of us in style."

Lola knew nothing would ever stop Nattie from telling her stories. It was her special time of glory to have center stage, exploit her exploits, and give her philosophy on life, love and sex.

"February 16, 1968, San Luis Obispo, the Pizza Pantry on Marsh Street. That's where I met him," Nattie began, blowing and popping her gum without it sticking on her face. "His friend Nick introduced us. We took one look at each other and we were paralyzed with ecstasy. I barely got out a hello."

"You?"

"Yes... Me! It was more than love at first sight. It had never happened before and it's never happened since. He swept me into his arms, walked me to the dance floor for a slow dance, French kissed me, and the rest is history. His name was Ron, a baseball player and engineering student from Cal Poly." Nattie lit another cigarette. "Ron was a Frenchman, too. Boy! Frenchman are the smoothest of them all. I should know. How many times I've tried them all. South American men run a close second, especially the ones from Rio. Anyway, Ron was six two, dark hair, white skin, and blue blue eyes the color of Avila Beach before pollution. Best kisser in the world. Damn! That's a lost art. It went out the door with common sense. I always told Ron he ought to open up a kissing school. I wonder what ever happened to him? Man oh man, could he kiss!"

It was impossible for Lola to tune out the sexy sounds and howls escaping the facial room while Nattie told her story. "I hope this is over soon," Lola said, blushing. "I can't handle another heart attack in here today."

"Not to worry, my dear," Nattie said, cutting Mrs. Scott's hair. "There's enough mouth-to-mouth resuscitation going on in that facial room to save everyone in the intensive care unit at Mercy Hospital."

Lola spiked Didi's bangs and sent her on her way.

"Thank you. Have a nice day," Didi said after she paid Lola and made her way to the front door.

"Thanks, but you gave me too much," Lola said.

"The extra was for the entertainment. Thank Raquel for me," Didi said, smiling. "And good luck to you, Lola. I'll keep a positive thought for the salon."

"Thanks."

"I think I'll go to my husband's office for lunch."

"Lunch?"

"Yeah, lunch," Didi said, wiggling her hips. "Plus he loves hearing the exciting stories of what goes on in here."

Lola watched Derrick, a mischievous look on his face, stroll over to the door of the facial room.

"Hey, what are you up to?" Lola asked.

"None of your business."

"It *is* my business."

"Just watch."

"You scoundrel," Nattie blurted out. "You're a fool to do the unthinkable."

"No problem." Derrick put his fist up as if he were going to pound on the door. "She'll sing after this."

"Derrick, don't you dare," Lola stated in a firm tone, outraged at his actions. "How could you think of such a stupid thing, let alone do it?"

"You bang on that door and you're dead meat, bubba baby," Nattie bellowed out. "I mean it. Raquel will strangle you with her bare hands for ruining the best orgasm of her life, and I won't jump in to help you this time. Hells bells, she's making history. Let her have a good time."

"Nattie's right. God knows how many lifetimes a woman waits for this kind of magic to happen. Back in Texas, you know, women have been known to string up a man for less. Raquel's a Texan by birth. You'd better watch it. You know how she gets revenge."

"It'll be worth it, ladies," Derrick said, arrogantly, "especially after that stunt with the flowers."

"There's no hope for you," Nattie said. "Revenge is blinding you. I can see it. I'm not going to say another word. You're on your own now."

Lola beelined over to stop Derrick.

"No, don't!" she yelled.

Lola was too late. Derrick repeatedly banged on the facial room door with all his might, slamming down so hard that the door and walls of the rickety old building shook as if hit by a ball and chain. Lola tried to grab his arm to stop him, but failed.

"Derrick... No!"

"It's cool, babe, calm down," Derrick said, continuing to hammer away with his clenched fists and breaking the door. "This will teach her not to mess with me."

Silence and stillness replaced the screams and banging. All Lola could hear was the loud tick of the grandfather clock, Nattie taking a deep drag from her cigarette, and the radio playing Donna Summer's "Love to Love You, Baby."

The cracked facial-room door had swung open. With an embarrassed look on his face, Francois rushed to the front door.

"I'll be back at six, Raquel. Make- up's great." Francois waved his hand, then unfastened the gold chain and cross that hung from around his neck. Throwing it to Raquel, he said, "I love you. Good-by everyone. It's been a pleasure. *Au revoir*."

Raquel, standing in the doorway of the facial room, caught the necklace and held it to her heart. Starry-eyed and smiling, she blew Francois a kiss.

"I love you, too, Francois," Raquel said, a sweet tear welling up in her eye.

"How thoughtful of him," Nattie smiled. "That is such a sincere gesture."

"You don't know the half of it, Nattie."

"I will."

Raquel immediately came back to the reality of what Derrick had just done. Nostrils flaring, anger streamed out from the depths of her soul. Lola sensed trouble.

Not surprising Lola, screaming from the top of her lungs, huffing and puffing, Raquel shouted outrageous obscenities. "Ugh! Derrick! I hate your guts. I hate everything about you. I just plain hate you."

"You love me, Raquel. Admit it."

"After I get through with you, buster, you'll be sorry you ever met me!"

"I know an outraged woman when I see one," Nattie said, "and Raquel's one. Stand back."

"Look at her face," Lola said, astonished. "She looks like a different Raquel. I've never in my life seen anyone so angry."

"She's hot enough to have steam come out of her ears. Ecstasy to agony in three seconds flat. Where's the camcorder? I have a pretty good idea of what's coming. I've got to get this trip on film." Nattie hopped to it, quickly grabbing the movie camera.

In a blind rage, like a mad dog in heat, Raquel, with ragged hair, mussed-up make-up, and wobbly legs, stormed towards Derrick. Panting, she grabbed his throat, swung him around, and cornered him between the wall and the shampoo bowl. Mouth gaping open, Derrick looked in shock.

"Slowly, I am goin' to kill you," Raquel seethed, slamming his head against the wall and pulling a patch of hair out of his scalp.

"Ouch!" Derrick screamed in agony.

"That pain is just a sample of what's in your immediate future."

Lola saw Derrick was taken by surprise, a surprise she knew he would never forget for the rest of his life. Lola felt sorry for him, she felt she must help in some way.

"Please, Raquel, calm down," Lola pleaded.

"Calm down? Are you kiddin'? No way. Not just yet. It'll be awhile before I'm done with this malicious piece of sludge."

Lola noticed that Raquel's anger gave her the strength of Superwoman. It frightened her. Not knowing what to do, she backed off.

With both hands clenched around his neck and sharp fingernails gouging his reddened skin, Raquel yelled and shook Derrick with all her might.

"How could you do such a horrible thing to me?" Sporadically banging his head into the shampoo bowl, Raquel continued. "You creepy maggot sonofabitch! I hate your guts! How could you do such a cruel thing? And to embarrass Francois like that? How dare you!" Raquel screamed. "I said how dare you! Just twenty more seconds! Ugh! Don't think you'll ever live to tell this story. Plan on a slow death."

"Ha! Ha!" Derrick caught his breath. "Did your French lover lose it?"

"How could he not after what you just did, you stinkin' rodent! You scared the hell out of us, bangin' on and breakin' that damn ol' door like a wild madman. What's with you anyway? I never dreamed you'd stoop this low. I'll never forgive you for this one," Raquel screeched while continuing to slap his face.

Lola shuddered. Derrick's skull hit the porcelain bowl, making a sound like a fist-sized rock hitting a cement floor. She saw Raquel was out of control.

"Raquel! Stop!" Lola knew she did not have the strength to pull Raquel off of Derrick. "You're hurting him!"

"Babe," Nattie grabbed Lola's arm, "let them work it out their own way."

"But I've got to try to pull these lunatics apart before something drastic happens. The way she slammed his head into that hard shampoo bowl, he could have a concussion."

"Don't interfere. She's got to get her anger out. Anyway, he's getting what he deserves."

"Maybe... But she's going to kill him! Just listen to his head crack. That sound gives me the shivers. I hate violence. I can't believe this."

"Get a grip. It'll take more than cracking his head on that bowl to crack that nut. Derrick's as hard-headed as they come." Nattie zoomed in more closely. "This is great. Look at his crossed eyes. I haven't seen this much action since old lady Russell caught me in her bed with her husband and her young gigolo. Hmmm... That's another story for later."

Raquel, who had well earned her reputation on the rodeo circuit, relentlessly mauled Derrick, kicking, chopping, and hollering ear-shattering sounds.

"You're lookin' sick, Derrick, but you haven't seen anything yet."

Lola stood in awe, her heart pounding, and watched the scenario. She felt confused and helpless, and wanted to cry and laugh at the same time while watching Derrick try, unsuccessfully, to defend himself.

"Cool it, Raquel," Derrick pleaded, trying to regain his composure, but could not. "Please forgive me. I'm really sorry." Adding fuel to the fire, he then said, "April Fools' Day."

"Sorry my ass! Who's the fool, bucko?" Raquel put Derrick into a head lock, knocked his feet out from under him, and began to drag him into the facial room. He was teetering like a newborn calf, scrambling for strength.

"Let me go, you wild, crazy woman! I said I was sorry! I'm not going to fight back. I don't want to hurt you."

"You already have, you maggot." Raquel hit him again, across his chest. Whop!

"What in the hell are you doing?" Derrick pleaded in agony.

"What does it look like I'm doin'?"

It was obvious to Lola that Derrick had never learned self-defense. She wished he had, especially now, because Lola feared for his life. Derrick never counted on tangling with Raquel.

Gasping for air, his arms flailed in the air. "Please don't mess my face up," he cried, whimpering. "Ouch! You're pulling gobs of hair out of my chest. I'm too much of a gentleman. I won't fight you."

"No way! You couldn't fight me if you had to. I used to wrestle steers back in Texas. Daddy always told me it was a good thing to learn."

Raquel yanked another patch of hair out of his head. "You'll be a chrome dome within minutes."

"Nattie, what shall we do?" Lola asked, her voice shaking.

"Let it take its course, meanwhile I'm getting some great stuff on film."

Raquel busted Derrick in the face again. Feeling helpless, Lola cringed at his pained expression.

"Since you're all that's around, I'm not lettin' you go until you finish what Francois started," Raquel said. "Now, drop your drawers and get your eenie-weenie up! Let's get this over with. Then afterwards, I'm gonna kill you... Just like the queen bee kills the worker bees."

"No!" Derrick began to cry, his male image vanished. Groping, he begged Lola and Nattie for help.

"What on earth is Raquel talking about?" Lola asked, astonished. "Drop what drawers?"

"Finishing the job," Nattie laughed. "Oh, this girl... She never ceases to amaze me. She's so cute. No wonder she's a rodeo queen."

"Raquel's delirious. Derrick's got to have a testosterone deficiency by now, plus he's barely capable of breathing at this point, let alone anything else. This is pathetic. Bizarre! No one will never believe this story."

"Yes they will. I'm filming it," Nattie said. "Cameras never lie."

"Nattie, we have to do something."

"Oh, look at his pleading doe eyes. Get a load of that look on his face. It's worth a thousand words." Nattie shook her finger at Derrick. "I told you so. I warned you. She's got the wrath of Thor. You're going to remember this incident for a long time. Probably will give you nightmares. May not date a redhead for awhile, either."

"You asked for that one, Derrick," Suzy said. "I thought you knew women better than that."

The front door opened. It was Jimmy, Raquel's one o'clock appointment. Lola was relieved that help had arrived.

"What in the hell is going on in here?" Jimmy asked, a slow smile covering his face.

Lola saw that Raquel and Derrick, thrashing wildly on the floor, did not notice Jimmy's entrance.

"Please, pull them apart," Lola pleaded, wringing her hands. "Hurry! Help settle this war. Oh Jimmy, thank goodness you're here."

"Great action. Keep up the good work," Nattie said to Raquel, still filming.

"Just look at that gal move. I see my fiery redhead has gotten herself into another brawl. Lucky for me it's just a half a guy this time." Jimmy strolled over to where Raquel and Derrick wrestled around on the floor. He grabbed their necks, pulling them apart, saying, "C'mon now, kiddies. The game's over. Time for recess."

"I never thought I'd be so glad to see someone in my life!" Derrick reached up and felt the bald spots on his head. "I don't believe you,

Raquel. Look! She's even pulled patches of hair out of my arms! You're mad. Bonkers! Out of your mind."

Holding his face, Derrick fled to the restroom and slammed the door. "You're nuts!" he yelled as he latched the door.

"Oh, Jimmy. I'm just so... so... Ugh!" Raquel whimpered as she dragged Jimmy into the facial room and locked the door.

"Whew." Nattie put the camcorder down. "Unbelievable! That exhausted me. Where's my glass of wine?"

"Human nature is so odd," Lola said, limp from the episode.

"Yup," Nattie said. "You'd better believe it."

"People's behavior patterns are too much. I must be from a more civilized planet."

"You're probably an emissary from Aldebaran," Nattie kidded.

"Where's that?"

"Way out, another planetary system."

"You work with someone for years," Lola said in a daze. "You think you know them."

"Believe me, you're never really going to know anyone."

"Why not?"

"Tides turn, so do people."

"Nattie! Don't be so negative."

"All in a day's work, babe. All in a day's work. Why, I could tell you stories that would curl your blonde, fluffy mane. I've lived to tell it all, too."

Nattie blew a big bubble with her bubble gum. It popped, laying a pink sheet across her face. "Damn these false teeth anyway... Haven't been able to blow a decent bubble for years."

Derrick sheepishly shuffled over to his client and continued blow drying Suzy's hair. "That woman is crazy. She's like a time bomb. You just never know when she'll go off. I've met a lot of women in my day, but I've never in my life ever met the likes of Raquel."

"Almost a short-lived life," Suzy added.

"Hey, Derrick, remind me not to call you if I ever need to be rescued."

"Save it, Lola," Derrick retorted with an angry glare.

"You'd better put some ice on that eye, Derrick," Nattie said, handing him an ice bag.

"Geeze... Unreal! And you women wonder why we men don't trust you."

"What's that supposed to mean?" Lola asked.

"What man in his right mind would trust a woman who bleeds for one week every month and doesn't die?"

"You're off of your rocker, Derrick."

Nattie handed Mrs. Scott a glass of wine. "Here, girlie, you need this. I'll bet you never saw action like this in your forty years at the library."

"I can't say that I have." Mrs. Scott gulped the wine, and shook her head from side to side. "I really can't. Raquel would be a great sparring partner for George Foreman." Mrs. Scott held up her crystal wine glass. "How about another? And please, fill it to the top again. Maybe I'll be able to taste the wine on the second glassful."

Nattie refilled her glass, grabbed a comb, and continued to fix Mrs. Scott's ivory-colored hair.

"I'm the best finger-waver in town. You young squirts think you know it all. It's all been done before you were even born. Nothing's new. You'll understand it all by the time you get to be my age. Experience does come with age you know. When you're young, you're sharp. But when you get to be my age, you're sharper than ever."

"I never dreamed Raquel had that kind of strength," Derrick said, still trembling from the trauma and excitement.

"Shows just how well you know women. Think about that, boy." Nattie popped her bubble gum. "Face the truth, admit your error, take your licks, and repent. Then get on with your work."

"Like the great Oscar Wilde said," Derrick stated, sipping the coffee Nattie had doused with whiskey. " 'Experience is the name everyone gives to their mistakes.' "

Chapter 12

Lola watched Marissa blow in like a gust of wind. She looked sophisticated dressed in a tailored white silk Christian Dior suit, red high heels, and smelling of rich perfume. Sunlight caught in her diamonds and flicked specks of light on the wall, matching the sparkle in her amber-colored eyes.

"Hello, everyone!" Marissa sang out. "Good afternoon, darlings. I've arrived."

"You should have arrived years ago," Nattie taunted.

"Oh, Nattie, thank goodness some things never change." Marissa brushed her wild, long hair behind her shoulder.

"Well, good afternoon, stranger." Lola smiled and stood up. "Welcome back to reality."

"Thanks, it's wonderful to see you again. It was so difficult to leave paradise. And who says Hawaii isn't reality?"

"Great suntan," Lola winked. "How was the hula?"

"Fab... Oh, girl, did I ever dance. My month in Hawaii went by too fast, but I've missed our weekly visits." Marissa pointed at the sign on the front door. "No yuppies allowed. That's a clever April Fools' Day joke."

"Oh, believe me, it's no joke. I put that sign up a week ago. Yuppie mentality nauseates me. Materialism doesn't work. I refuse to do their hair any more. I'm not into shallow materialistic lightweights who talk about false fingernails and white Zinfandel for the duration of a haircut." Lola shook her head in disgust. "Idle talk went out with the 80's. Anyway, like the saying goes, if you're not in tune with someone, you'll never please them. I'm not into pleasing pigs. Human beings are more my speed."

"Don't worry. We'll talk about my vacation today."

"We'd better because you're a borderline case, half human, half yuppie-pig."

"Testy. Testy. Got a problem? I'll be your shrink today."

"Call me next week before you come in. Bertha's being stubborn about signing the lease."

"Hasn't she signed that yet?" Marissa threw her multi-colored leather handbag on the sofa. "What's the latest scoop?"

"She's enjoying dangling me like a fish on a hook. By midnight tonight, she'll either pull me in or throw me out to sea. You may have to come and get your hair done at Carey's."

"I'll go anywhere you are. I'd go to your kitchen sink if I had to."

"I've done some of my best work at kitchen tables."

"Haven't we all? No, seriously, I know it will work out for you. It always does. The universe provides well for you because you're one of those special people." Marissa pointed her finger towards Lola. "C'mon, it's time for you to practice what you preach. Your daily prayer is 'thy will be done,' so let go, and let it happen."

"I'm trying. It's just that it's a crucial and difficult time for me right now."

"Whoever said life was easy? Fun, interesting, creative, lots of surprises, and hard work? Yes. But easy? No."

"Let's get your shampoo going," Lola smiled.

"Great bouquet," Marissa said, seeing the bouquet of tulips. "I got one exactly like it this morning. I'm going to the florist after I leave here. I need to know what splendid hunk sent the flowers."

"What are you talking about?"

"The card just said 'thinking of you.' With all the fascinating, playful men I know, the process of elimination would take too long." Marissa breathed in deeply and swished her hair around. "I must admit, I do date clever men. This is a noteworthy April Fools' Day joke, one that will call for a reward."

"Yeah, I can see that. Some lucky guy's going to get it good."

Lola watched Raquel gloat and noticed that Nattie kept her big mouth shut for a change and went on with her work.

Lola told Marissa of the day's happenings, and she lapped it up like a kitten laps milk. Just as Lola finished Marissa's shampoo, the telephone rang.

"Go ahead and sit in my chair while I get the phone," Lola said. "It's probably one of Derrick's fans."

Marissa paraded by Derrick, puckered her painted red lips, and blew him a kiss. With no sound coming out of her mouth, she asked, "Where did it land?"

In mid-air Derrick pretended to grab her kiss and slapped over his mouth.

"This will be good for sweet starters," he whispered.

"Good afternoon," Lola said. "Contemporary Hair Design. May I help you?" There was a brief pause. A puzzled look came over Lola's face as she listened to the person on the other end of the telephone line. "Just a minute please."

Lola excused herself and put the call on hold. "Derrick, I think there's a long distance call for you. The man has a heavy accent, and I can't understand a word he's said, except for your name. The connection's not real good either. Maybe it's from overseas."

"Tell him I'm busy and I'll get back with him later," Derrick coolly replied. He rolled his ivory colored silk shirt sleeves up, then continued to twist Anita's majestic brown hair into a high-fashion mermaid design.

Lola parlayed the message, hung up the phone, then walked to her work station which was next to Derrick's. She could tell that Derrick was irritated and that he had no intention of returning the man's call.

"What was that all about?"

"That guy has been bugging me for weeks. He wants to buy the patent on my new invention."

"Oh, I can tell you are going to be a very rich man," Lola snickered, knowing that Derrick had used his engineering skills to invent a vibrator that plugged into a stereo. He had boasted to Lola that Beethoven's *Fifth Symphony* was a favorite among his many conquests.

From the corner of her eye, Lola saw Derrick wink at Marissa. She ignored their secret communication, reached for her scissors, then asked Marissa what type of haircut she wanted.

"Jazz me up today, and make the bait more attractive. I have a hot date with a new man tonight. Lay off the spritz, please. Nothing too fixed looking, either. I don't want him to get his fingers caught in my hair."

"Consider it done." Lola parted the brunette's mahogany mane and began to design a new do for the vamp. "How many new hair-dos have I given you for every new man in your life?"

"That's why I come to you, Lola. You're talented, and you make me look sensational."

"Plus you know I'm not a cheap gossip," Lola teased. "You trollop, I could write ten volumes out of one week in your life."

"And just who are you calling a cheap trollop, you sweet tart? You don't do too bad yourself."

"Not any more. This is the 90's. Times have changed. It used to be we thought we'd die if we *didn't* have sex."

"You've got that right. No more fast flings for me either. The next man in my life will have to put in a thousand hours before he can hold my hand."

Rock music blared, hair dryers blew, and the smell of hair spray permeated the air. Lola whistled like a songbird while concentrating on her work. She felt the warm aliveness of her salon, her home away from home, and she was comforted.

"Time to relax, darlin'," Raquel said, laying Jimmy back in the shampoo bowl. "And let my fingers do the walkin'."

"How about going parachute jumping with me again this weekend?"

"Jimmy darlin', give me a rain check, *s'il vous plait.* That means 'please' in French."

While waiting for Mrs. White's hair to dry, Nattie downed three glasses of wine, then began to devour a roast beef sandwich.

"I'm starved. My stomach thinks my throat's been cut. This sandwich sure hits the spot."

Lola glanced at Nattie, sitting in her styling chair, eating.

"Nattie, there's a long dark hair hanging from your sandwich. Pull it out."

Not paying attention to what Lola just said, Nattie took another big bite.

"Gross, Nattie," Derrick said. "Show a little class."

"I *am* a class act." Nattie smacked her lips. "It's hard to improve on perfection." She chomped some more.

"Ewww... It's hangin' from your mouth now," Raquel said. "Grossin' me out!"

Lola walked over to Nattie and grabbed the strand of hair from her lips.

"You know, kiddies," Nattie said, "before beauty school, if I'd find a hair in my food, I'd throw the entire plate of food away. Nowadays, if there isn't hair in my food, I think something's wrong."

"Nattie, please!" Raquel said. "You're somethin' else."

"So, buy me a present," Nattie teased.

"How was your trip?" Lola said, walking back to Marissa.

"Sensational. Hawaii is a place where nothing else matters. It was like living in a heart-warming movie. Boy, I really needed a good rest. Working in real estate has taken its toll on me. I hate to admit it, but at thirty, I'd burned out. I got to the point that I shook every time the phone rang. My heart palpitated one night, and it scared the heck out of me. Going to Hawaii was the greatest prescription my doctor could have given me. I feel like I've been reborn, given a second chance."

"It's the island of love, so peaceful and gentle."

"Yes, and no stress. It's hard to put it into words, but my burdens lifted off my shoulders as soon as I walked off the plane."

"It's the lavender aura in the air," Lola said. "That's why they call it paradise."

"It is a very special land, kind of sacred, like a holy church filled with ferns and palms and miles of sandy white beaches. The cloud formations were exquisite. I couldn't have arranged them more beautifully than the angels."

"And?"

"And what?"

"The spicy particulars. What do you think? We only have an hour, so out with it."

"Well, I couldn't sleep the first night, hadn't unwound yet. So I went down to the shore a little before sunrise, walked a couple of miles, then sat in the sand. No one was there except for a tall, willowy Hawaiian guy in the distance. Oh, glorious is the sea. Sea gulls flew all around, mild waves kissed the shore, sounding like music, and the early morning sun soothed my soul. Palm trees swayed in the gentle wind. The wet sand was cool to the touch," Marissa said, a faraway look in her eyes. "It hit me like a ton of bricks how far I had grown away from nature, our source of life! Then I got angry with myself for having let my life get so out of balance to the point that my health was at stake. As sharp as I am, I can't believe I didn't see it coming."

"You didn't tell me you were ill," Lola remarked.

"Just the stress-related stuff. You know, headaches, stomach problems, the usual."

"What blinded you?"

"Money, power, and the idiotic desire to keep up with the Joneses. It's a process that didn't happen over night. It crept up on me over a period of years. Then one day I looked into the mirror and I didn't like what I saw. Unconsciously, I had yearned for all the wrong things," Marissa said. "I promised myself that I would do something about it."

"Hallelujah. I'm glad you've seen the light. I've worried about you at times," Lola said. "Keep in mind, materialism is the ultimate vulgarity."

"If you had said that to me one month ago, I wouldn't have believed you. Every cell in me knows that now. I've done a lot of thinking and have made new resolutions for my life. I cleaned out my mind so my heart can heal. Peace is not something that comes from the outside. It's all within."

"I'm proud of you, for catching it in time. It's usually not until we've had a great fall and have become extremely troubled in the soul that we're ready to appreciate the unadorned simplistic life."

Lola fondly remembered her special vacations to Hawaii. She had felt like an uninhibited child in a playground; swimming, canoeing, and riding the waves. Besides Yosemite, Hawaii was a wondrous place where Lola took much delight in becoming one with nature.

"That's right," Marissa said. "Who ever dreamed the simple life would be filled with contentment, peace. I've never felt so alive and creative in my life. I'm even back to sculpting again, and you know how long it's been since I've taken the time for that."

"Terrific. Knowing you, you'll stick to it, too. Anyway, you'd better, or you'll get old before your time, and God knows that's the last thing you want."

"*Moi?*"

"Yes you. None of us are above it. Now, get on to the good stuff."

"I sat with my eyes closed, laid my head on my knees, and released a cascade of tears I didn't know I had. I don't know how much time passed, but all of a sudden, I felt a loving hand on my shoulder and a tender kiss on the back of my neck."

"That's pretty far-fetched. Sounds like a scene from a movie."

"The entire scenario felt like being in another time in space."

"Didn't this all startle you? The stranger and all?"

"No, it's a funny thing. As uptight as I had gotten in my stressed-out life, it didn't. Plus I was exhausted."

"Who was the mystery man?"

"He was the Hawaiian guy, the kind of man you leave the lights on for. When he sat behind me, his peaceful nature kept me from feeling his approach."

"Boy, you were more numb than I thought."

"I was, but I'll never be again."

"Good. Anyway, tell me more."

"He embraced me, then wiped the tears from my face. Not saying a word, he hugged me tight and sang a loving Hawaiian song. I got lost looking into his incredible face, I couldn't get enough of staring into his deep dark eyes, a space of infinite peace. A look of intense, clear light poured through his eyes into mine. I felt he read my soul while gazing into mine. He exuded gentle serenity, so loving, in an unconditional way like Granddaddy loved me. I automatically trusted him."

"You?" Lola said. "Trusted someone?"

"Yes I did. Don't you think it's about time? I can afford to trust someone now that I'm balanced and in tune with myself. I can actually feel again."

"I've been waiting to hear that for a long time," Lola said. "And?"

"Bathed in beauty, we swam and frolicked in the waterfalls. Beneath the sun, and beneath the moon, he kissed me over and over all over."

"Wow! Talk about Hawaiian hospitality. This is better than a romance novel."

"I joined his dance through life and he took me to his private cove and made love to me for a month. I thought I had made love before, but I was just being screwed. I lost myself in his sweetness and got in touch with the Marissa I had so foolishly thrown away. Walking with him, our footsteps became like a drum beat that harmonized with the heartbeat of Mother Earth. Every day, miles vanished under our feet. Hand in hand we walked along the water's edge, not speaking much, just enjoying the grace and solitude of quiet days and nights. It's amazing how two people can communicate without using words. I didn't find the Hawaiian people to be verbal."

"They don't need to be. One look or gesture says it all," Lola said. "I guess a person naturally knows and does these things when he honors and stays living close to Mother Nature."

"A moment in the soul will last forever," Marissa said, dreamily.

"He does sound like a natural man."

"Yes, he is. You know, I finally met a man who was worth shaving my legs for, and he didn't care if I shaved them or not."

"You're too much."

"I try. Anyway, he made my trip very special. My eyes are open now. I'll never be the same, and I'll no longer live in a hell disguised as heaven. I'm so ashamed of myself for being so greedy and selfish."

"Marissa," Nattie butted in, "in my day, we'd call your kind a tough broad. You'd better thank your lucky stars that you met that Hawaiian guy to soften you up. The rate you were going, you would have ended up with an exterior as resilient as an army tank. Boy, talk about divine intervention. This is a classic case."

"I didn't realize I was so obvious." Marissa's face looked hurt.

"It's all behind you now, babe. Just go forward, you're on a better path now."

"Thanks, Nattie," Marissa said. "I feel I've been given a new lease on life."

"Trust me, you have." Nattie shook her finger at Marissa. "You were one of the lucky ones. You must have earned that grace somewhere."

"I guess," Marissa said. "At first I felt bad about not fitting in with my old friends when I got home, but now I realize it's for the best. They weren't true friends anyway, just selfish users. New beginnings are wonderful. I'm flowing into it. I will never go back to my hectic, limited lifestyle."

"I'm glad for you. But you'd better go back and visit your Hawaiian delight," Lola said. "Love from a pure, clean heart always gives us strength."

Marissa's words, "New beginnings are wonderful," filled Lola's mind. She wished she could release her fear of starting over again from scratch and find joy in a possible new beginning. She was very pleased and secure with her new relationship with Craig, but she wished Bertha would hurry and sign the lease.

"You know," Marissa continued, "I used to think that I had to cleanse and purify my heart, mind, and body with all these different processes that take forever, but after my month in Hawaii, I see it all differently now."

"I know what you're going to say, but say it anyway."

"Oh, Lola, I know you know, because you live in the spirit of the universe. I can see it clearly now, and it's easier to do than I thought. While in Hawaii, I received so much goodness, and filled myself up with positive, healthy living and loving, that all the negativity dissolved by itself."

"It's naturally easy to release bad feelings in a nurturing environment."

"Yes, and it was a relief to receive a healing and know that I am whole again. My parents are still celebrating. Daddy surprised me and took me shopping yesterday and bought me the silver Rolls Royce that I've always wanted."

"Well, congratulations! You've had your eye on a car like that for years."

"Daddy says he trusts me now, and he and Mother are so happy to see zest and zeal in me again. Our relationship is so much better now. For the first time in years, we're communicating. No more tension, just a nice comfort zone. I'm finally understanding and accepting their love, and I'm grateful that we're a family again." Marissa let out a satisfying sigh. "The whole world is at my fingertips, and I know it."

"You're growing up, kid," Nattie said, "and building character."

"I'm happy for you," Lola said, remembering the incident earlier that morning with Judge Garrett and his mother. Lola was glad that Marissa would not have to carry the burden of guilt like Judge Garrett had carried for so many years.

Lola noticed that Raquel had finished Jimmy's haircut.

Whispering to Marissa, Lola said, "That's Jimmy, the exhibitionist I've been telling you about. He's a stunt man and he loves to preen for the women. Now, watch his style. He does this grand routine every time he comes in here. He loves to show off his gorgeous body."

"Well," Marissa said, putting two thumbs up. "That's a body to show off. Talk about a tight ass and long, Tarzan legs. He sure does justice to those threads. It's sinful."

"No, it's heavenly," Lola said. "The more clients that are in here to see him parade around, the happier he is."

Jimmy, acting cool and playing dumb to the fact that everyone in the salon was gawking at him, took his T-shirt off and shook it as if to shake hair from the neckline.

"Thanks, doll," he said in a low, sexy voice. "Great job. Luv ya, Raquel."

Jimmy rubbed the T-shirt around the back of his neck to remove cut hairs that Lola knew were not there. She had seen many show-offs in her day, but Jimmy was the most obvious with his extravagant style.

He snapped and crackled his T-shirt six times, like a round of gunshots, shaking the supposed hair from it. Promenading up to the reception desk, he handed Raquel a fifty dollar bill for cutting his half-bald head then flipped her a silver dollar.

"That's for good luck, good-lookin'. Be in touch. *Ciao*, baby."

"Thanks, darlin'," Raquel winked. "Luv ya."

"Anytime." Jimmy winked back, glanced around the salon, then slowly strutted out of the front door. "I'm going to hold you to that parachute jump."

"You're on," Raquel said. "I love to fly high."

"Oooooo..." Marissa said. "He definitely has a way of his own."

"You've got to give him credit for that," Lola said.

"Yes, I do admire individuality," Marissa said. "So what went on in town while I was gone?"

"You missed the seminar of seminars." Lola lowered her voice to peak Marissa's interest.

"You mean another one of those new age higher-consciousness classes on letting go and lightening up?"

"Yes. This course would have made your day," Lola said, facetiously.

"I've met too many of those metaphysical airheads who go from seminar to seminar in search of truth and enlightenment. They live in a shallow world of illusion, but their phenomenal egos make them think they live in a profound reality. They're so open-minded their brains fell out. Their intentions are good, but their follow-through is for the birds. There's nothing centered or solid about any of the ones I've met. What they really need is a good dose of common sense and a big shot of integrity."

"And a good month of loving in Hawaii," Lola teased. "Maybe you should give a class and save those poor meandering souls."

"Please! Give me a break. I'm successful because I walk my talk. Like Daddy always said, 'the act is the fact'."

"One thing about you, Marissa, you do walk your talk."

"I know to stay focused and grounded, so I naturally end up in the right place at the right time, with the right people. Anyway, did you attend the seminar?"

"Ha! No way! I wouldn't be caught dead in a class on pelvic release."

"Ah... Excuse me?" Marissa's mouth hung open. "Run that by me again, only a little more slowly this time."

"What are you two talking about?" Derrick asked. "Why don't you say it a little louder?"

"Don't move too far to the left, Lola," Nattie said, "or you'll step on Derrick's ear."

"You're like a nosey old lady, Derrick," Lola said. "You never give me privacy with my clients."

"That's because I love to listen to your lewd trash," Derrick quipped. "You and your clients have given me great material for a best seller."

"Lot of good it will do you," Raquel sneered.

Lola felt the tension in the air between Raquel and Derrick. She felt helpless, not knowing how to ease the ill feelings between them.

"Cool it, Raquel," Derrick said, trembling with anger. "I've had more than enough of you for one day."

"And I've had enough of you two kids for a lifetime," Nattie said, shaking her fist. "Either shape up or I'll ship you out. And I mean it."

Lola sat on her cutting stool, rolled around near Marissa's ear, and said softly in a teasing tone, "You heard me right, frigid lady. For a mere $1,500, you could have taken the class and learned how to release your pelvis."

"I've never heard of anything in my life so stupid and outrageous! Blind fools... Leave it to those bed-hopping idiots to come up with this," Marissa stated. "It's absolutely absurd, and they have the audacity to think they're spiritual beings attaining enlightenment. Ugh! Just when you think you've heard it all."

"Why, I think it's worth every damn dime if that class can help warm up a hung-up ice cube." Nattie put her two cents worth in. "Everybody needs help in a different way."

"Nattie, you have great hearing for a woman of your age," Derrick said.

"I have everything great, baby, and don't you forget it. I was wiser than you when I was half your age."

"For $1,500, I'd rather have an emerald necklace," Raquel said. "Derrick, maybe you can assist the instructor for that seminar and help those hungry, horny women. They may settle for your three seconds of expertise. Spread around what little you've got, whatever it is that you have, or have left. You know, girls... One of the things that's great about bein' a virgin is that she hasn't been disappointed yet."

"The day's not over yet, Raquel," Derrick threatened. "Just remember that."

"I'll get that tape from you yet, bubba," Raquel said. "One way or another."

"Don't you two start in again," Nattie said.

Lola explained to Marissa that the instructors go from town to town while sexually frustrated women flock to their door, checks in hand. One look at Marissa's expression and Lola knew she was ready to spew out her philosophical wisdom.

"Those brain-free women definitely function from below the belt; plus I think they're a couple of quarts low, a little left of center. If they were smart they would take that $1,500, get fifteen twenty-year-old studs, give them each $100, line them up and screw them one at a time." Marissa blasted, "And if that doesn't work, they can borrow Derrick's vibrator!"

Caught off guard by Marissa's statement, Lola raised her eyebrows and asked, "How do you know about Derrick's vibrator?"

"Well, how do you know?" Marissa said, coyly.

"He's been my working partner for six years! I know everything about this ladies' man. I even know about the hooks in his nipples."

"Not everything... You don't know it all." Marissa could not mask the smirk on her face.

Lola flipped her scissors around her middle finger as if it were a loaded pistol. She pointed the tip towards Marissa, then asked, "Tell me, you painted chippy. How did you like Beethoven's *Fifth*?"

"Never mind. Ten volumes a week for you is enough! Da, da, da, daaaa..."

Lola loved the lively shop talk but she was burdened with worry about Judge Garrett. She glanced out of the window across the street and saw an elderly, white-haired gentleman who looked like the judge. Lola said a silent prayer for Judge Garrett's fast recovery.

Chapter 13

Lola telephoned Mercy Hospital and spoke with Judge John Garrett's wife on the phone.

"I'm so relieved to hear he's resting comfortably and that he'll be all right. Yes, I'll be over to see him soon. You take care, too. Good-bye."

Lola hung up the phone and relayed to Nattie and Raquel what Mrs. Garrett had said.

"Judge Garrett is out of intensive care and resting nicely. Mrs. Garrett said he was so peaceful and that he had a pleasant smile on his face."

"I'll bet," Raquel said. "Is that why y'all said, 'yes, he is a happy man with a great disposition.'"

"Well," Lola said. "He is."

"Ahem..." Nattie said. "Is that what it's called?"

Derrick greeted his client Crissi and kissed both her cheeks. "Hi, doll. Hey, how's the tennis pro? Stand back, let me feast my eyes. Ohhhhh... So good, darling, your eyes are so beautiful and you've captured my heart."

Lola laughed when she recognized Francois' romantic words coming out of Derrick's mouth.

"Just sweep me off my feet with those words," Crissi said, puckering her lips. "Anything for you, Derrick... Anything."

"Let's get your bleach touch-up going."

"Oh, I have all day, Derrick."

"You may, but I don't. It's been a weird day, and I'm outta here ASAP."

"But, what about..." Crissi glanced towards the facial room.

"Later, babe... Later."

"But..."

"I said later." Derrick kissed her cheek and hugged her to his body. "Trust me, I'll make it worth the wait."

Lola stood with Raquel and Nattie at the reception desk and talked about the day's events while waiting for their next clients to arrive.

"Thank God this day is almost over," Lola said, still feeling the tension of the day's happenings. "It's been a real lulu. I pray Bertha pulls through and signs my lease. She's just got to. So much of me is in this shop. This building isn't as old and rickety as she says it is."

"Yes it is," Raquel said. "Even a mild storm could blow it over."

"Hush," Nattie said. "Just because something's old doesn't mean it's no good."

"Her saying she wants to live in that retirement home has got to be a lie," Lola said.

"It is," Nattie agreed. "She'd die in a sterile environment. Germs give that woman her will to live."

"She'll pollute the rest home," Raquel blurted out. "They'll kick her out the first week for belchin' and passin' enough gas to fill the Goodyear Blimp."

"Don't stress yourself out, Lola, you'll deplete the minerals in your body and age before your time," Nattie said. "Trust me. It'll work out for the best."

"You're usually right, but this time I have my doubts. It's so close, yet there is a timelessness about the whole thing. I can't quite put my finger on the vibes." In despair, Lola looked down. "That's why I'm so antsy. I'm uncomfortable not knowing for sure, and I hate the idea of having to start over again."

"You're old enough to be over that trip. Being so attached to this salon makes you fearful, causes anxiety." Nattie rubbed creme on her hands. "You listen to me, and trust."

"We usually waste more energy worryin' about a move than we would if we moved," Raquel said. "Nothin' like a good challenge to get our spirits in high gear. Just gotta do it, sugar."

"Yeah! Like Francois," Nattie whistled. "Hubba, hubba, zing, zing, zing! Baby, he has everything. Girl... Man o' man, you can sing it out! His family jewels must have been some real gems to make you bellow out like an opera singer."

"Forget family jewels. We're talking more like Fort Knox! Oh... I get goose bumps just thinkin' about him. I can't wait to see him again. I love him so much, I'm burstin'. Glad he's already called me; it's a good sign. The commercial went real good."

"I didn't know you were a screamer," Lola said.

"Neither did I," Raquel giggled. "Ahem... Believe it or not, we have lots of other things in common."

"Yeah, sure," Nattie said.

"We do. Honest... Even though we just met, we have a feelin' of completion with each other. It's a nurturin' comfort zone," Raquel said, a smile of satisfaction on her face. "He's so easy to talk to."

"Déjà vu." Lola hugged Raquel. "I believe you, and I'm happy for you."

"We're gonna go to Mama Corelli's for dinner after work."

"That's great. Craig and I are, too. We'll have to dine together," Lola said.

"Mr. Jenkins and I will join you too. We'll all do dinner," Nattie said. "Get ready to celebrate."

"Who is this Timmy guy who's comin' in next?" Raquel said, pointing to her appointment column.

"Spencer's nephew from New York City," Lola said.

"New York City! Oh, my kind of place. Is he real cute and everything?"

"He looks like Spencer."

"Ugh. That explains it. Say no more. He'll probably give me the creeps like his uncle does. I hate cuttin' the old pervert's hair. He breathes funny and stares at my boobs the entire time."

"Spencer only has a few strands of hair," Lola said.

"A little dab of Mop'N'Glow should do the trick," Nattie laughed. "You should get a chamois and polish and buff his chrome dome up real good."

"Yeah," Raquel said, "and end up with a glob of lard on my chamois? No thanks. All of his bucks could never buy him a microgram of class."

"It's a fast buck, babe," Nattie said. "Accept it. It's all a part of this exciting beauty business. When you work so closely with the public, you have to expect all kinds of behavior. Detach emotionally and do the best you can."

"That's why most of us hairdressers are a little jaded. We've worked too closely with too many weirdos," Raquel said.

"Hey, we're hairdressers... Beyond being human. If you're lucky, you'll survive and end up a tough ol' bird like me. I've learned through experience how to relax and take things in my stride. It takes quite a bit to ruffle my feathers. I'm a very tolerant person. I have a tremendous amount of patience. Like I always say, it's all in a day's work. Anyway, you've got to be a little zany to work in a crazy profession like this. Hairdressers are the women's bartenders, you know. Hey, listen!" Nattie snapped her finger. "Do you know the four animals a woman shouldn't do without?"

"No, Nattie," Raquel asked. "What?"

"A jaguar in the garage. A stallion in the bedroom. A mink in her closet. And a jackass to pay for it all. Ha, ha..."

"I love your jokes, Nattie." Raquel roared with laughter. "Your pizza man keeps you well supplied."

"You've got that right, babe."

"It's an insult to my integrity to even laugh at your silly jokes." Lola shook her head. "I don't know why I do."

"Because they're funny," Raquel said. "That's why... We all know a beauty salon wouldn't be a beauty salon without jokes. You've gotten so serious lately. Now, sugar, lighten up at least enough to make it through the rest of the day. We're gonna have fun tonight."

Lola saw that Nattie had that look on her face, the look that said she was on a roll to tell more jokes. When that happened, Lola knew there was no stopping her.

"Did you hear about the three sexually frustrated men who had been up at the icy North Pole without a woman for six months?"

"Out with it, Nattie," Lola said. "Get it over with."

"No, no, you'll like this one. Now listen... The guy from Paris got the bright idea to mail away for a plastic, life-sized blow-up doll. The guys from Los Angeles and Fresno agreed it was a great idea. They checked the mail every day for two months. Finally Sheila arrived. They blew her up, then pulled straws to see who got her first. Francois, the Parisian, took Sheila into the bedroom. Kiss. Kiss. Plastic passion, *mon chérie*. Smooth as silk. Twenty minutes later he came out and told his friends how great the lovemaking was. Then Craig from Los Angeles went into the bedroom. Smooch. Smooch. What a way to go. Bench press the bundle. Heavy breathing. Forty-five minutes later, he came out, telling his friends it was worth the wait. Now, Derrick, the guy from Fresno, was so excited because it was finally his turn to fool around. He went into the bedroom. One minute later, he came out, a baffled look on his face. His friends, astonished, asked him what had happened. 'I don't know. I laid down beside her, kissed her, bit her on the neck, and damned if she didn't hiss and fart and fly out the window.'"

"Real funny, Nattie," Derrick said. "Just bash me all the more."

"Oh... You were born to be bashed," Nattie teased. "April Fool."

Lola felt Derrick deserved the jokes that were being played on him and that he was getting a taste of what he usually gave to others. Everyone in the salon was laughing when the front door opened.

"Flowers for Raquel Warner."

Raquel rushed to the delivery boy and grabbed the long gold foil box out of his hands.

"Oh! Thank you," she said, flipping him a silver dollar as he left. "I'm so excited, I just know it's from Francois. He's such a honey bunny. Doesn't waste much time, either. My kind of man. I've waited for my RPM for too long, but after today, I know it was worth the wait. Oh! I can't wait to get my hands on my prince charmin' again."

"Here, open this." Raquel, her hands shaking from excitement, gave the card to Lola. "I can't wait too much longer to feast my eyes on the roses. Francois knows I love long-stemmed roses."

"Hurry up, I don't have all day," Nattie said. "My next client is walking in now."

"He asked me what my favorite flowers were. I knew he'd send me white roses, but I didn't realize he would send them so quickly." In anticipation, Raquel's fingers trembled while she untied the gold lace bow.

"He's definitely a man of action, just the kind of guy you need," Lola said.

"To say the least, " Nattie said. "I hope it works out between you two. God knows, and the entire neighborhood knows, that you love-birds got a great start. Now, rip that bow off!"

"Oh, Nattie.... My stomach's a-flutterin'. I'm so excited. Romance is so thrillin'." Raquel flipped off the box top, lifted the tissue, and gaped into the box. Standing like a mannequin, stiff and speechless, an appalled look curtained her face.

"No!" she screamed. "It can't be. No, no, no... This isn't happenin' to me."

Lola peeked into the box, saw the bright lime-green fourteen-inch dildo, and laughed uncontrollably.

"I love it. I love it! This is so great... It's classic." Without delay, Lola opened the card and read aloud, "Thinking of you."

"Oh, I love it. Just when you think you've beat them... Ha!" Nattie held her stomach and roared like a laughing hyena. "That's what's so great about life. Just when you're so positive that you know what's next, something comes in from left field."

"I told you George would know it was you," Lola said.

"You called and told him, didn't you?" Raquel demanded.

"No I didn't; I swear I didn't."

"Yes you did, Lola. There's no way he could have found out."

"I have never lied to you or anyone, and I'm not about to start now, especially on a silly matter like this. Now, did it ever cross your mind that you may not be as shrewd as you think you are?"

"No way! Never! Never, never, never..."

While walking back to the shampoo bowl, Nattie told Mrs. Gordon the details of Raquel's backfired April Fools' Day joke.

"Youth," she said. "There's nothing like it. These kids have got a long, fun road ahead of them. If only they would learn to relax, go with the flow, and get the full value out of their experiences. Life is a journey, to be enjoyed."

"Yes," Mrs. Gordon agreed. "Life is like a treasure hunt, only the map gets left in heaven."

"Does it look familiar?" Lola snickered, unable to refrain from laughing so hard.

"Gateway Boutique, Hollywood and Vine," Derrick said.

"Shut up, Derrick," Raquel said. "I don't need your lip service. You're still on my hit list. I hate your guts more now than I ever did. To think I once liked and trusted you. Boy! Was I ever wrong. I promise I'm gonna strangle you again before the day is over."

"Please," Lola said, "not on shop time. Once is about all I could live through in one day. Lucky for you Jimmy came in and kept you from killing Derrick or you'd be on your way to the poky right now."

"I still can't believe he did what he did." Raquel yelled out, with exasperation, "Yes! It looks familiar! The damn thing looks too familiar! How on earth did that creepy George know it was me? I covered all the evidence. Remember? I'm the Sherlock of the bunch. It's gotta be a lucky guess on his part."

"Yeah, sure. You're such a readable book," Derrick said. "Evidently he knows you better than you think he does."

"That's a disgustin' thought. You should've kept it to yourself. You've already inflicted enough misery on me today. How much do you think I can take?" Raquel threw the gold box with the lime green dildo in it onto her work station. "I can't believe he knew it was me! And then to tantalize me by sendin' everyone and their sister a bouquet with a note sayin' 'thinkin' of you.' And Maria and Marissa! What nerve! How dare him! Boy! Today has been one of those days. I need to be somewhere else. I wish it was dinner time."

"Me, too," Derrick said, feeling his bald spots. "I have a horrible headache. I wonder why?"

"Me, too," Lola said. "Mimi will be in next. By the time I give her a permanent, and blow-dry Janice's and Patricia's hair at 5:30, my day will be over. With any luck and three sane clients coming in next, not much else can go wrong for me today."

"You'd better hope not, sugar. I don't think any of us has tolerance for any more trauma."

Lola was in awe of the day's happenings. She had laughed and had cried and had felt feelings that she had never felt before. She looked forward to sharing her thoughts with her dear client, Mimi, a gracious, elegant, international woman who wore her wisdom lightly.

Lola hugged the elderly, lovely woman when she arrived.

"It's so good to see you again, Mimi. I've missed seeing your happy face every week. C'mon, let's get you started."

Mimi, a nurturing and wise godmother to all, had been Lola's favorite client for the past six years. Their love, friendship, and respect for each other continued to grow strong. Like Lola's mother, Mimi's husband had recently died a painful death of cancer. Lola was grateful that they had helped each other through their rough times of dealing with sickness and death. At times they were all each other had, but Lola knew it was enough.

"I've missed your sweet face too, dear heart. I had a lot to deal with after André passed away. I got our San Francisco business in order, then I sold it."

"Good, that's just one more pressure off of you. I'm glad to see you've gained your weight back. How about joining all of us for dinner at Mama Corelli's later on?"

"Thank you. I'd love to, but I'll have to take a rain check. I must get things ready for my early flight to Switzerland tomorrow."

"How long are you staying this time?"

"Two months. It will be nice to spend time with my son and his family again. I so love the countryside. To entice me back, they bought me a beautiful Lippizaner horse. Dressage was such a big part of my life as a young woman. It will be nice to get back to it. I'm thinking of moving there permanently now that André is gone, and I'm going to take you with me."

"That's a deal. And you can teach me dressage."

"Of course, my dear, it would be my honor and pleasure."

Lola watched a young man, who looked like Spencer, enter the salon. From his slovenly appearance, Lola hoped Raquel would have the patience to deal with Spencer's nephew, Timmy.

"C'mon, I don't have all day." Raquel arrived at the shampoo bowl ten feet ahead of Timmy.

Like a rolling bucket of slime, walking at a snail's pace with loose-jointed awkwardness, Timmy tugged his feet along.

"My uncle was right! You *are* a real knockout," Timmy said, rubbing his hands together. "Redheads turn me on."

"I'd hate to even think what else turns you on. Now, set your fat butt down and cut the flattery crap." Raquel didn't bother to put his feet up on the foot rest for his comfort. "Ewww! You have dandruff all over your shoulders."

"Oh, that's no big deal." Timmy brushed his shoulder, white particles flew through the air. "Just another part of life."

"Maybe for you, buster," Raquel said. "You're here for a haircut, and that's it. If it wasn't for your uncle, you'd have never gotten an appointment today."

"Yeah, he opens lots of doors for me."

"Someone can open a door for you, but it's up to you to stay in the room."

"No problem."

"There better not be."

Lola could tell from the sour look on Raquel's face that she was repulsed by Timmy. He seemed to be more of a grungy slob than his uncle. His jiggly belly, bulging out between the buttons of his wrinkled white cotton shirt, flowed over on to his stained navy blue polyester pants. His black beady eyes looked like buttonholes behind his thick-rimmed glasses. His curly hair, matted and dull, looked like a scouring pad.

Even though Lola felt empathy for Raquel, she could not help but chuckle while watching Raquel try not to touch Timmy when she put the towel and plastic drape around his neck.

"Poor Raquel," Lola said. "Timmy's worse than his uncle. I would have never booked him if I had known."

"Oh, dear... How were you to know?" Mimi said. "He is a fright."

"She'll never forgive me for this one, especially after all that's happened today."

"Let Francois be your ace in the hole. Love conquers all."

Raquel stood at arms length away from Timmy's body. Only her fake fingernails touched his scalp during the shampoo.

"Pewww! Looks and smells like somethin's died on your head," Raquel said. "We're almost done."

"This is so great," Timmy said. "I could lay here all day."

"Just try it, fool, and I'll call the dog pound."

"I love you to talk mean to me."

"You're disgustin'," Raquel exclaimed. "I'd slap you silly but you'd probably enjoy it. Ugh! And that face of yours... And wild eyes! Ugh! You're frightenin' to look at."

"I like being different," Timmy said. "I lucked out."

By the way Raquel had her nose tilted up and away, Lola figured Timmy must be giving off a terrible body odor.

"The oil from his scalp must smell rancid," Lola said.

"Oh, dear," Mimi said. "I wouldn't doubt it if that's all that smelled on that guy. He and Bertha ought to get together."

"Mimi, that's the fastest shampoo Raquel ever gave, and I don't blame her one bit. I wouldn't want to touch that creep either. Mark my words, she'll have his haircut done in five minutes flat."

"Poor child. You know I'm not one to judge, but from the looks of him, he's living proof that ignorance is rampant. It's not easy working with new clients or strangers off the street."

"No, it's not. But wonderful people like you make up for the few idiots we have to put up with."

"You're such a dear, Lola," Mimi said. "Who will be at the dinner party tonight?"

"All of us in the salon, a few new friends, and the new joy in my life, Craig."

"Craig?"

"Craig Michaels. He owns the gym down the street. He's a great guy, kind and thoughtful. I'm looking forward to being with a clean-hearted man who will actually talk to me and not at me. I've told you about Craig before."

"Oh, yes, I remember. Beautiful specimen. He's a fine young man, very attractive if I recall correctly. Nice family." Mimi's eyes twinkled, eyebrow raised. "If he's anything like his father, you're in for a real treat."

"Really?"

"Yes, Craig's father was one of André's golfing partners at the Bel Air Country Club. Wonderful man, fabulous dancer, too. He and I did a fancy tango one night at the Mardi Gras."

"How fun. What a small world. It's reassuring to know that you know him. What's Craig's mother like?"

"Lovely lady, wise and loving. As a mother-in-law, she'd be any woman's dream," Mimi said. "Is Rick still history?"

"I hope so. Love wasn't enough to sustain that relationship. I can't take much more pain, and I refuse to stay in a relationship where there's no fidelity, especially nowadays. It's beyond being a moral issue."

"You don't have to," Mimi said, touching Lola's arm. "It's your prerogative. Just remember, you're the captain of your own ship. Don't bat an eye when you throw a hurtful person overboard. You'll just be making more room for good, sincere people to take his place."

"You are so right on, Mimi; you always have been."

"There is a good future with an ethical man like Craig. I'm delighted for you."

"Thank you, Mimi," Lola said. "I think so, too. Being with him feels right."

Lola continued to wrap the permanent-wave rods in Mimi's hair. Disco music from the radio spiraled around Lola while she hummed the tune. Giggles came from the shampoo area.

Derrick shampooed the bleach out of his client's hair and playfully sculpted breast shapes out of the mounds of white lather.

"I love the way you tease me," Trixie cooed.

"Darling, you know it gives me great pleasure to please you."

Nattie finished cutting Mrs. Gordon's hair. Moving to the beat of the drum, she danced while rolling rollers.

"I'll whip this set out in no time flat. I'm still the fastest beauty operator in the West."

Lola couldn't help but hear Raquel try to be polite and carry on small talk with Timmy. His sniveling voice was assaulting to Lola's ears.

"I've never heard anyone talk with such an annoying utterance as his."

"Let's hope we never do again," Mimi agreed. "I'd rather listen to fingernails scrape a blackboard."

"So, Timmy, how do y'all like Los Angeles?" Raquel asked.

"Groovy. I love it," he replied with an irritating nasal whine. "It's a happening place. I spend my days at the beach and my nights at dance clubs in Hollywood. This trip has been a nice change from my boring job. But it's work, and it's what I'm good at."

"At least you're good for somethin'."

Lola shook her head, knowing Raquel was reaching her tolerance level. The statement she had just made to Timmy was not a Freudian slip.

"What does an action-packed babe like you look for in a romantic relationship?" Timmy asked.

"Ugh! Every question you ask adds fifty bucks to your bill," Raquel said, a soured look on her face.

"That's no problem, beautiful... My uncle's paying for it anyway. Are you a good cook? I expect to come home from a hard day's work and have a meal on the table. Plus, I like exotic dinners, oysters and all... Got the idea?"

"That's a hundred bucks more added to your bill."

"Cool... It's worth every penny. You and I will have a great time. I love your sensual, long fingers. I hope you're a sexpot who likes to scratch backs."

"If I scratch you, I guarantee it won't be your back."

"Cool."

Raquel frantically snipped, throwing hair everywhere. Lola saw that her patience was running thin.

"Ugh!" Raquel exclaimed. "You're an obnoxious disgrace to all of mankind."

"Go with the jungle magic of it, babe," Derrick sneered.

"Shut up, Derrick," Raquel said. "You're not helpin' matters."

"Raquel, do you cut men's pubic hair?" Timmy squeaked.

"Ah... Excuse me?" Raquel said, revolted.

"Do you cut men's pubic hair? I'd really like to know."

"No way, you ugly freak," Raquel said, keeping her cool. "I wax it out, and I rip the wax real, real slow. Sadomasochistic pig men who want that are usually into pain."

"Wow, good answer. Far out." Timmy sat with a silly smirk on his face, his breathing became deeper and more rapid. "Hey gorgeous, what gets your fires stoked up?"

"Please! Just shut your big, filthy, foul mouth," Raquel said. "You're a sicko!"

Raquel excused herself and walked across the salon to Lola and Mimi.

"Do you believe this?" Raquel said, wiping her forehead. "I'd like to mash the sonofabitchin' dirt bag piece of shit in his ugly mug with a two-by-four. Why, if I had my bull whip, that maggot would be hamburger."

"I don't blame you," Lola said. "Take his cape off and get rid of the scoundrel. Don't think twice about finishing his haircut. That ignoramus won't even know the difference. We're not going to book his uncle anymore either."

"Lola..." Raquel whispered. "That animal is doing you-know-what to his you-know-what under the cape."

"Do you mean to say that fella is playing with himself under that drape?" Mimi asked, gasping for air. "Why, I never imagined such an indecent incident could take place."

"Naw!" Lola said. "Are you sure?"

Raquel, eyes wild, not uttering a word, nodded a firm yes.

"What an uncouth dope," Lola said. "We haven't run across this for quite a while. I just hate it when people do that. It's such a violation."

"People?" Stunned, Mimi asked, "Just men do that... Or men and women?"

"Both. Isn't it disgustin' that we have to be subjected to such perversion?"

"Oh, dear, dear me," Mimi sighed, in shock. "Yes, it is a sickening assault. They have no morals."

"Now y'all listen to me," Raquel said, fluffing her hair. "You and I both know I can handle this situation, but, for the fun of it, let's sic Nattie on Timmy and get some sweet revenge out of the deal. Y'know how theatrical Nattie can be."

"Indeed we do," Mimi laughed.

"Great, we'll go for it," Lola agreed. "Nattie will give the creep what he deserves."

"Probably more than he ever bargained for."

"Hopefully," Mimi said. "He deserves to be castrated. Shame on him."

"This should be entertaining," Lola said, "because Nattie turns into an explosive, rabid dog when she knows someone has been violated. I'll get the camcorder. I might as well film this. It's not an every-day occurrence. Plus we'll have proof we didn't make up this far-fetched story."

"We'll name the flick 'Nattie in Action,'" Raquel said, rubbing her hands in anticipation.

"Great!" Mimi's eyes sparkled. "Another unbelievable story to tell my friends. This tale will be circulating throughout Europe by tomorrow night."

Lola calmly strolled over to the camcorder. Raquel cleared her throat and poised herself.

"Nattie, darlin'..." Raquel said in a confident, loud, stern voice. "Jackhammer... Chair number two."

Nattie instantly cocked her head like an inquisitive parrot. Her look intense, wildfire shimmered in her eyes. The rage within her caused her eyes to glare and become more watchful. Immediately prepared for battle, Nattie's nostrils dilated like those of a frantic lioness protecting her cubs. "I'll be right back, dear." Nattie handed the comb to Mrs. Gordon. "I have a little something to take care of. It won't take but a minute. You can trust me on that. Relax and enjoy the show."

"Oh, dear." Mimi sat quietly in anticipation, wringing her hands.

Derrick, unaware of what was going on, still sculpted breasts out of the rich lather in Trixie's hair.

"Feeling good, baby?"

"Yeah," Trixie said. "Meow..."

Timmy slouched in the chair. With a silly grin and in a blissful state, he impatiently awaited Raquel's return.

"I'm still waiting for you, Raquel, my little chickadee," Timmy crooned.

Lola, angered at Timmy's behavior, zoomed the camera in and filmed Nattie nonchalantly strolling near Timmy's back. All of a sudden, Nattie's hand, looking like a blur of light, moved quickly towards the plastic drape that covered Timmy.

"Hiiiiiii-yyaaaaahhhhhhhhhhh!" Nattie screamed at the top of her voice, making sounds that were bigger than she. "Aaaaaaaaaaaaaaeeeee! You sick jerk! This is *war!*"

Yanking the drape from Timmy's neck, she exposed him. "You pervert! Just look at you. Ugh! Lola, zoom in on this."

His stumpy fingers were still around his stiff penis. Frozen from shock, his body was rigid. Beginning to whimper, he sounded like a wounded rat.

"Ah, ah..." Timmy cried out. "What are you doing?"

"Nail the sucker, Nattie!" Raquel hollered. "Show no mercy!"

"Knee his nuts!" Mimi whooped. "Knee the bastard's nuts."

Zooming in close, Lola tried to keep the camera focused and still while laughing uncontrollably.

"This movie will look like I took it from the front seat of a roller coaster."

"Hey everyone, look at the sexual deviate, fiend sonofabitch!" Nattie started her verbal abuse. "Why, if it isn't needle dick the bug fucker! You breathing piece of stinkin' shit! How dare you take advantage of a virginal, virtuous girl like Raquel! Where's my scissors? I ought to slice your balls off. In fact, I think I will!"

"No! I, I... I'm innocent," Timmy cried, trying to get out of the chair.

"Innocent my eye, you SOB maniac. There's nothing innocent about you. You're just plain stupid." Nattie wrapped her arms around his neck and anchored him into a headlock, then pushed him back into the chair. "You're like a sittin' duck, now, buster. Huh! Innocent he says?"

Clutching and twisting his ear, Nattie reached for the fourteen-inch lime green dildo on top of Raquel's work station. Slinging it around, she whopped him upside his head, then whacked his blubbery back. "How about that?" Nattie asked. "I said, how about it?"

"You're hurting me," Timmy screeched. "Let me go."

"Hurt?" Nattie said. Whomp! "Great! I guess I'm on the right track." She grabbed, pinched, and twisted his ear again. "You haven't seen or felt nothing yet."

With the dildo as her weapon, Nattie smacked his head again and again. Timmy's glasses fell to the floor.

"Ugh, my glasses, where are they?" Timmy pleaded. "I can't see without them."

"You won't need them where you're going. They'd burn in hell, anyway." With the heels of her white leather boots, Nattie stomped Timmy's glasses to smithereens while continuing to whip him fiercely. "Like the pain, crybaby? How about a fast wax job?"

"Nooooooo..." Shrieking hysterically, Timmy wailed out like a lacerated vulture. His eyes crossed, he gasped.

"Aaaaaaaaaa..." Timmy raised his arm, striking at Nattie, slicing the air with a wavering karate chop and missing as she quickly ducked.

"I'm a senior citizen." Nattie walloped him again. "Assaulting the elderly, huh? Take this."

Whup!

"Take that."

Bam! Bam!

"How dare you try and hit a sweet little old lady like me."

Bang!

"Now listen good, jerk, anyone who lives as long as I have deserves respect."

Whop!

"Think about that, punk."

Lola figured the force of the dildo hitting his head had rattled his brain. She kept the camera rolling. The red welts on Timmy's body darkened by the second. With his zipper still down, Timmy groaned out in agony and ran towards the front door.

"You crazy lady! Don't hurt me anymore," Timmy pleaded. "My glasses... Ugh."

"Understand this, you scum-sucking pig! I can snap your neck clean."

Lola panned the camera, keeping it on the action. She had never experienced anything like this before. The violence frightened her, but she knew Timmy was getting what he deserved.

Nattie was at Timmy's heels, dildo in hand, still swinging hard.

Whup!

"And that was for your pervert uncle." Nattie belted his flabby ass, sending quivering ripples of polyester up and down.

"Your uncle will hear about what you did. I'll make sure of it," Nattie yelled. "The entire world will hear about this! We're going to sell this video to *Inside Edition*. You and your needle dick will be on every television set across the country!"

"Please make her stop," Timmy cried out to Derrick.

"You're on your own freak," Derrick said.

Timmy fled, stumbling and falling in the gutter while attempting to run across the street.

"I'll get you for this," Timmy threatened. "I mean it!"

"Yeah, you and who else?" Nattie barked back.

"You're crazy, woman!" Timmy cried, still sniveling and gasping for air. "You Californians are nuts!"

"Take a long hike off a short pier, buddy." Nattie turned around and faced everyone. "Hells, bells! I wasn't finished with the loser yet. Boy! Talk about a tight fight with a short stick. The idiot got lucky and got away. I was just getting ready to put the nincompoop in another headlock and flip him over."

"Nattie, you're too much." Lola kept the film going.

"I hate to admit it but, in a sick kind of way I actually enjoyed that. Was good exercise. Where's that bottle? I need a stiff drink."

"Good for you," Raquel said, handing her a bottle of Jack Daniels. "And thanks for coming to my rescue."

"I've never seen such an ugly dick in my life." Nattie took a long swig. "Bad genes, it's got to be. Some sexually abused woman must have put a curse on the men in his tribe a thousand years ago."

Everyone laughed hysterically, sounding to Lola like a laughing track on a sitcom.

"Bravo, Nattie; y'all out did yourself this time," Raquel said. "You deserve an Academy Award for that winnin' performance."

"Splendid indeed," Mrs. Gordon said. "You're good at everything. It's thrilling to watch you in action. Why... You punished him more than the authorities would have."

"I know. I made sure to. Those bumble-dickin' guys down at the station would have just laughed and let him go."

"Good show, Nattie, good show." Mimi stood and cheered. "I just love coming in here and getting my hair done. You characters really know how to cut up and keep the juices flowing. Justice has always prevailed in this salon. That amount of revenge was enough to satisfy me. How about you, Raquel?"

"I'm satisfied. I'm glad it's over, and I'm glad it's all on film. Plus I'm rid of ol' man Spencer forever," Raquel said. "Nattie, you're quick and tough. I'm so dang proud of you."

"Me, too," Lola said, hugging Nattie. "Nice job. You did some pretty fast footwork there, let alone everything else."

"You're damn right I did. I've still got what I was born with, babe."

Lola could see that Derrick could not wait to state his opinion.

"I think you crazed women have gone bonkers. Obviously a good screw isn't enough to calm any of you down. Maybe the stars in the universe have caused your hormonal frenzy. I'd say it could be PMS, but Nattie's too old to have periods. You must have all eaten something bad, or maybe it's the full moon or a weird epidemic."

"Fool, what are you talkin' about?" Raquel asked.

"Nattie, you mutilated that poor guy." Derrick stood erect, as if defending himself. "Give the bloke a break. He was just having a good time."

"Good time? At my expense?" Raquel glared at Derrick, throwing daggers sharp as razors. "You're as dense as a stinkin' slab of meat."

Lola was outraged at his statement, too. She opened her mouth and lambasted him. "Derrick, what on earth are you using for a brain? That guy was a sick pervert. I'm surprised at you!"

"We all know Derrick's pea brain is below his belt," Raquel said.

"Derrick," Lola said, "you have no filter between your brain and your mouth. How can you condone what that idiot did?"

"You two button your lips, or I'll button them for you." Nattie pointed her finger at Lola and Raquel. "Now, get on with your work. Detach and move on. Just remember... Men think in black and white... Women think in color."

Lola went back into the supply room and laid in her comfortable chaise lounge. It was satin cool and smooth to the touch, and she questioned when the day would be over.

Lola closed her eyes, daydreamed of Craig, took a deep breath to regain her composure, and relaxed. Within a few more hours, Lola would know her fate.

Chapter 14

Lola, sitting at her work station, watched Nattie finish rolling Mrs. Gordon's hair and put her under the hair dryer, then noticed Dorothy walking in hunched over her walker, struggling to push it because of the excess weight she carried. As usual, Dorothy greeted everyone with love in her voice.

"Hello dear ones."

"Hi, Dorothy," Lola said. "Good to see you."

"Thank you, honey. It's always a pleasure to see your lovely face."

Nattie took Dorothy's purse and set it on the marble shelf. "Keep on rolling, Dorothy. Roll it on back to the bowl, and I'll get your shampoo going."

"How's your day today, Nattie?" Dorothy asked.

"Moving right along. Got some good stuff on film. I'd tell you all about it, but I don't think your heart could handle all the excitement."

"You're probably right, dear. I haven't been feeling well lately. Heart palpitations and all, you know the story."

"I know it too well. If I could take your pain away, I would. You're my friend. I hurt when you hurt."

"I've been lucky to have your friendship, Nattie. I've loved being your sidekick all these years. We're a good team."

"I'm the lucky one. You're one gal who knows how to party hearty."

"I used to be a wild and crazy gal, but look at me now."

"You're still the greatest," Nattie said. "Oh, the comical lines you used to come up with and the situations we got into. We were like

Lucy and Ethel. Babe, you used to have everyone laughing so hard we'd have to gasp for air."

"Those days were the best."

"They were, but these days are good, too."

Over the years, Lola had watched Dorothy decline from a healthy vital character into a weakened, sickly woman. It saddened her to see such a wonderful person in so much torment. Lola knew it was hard for Nattie to keep up a positive exterior for Dorothy, but they were best of friends, and Lola knew that Nattie valued her true friends more than anything in the world.

"You look good, babe." Nattie patted Dorothy on the arm.

"I'm a freeze-dried apple. I look good on the outside, but I'm dust on the inside. My daughter's taking me to the doctor after I leave here."

"Your daughter's a real gem. I know you're grateful to have her."

"I sure am. Nattie, do you ever regret not having had children?"

"None of my husbands wanted them."

"Did you?"

"Yes, I sure did. I even got pregnant one time, but my husband beat me up and forced me to get an abortion."

"But why? Why didn't you have the baby anyway?"

"I was eighteen, young, scared, and stupid. No one to turn to in those days. I was terrified of him, especially when he drank. He drug me to some dark back alley, remote and filthy. I remember it like it was yesterday. The room was cold and dirty, a merciless expression covered the so-called doctor's face, and that smell..." With a faraway look in her eyes, Nattie rubbed the goose bumps on her arms. "Something from so long ago is still so alive in me today."

"Of course, dear," Dorothy said. "Nattie, I'm so sorry you had to live through that horrible trauma."

"It could have been worse. At least I'm alive to talk about it."

"Life can be so beautiful, if only people would be good to each other."

"Geezzz... What we did for love, or what we thought was love. You know how those days were, the dark ages, when we were a man's property. What he said went and we did as we were told, or else. I never could conceive again."

"My God, what we humans have endured. Nattie, you know you're like a second mother to my daughter. You were always there for Julia when I couldn't be."

"Yes, I love Julia like she's my own. She's filled quite a gap in my life."

"I'm still waiting for civilization to become civilized. Remember how obedient we were to our controlling, demanding husbands? I'm glad those days are gone. At least the young girls of today have choices and support for their decisions."

"It's been awful to carry the guilt and pain, there's been no getting away from it for me. For forty-five years, I've missed the wonderful child I never gave birth to. But I have to look at it this way; a mother is a mother whether she has children or not."

"Yes, I agree, and you've mothered us all," Dorothy said. "Lots of women who do have children aren't good mothers."

"That's for sure. Unfortunately we see it all the time."

"Speaking as a mother with a grown child, do you know what I miss the most?"

"No. What?" Nattie asked.

"I'm grateful that my daughter is married to a wonderful man, and that they have three healthy, beautiful children, but for once I'd like for her to come home, sit with me, and with no one around, just visit. I could cook her favorite dinner. I would love it if Julia spent the night and slept in her antique canopy bed, so I could peek in on her while she slept, like I did when she was our little girl. Quality times with her would be invaluably special to me."

Lola's mind flashed back to a day back on their ranch when she and her mother had lunch on the veranda in the springtime sun and watched the newborn colt frolic with his mother in the pasture, laden with lupine and poppies. It was a special moment they bonded and shared their love for horses, and their time.

"You know, Dorothy," Nattie said, "throughout the years of my hairdressing career, you can't imagine how many times I've heard that request from parents. It's a universal desire."

"Really? I thought I was alone in my wants."

"Don't flatter yourself. You've been at the dinner table too long. No one is alone in anything they think or feel. You're not the first, and you won't be the last mother to ever want that exclusive time with your child. You're going to die wishing for that, most mothers do. Lots of kids are unaware of their mother's desires. I'm sorry to say, but by the time the children wake up, it's usually too late. Most likely they'll be in the same boat some day. When they have their own kids, or when they don't have a mother to call. Now, lie back and relax. I'll give you a heavenly shampoo and make you feel better."

"I look like a worn-out old sheep with this long hair. Please give me a haircut today, too."

"You've got it, babe. A new do will make you feel like a million bucks."

"You've always taken such good care of me all of these years, and we've had hilarious, fun times together. Thank you, Nattie. I appreciate your kindness. You've been a good friend to me, closer than my own sister. You never picked on me. So many people are takers. You don't even bat an eye when you give so freely."

"I've enjoyed you too, Dorothy, and your family parties have been a ball. You're always good for a laugh, and a donut."

"Thank you. We've shared a lot during our years together, ups and downs."

"Yeah, more ups than downs, and more tears of laughter and joy than tears of sorrow. C'mon, let's get going. We're getting too sentimental. I'm going to give you a new hair-do today. That'll pep you up."

"Losing weight will pep me up."

"You will, Dorothy."

"I tell my doctor that my body is a home of the Lord and I'm making a mansion out of it." Dorothy winked at Nattie. "Nattie, remember your third husband?"

"Arnie?"

"He was sure a great dancer."

"Yeah, you two danced together like Fred Astaire and Ginger Rogers," Nattie said. "Too bad that was all he was good at."

"Remember the night we met Clark Gable at the premiere in Beverly Hills?"

"How could I forget?" Nattie swayed as if on a ballroom floor. "Clark was bigger than life itself. We swooned when he nodded to us and said hello. Now, there was a real he-man! Wow!"

"We were mere children then. Seems like yesterday."

"We were young and beautiful." Nattie scratched behind her ear. "You had a better figure than I did."

"Glamorous Hollywood Dollbabies, that's what they called us. I really do have a spectacular body under all this gooey fat." A joyful glint sparkled from Dorothy's eyes. "Our clothes were the highest style. Our jewels dazzled. Everyone referred to us as fashion plates."

"We were, and we still are. Call it like it is, babe. You know, the kids of today look at us as old ladies, but they should realize that we were young and beautiful once, and that they'll be in our shoes some day."

"Oh, Nattie," Dorothy sighed, "remember that day we had so much fun being extras in a movie."

"Yeah, at MGM. I loved having lunch in the commissary. All the superstars were out that day... Cary Grant, Katherine Hepburn, John Wayne, Elizabeth Taylor... We looked fabulous, and people treated us like we were movie stars. That's the day I met my fourth husband."

"Ray?"

"Yes, the second rate actor." Nattie rolled her eyes. "He was a good looking son-of-a-gun, and a good dresser. I must admit, he got us into some exciting parties. We knew the gossip before it hit the newspapers. The last party I went to with him is where I met my fifth husband."

"Was he the one who loved to skinny-dip?"

"Yeah, especially in Tahiti. Our sex was so good, he decided to spread it around."

"Nattie, between you and me, we've enjoyed more laughter than a thousand clowns."

"Yes, and I look forward to lots more, for a long, long time."

"Me, too. Go easy on me today, though, and hold the real funny jokes till my heart gets stronger."

Lola watched Nattie pat Dorothy's arm with tenderness and thought about the enjoyment she had in her own life while listening to Dorothy and Nattie reminisce. She marveled over their long-lasting friendship, and their love and respect for each other. They were positive role models for Lola.

Lola applied permanent-wave solution to the rods in Mimi's hair, set the timer for twenty minutes, then changed the radio station over to country and western.

"One cup of coffee, coming up," Lola said.

"Thank you, dear," Mimi said. "I just love that song."

"Me, too," Lola said. "Willie Nelson's the best."

"Sing it out, Willie!" Nattie whistled along with the song. "Sing it like only you can."

Lola smiled, remembering the fun times on the movie set with country and western superstars.

"How about meeting me at Mama Corelli's for dinner at six?" Derrick said, cutting his client's hair.

"You're on, sweetie," April, the sultry blonde moaned.

"Then afterwards we can play with more lather... And leather."

Listening to Derrick spew out several of Francois' romantic lines, Lola laughed.

"Hi Connie, how's it goin' today?" Raquel greeted her next client, a baby-boomer with bobbed hair, crispy white blouse, and a plaid skirt.

"I wish I could say I was fine, healthy, and happy... But I can't. I gave myself to the world, and it's chewed me up."

"What's wrong? Got the blues?" Raquel asked. "Come and join us for dinner tonight. We'll have another fun time, sugar. Lots of laughter cures all. That's just what you need. In fact, it's what you've needed for a long time."

"Stress is getting the best of me. I really do try to relax, but I feel like I'm a maniacal mouse on a treadmill going nowhere. I don't mean to be a driven workaholic, but I have this thing about over-achieving. I hate it that depression is getting to be a way of life. Must be bad karma."

"Don't interpret karma as punishment. I'd rather think of it as kind of a lesson to make me see reality more clearly."

"I guess illusions have to be popped, but how do people cope?" Connie asked. "How do people make it through life?"

"We persevere, and when we get desperate enough we manage to pull on strength from deep within. What other choice do we have, sugar?"

"Not much."

"Prayer helps. Let your little cherubs go before you and pave the path. My mama always told me that when I was just a cute little thing... It works."

"No one hears my prayers anymore."

"Don't kid yourself, cherubs even cover their lunch breaks. It's you that's not relaxed and open enough to let good stuff into your life."

"I remember a time in my past when I was so blessed and flowed freely through everything in life."

"If you did it once, cissy, you can do it again. Desire good things with all of your sweet little ol' heart. Hey, Connie, let's wash this gray away and make you a blondie. Then you can just sit around and look pretty all day long."

"The bleach would probably destroy my brain cells. Would you believe that yesterday I found a gray hair in my eyebrow?"

"Then let's color it all chestnut brown with tints of golden highlights."

"I wish that changing my hair color would take care of all the change I have to do."

"It's a beginnin'," Raquel said. "We all have to start somewhere."

"I just came from my therapist's office. He suggested that I take a one-month leave of absence from my job at the television station."

"Sounds like a good idea. Do it for yourself and for your husband and children. Your family needs a healthy mom." Raquel rubbed behind Connie's neck to calm her trembling body. "Your fists are clenched. Loosen them up and relax a little. There's no threat in here, and if there is, Nattie will take care of it."

"I didn't realize they were balled up. No wonder the circulation in my hands is so bad."

"How about a nice cup of herb tea to calm you down a little?"

"Thank you. Orange spice sounds good. Don't forget my tea-spoon of honey."

"Do I ever?"

"No. This is one nurturing place I can come to where the rest of the world doesn't exist. The television station is a twenty-four-hour-a-day madhouse. You're fortunate to work in a pleasant, peaceful environment."

"Yep. We try and keep it like that. We try real hard," Raquel said. "Some days we actually get lucky."

"Yes, like right now."

"The days of livin' from day to day are over. Life is forcin' us to learn to live hour by hour."

"I guess minute by minute will be next."

"I hope not for awhile."

Overhearing Raquel and Connie, Lola laughed and reminisced about her days as a hairdresser. She had never thought of the salon as a non-threatening, stress-free environment but was grateful that her customers did. Clients' short time in the salon did not allow them to see the full spectrum of the beauty business. Hairdressing entailed much more than playing with hair. Lola knew that any time a person physically touched someone and dealt closely with people's egos and emotions, anything could happen. And it usually did. Today had been proof of that.

"Wake up." Nattie shook Dorothy's arm. "Your shampoo is over."

Lola noticed that Dorothy did not move.

"Wake up, girlie." Nattie shook her again. "Your shampoo is over. Good things can't last forever."

Lola became frightened when she saw an alarmed, terrifying look cover Nattie's ashen-colored face. Nattie picked up Dorothy's arm, then let it fall down hard.

"Dorothy, this is a sick April Fools' Day joke. It's not like you to do this. C'mon, now, get up and let's get on with life." Nattie stood stiff. "You're scaring me."

"Is Dorothy passed out?" Lola rushed over to them.

An awful noise and smell came out of Dorothy's mouth.

"Uhaaaaa..." Dorothy moaned, then lay still, limp like a rag doll.

"Lola, call 911, fast!" Nattie yelled.

"My God! What's happening?" Lola pleaded. "What is wrong with Dorothy?"

"She's gone," Nattie said, closing Dorothy's eyelids.

"But what do you mean she's gone?" Lola began to tremble.

"Died... Her belly's already swelling," Nattie said, gently stroking Dorothy's face. "She's no longer of this world."

"No pulse?" Lola gasped.

"No..."

"It can't be," Lola cried. "No... It just can't be!"

"Yes, my dear, Dorothy left us and went to the Kingdom of God. Look... She died with a smile on her face. Sweet acceptance," Nattie said, laying a sheet carefully around her body. "What a way to go, Dorothy. Little did I realize that my heavenly shampoo would send you off to Heaven."

"What do you mean? She can't just die like this," Lola cried, watching in horror.

"She did." Nattie fought back her tears. "Dead! She's died on me! How dare you leave me like this, Dorothy! We were supposed to grow old together, and rock in rocking chairs, and laugh forever." With sorrowful eyes, Nattie turned to Lola. "I needed her friendship. We've been together for forty years. She's the one stable friend I had in my life. If anything went wrong, I always knew I had Dorothy. Now she's gone."

"I'm so sorry for you," Lola said.

"That's it!" Nattie burst into tears. "I'm retiring. Today is my last day. I've heard of stories like this throughout the years, but I never thought it would happen to me. And my sweet Dorothy, of all people."

Lola dialed 911, her hands shaking.

"Please send the boys down again, Butch, and pronto. Dorothy's died. It's been a rough day."

Tears welled up in Lola's eyes. She began to cry because she felt helpless and saddened that their dear customer passed away. She had empathy for Nattie who tried to be strong, but Lola knew the softness she carried.

"How could you not know Dorothy died?" Derrick asked. "Didn't you notice her breathing stopped?"

"No, I never look at my clients' when I shampoo them. It's not as if rigor mortis had set in yet," Nattie said. "I put my fingers in automatic drive for the shampoo and daydreamed about my date with Mr. Jenkins tonight. He's a pretty sexy old guy, you know... I was wondering if he could get it up and keep it up, or if I'd just have to roll it in. Sex therapists say it's good to daydream about sex. Boy! Talk about a nightmare bringing me out of a blissful state. Dorothy really did it this time. The greatest gal in the world, had a lot of class. She died in style. As good as my shampoos are though," Nattie said, wiping the tears from her eyes, "I think she would have rather died eating a chocolate fudge cake with a half gallon of vanilla ice cream on the side. She never bothered to put ice cream in a dish. She'd just get a big spoon and eat right out of the container."

"Food is what she loved. That's what she was taught." Lola put her arm around Nattie.

"I know, and she agonized over it and never could beat it. Dorothy looked to food for comfort and reassurance because her mother and nanny plea-bargained and nurtured her with gourmet cooking. If she wasn't eating food, she talked about food. When I'd tell her I was in the mood for Italian or French, she thought I meant food!"

Lola knew babbling was Nattie's way of releasing anxiety. She felt Nattie's mind had slipped into another space, taking no comfort from anyone.

"This was the straw that broke the camel's back," Nattie continued. "My back! I've really had it now. The nerve of her to die on me like this. Always said she had an iron gut, but it growled loud enough to wake the dead. She'd put coffee in her sugar. She'd even eat what everyone else at the table didn't eat. One night she put nine pats of butter on the last piece of sourdough. Her eyes would get glassy when she'd look at food, no matter if it was salty, sweet, greasy, or burnt. Her eyes would light up, and she'd salivate every time the waiter brought another course. I always joked to her that I'd never go out in public to eat with her again. Well... I guess I won't have to worry about that any more."

Nattie pulled the sheet over Dorothy's head, then wiped the tears from her cheeks.

"I already miss you. I love you, Dorothy. Thanks for being my good friend for so long. Hey, lady... We did it right, didn't we? Our friendship lasted a lifetime because we were loyal to each other, never any judgment. Never a jealous moment between us. We were always happy for each other's good fortune." Nattie wiped more tears. "I'll see you in Heaven when my time comes. Meet me at the gate. Be sure to tell Clark Gable that I get the first dance with him when I join you all in the Grand Ballroom. I hope Harry James is playing the big band sounds. He was the greatest big band leader of all time. We always loved him, didn't we Dorothy? Yeah... We always loved Harry."

Lola's heart felt Nattie's pain as she held her close, sobbing. Her mind swirled in thoughts of the day's events, and she prayed for grace. Nattie had always joked about retiring, but now with Dorothy's death, Lola knew Nattie was serious about really wanting to end her career. Lola felt that maybe it was time for a new chapter in Nattie's life, too. Yes, Lola thought, life was full of new beginnings. It became more evident all the time.

Lola noticed that Mrs. Gordon continued her deep sleep and snoring under the dryer, and saw that Nattie was heart-sick and tried to cover her feelings.

"Ol' Gordon could sleep through an earthquake," Nattie said, trying to divert her mind. "That sweet woman will never suffer from stress-related problems."

Mimi, wringing her hands, offered to help, but there was nothing to do. "My heart goes out to you, Nattie. Loving friendships are what makes life rich. You and Dorothy were always like two kids in Candyland. The rest of the world did not exist when you two laughed and played."

"Poor Dorothy," Lola said, feeling the solemnness that death brings. "We must call her family."

"I'll call her daughter right away."

"Thanks, Derrick."

"This is unreal. Ugh! That awful sound she made. What was that?" Raquel hysterically shouted. "I've never been around a dead person before. Oh, dear sweet Dorothy! She was such a kind lady... A sugar of sugars. We all loved her so much. Her family will be just devastated to the max." Raquel's tears streamed down her face, her body shook. "Ahhhhh... I think I'm gonna be sick."

"Get yourself together," Nattie said. "This is no time to fall apart."

"Times like this separate the men from the boys," Derrick said.

"Time will tell what you'll do." Raquel darted her eyes towards Derrick. "It won't be hard to guess what side you'll end up on."

Uneasy, Lola wished there was something she could do to ease the tension between Raquel and Derrick.

172

"Uh, uh, uh, uhhhh..." Connie choked loudly. Suddenly, her head flicked back uncontrollably. Jerking spasmodically, she flailed to the floor.

"It's a grand mal seizure," Nattie blurted out. "I've seen them before." She quickly grabbed a hairbrush and put the handle into Connie's mouth. "This should help a little."

Convulsed in pain, Connie flip-flopped on the linoleum. Terrified and awestruck, Lola ran to help.

"Lola, you call emergency," Nattie ordered. "Derrick, push the furniture out of the way." Nattie, turning Connie on her side, kept an eye on her. "We'll make it through this, babe. Just stay calm."

Lola dialed 911 again.

"Oh! Butch. Send another ambulance. Fast! Our client's having an epileptic seizure." Lola paused to listen. "No! I'm not kidding. I know it sounds unreal. I'll remember this horrid five minutes for the rest of my life. Today's ending up to be more than I can handle." Still crying, Lola pleaded, "Hurry, Butch. Please hurry."

"I didn't know Connie was an epileptic!" Raquel said, rubbing her temples. "Hairdressers are supposed to know everything. She should've told me. Maybe then I could have been better prepared."

Lola opened the door for the paramedics, arriving one ambulance after another. She watched them administer to Connie first, then lift Dorothy up, over, and out on the gurney. Lola was distraught but she knew she must stay strong, at least until this ordeal was over.

Lola noticed Raquel looking faint, her skin turning white as snow. With her eyes bugging out and her head falling to the side, Raquel's body went limp.

"Raquel?"

Spineless, Raquel fell to the floor, unconscious.

"Raquel!" Lola rushed to her friend and knelt by her side. "What's wrong?"

It broke Lola's heart to see Raquel lying there, defenseless. She threw a towel over her exposed, sprawled-out body. At that moment, in her mind, Lola forgave Raquel for all of her wrong-doings throughout their years of working together. When confronted with death and sickness, Lola realized the aggravating things Raquel did were trivial and that their friendship meant more than anything.

"Derrick! Hurry! Help me with Raquel!" Lola said. "We're out of smelling salts. What shall we do?"

Derrick rushed to Raquel and knelt next to Lola.

"I don't know why I'm trying to help her," Derrick said.

"Yes you do."

"No I don't. Get real... Just look at the holes in my hair. It will take months to fill in."

"Forget about that. Now do something before I scream."

To Lola's surprise, Derrick leaned over and kissed Raquel on the lips.

"That should bring her out of it," he said.

Lola, appalled and disgusted with his behavior, rapped his shoulder with the back of her hand.

"You idiot! This is no time to play Prince Charming! It's going to take more than your kiss to wake her up. You don't have to keep proving you're a jerk. Now do something. Quick!"

"Today must be 'Bash Derrick Day.' I'm trying my best. Go easy on me. I'm only human."

"Sometimes I wonder."

With his fingertip, Derrick tickled the rim of Raquel's nostril. Awestruck, Lola watched in dismay.

"Raquel."

She didn't respond to him. Derrick stuck his finger up into her nose and wiggled it hard. "Wake up, Raquel."

"Are you nuts?" Lola asked. "Just what do you think you are doing?"

"Trust me."

"What choice do I have?"

"Mmmmmm..." Raquel murmured, laying still.

"You are *gross!*" Lola said, irritated with Derrick's performance. "Why on earth are you putting your finger into her nose?"

"Because I don't have a fire cracker."

"Huh! This is no time to be clowning around like that." Lola shook Raquel's arm, trying to awaken her. "Wake up."

"This will do it." Derrick inserted his finger into her nose again. More intensely, he shook his finger hard against the inside wall of Raquel's nostril.

Quick to come out of her unconscious state, Lola noticed that Raquel's eyes popped open and expressed rage.

"How dare you," Raquel screamed, trying to sit up. "You're really battin' them today... Tickin' me off... And furthermore, get your filthy finger out of my nose before I break it!"

"But it worked," Derrick said. "What more could you want? I got the job done, and you're still not satisfied."

"Dimwit."

"Compliments will get you everywhere." Derrick kissed Raquel's forehead. "You'll be OK. I see your sense of humor is already back."

Derrick lifted Raquel, carried her to the facial room with Lola and Mimi close behind, and laid her on the bed.

"Oh, Raquel. I feel so bad for you." Lola put a soft blanket over her.

"Stay relaxed, dear, you'll be just fine shortly." Mimi laid an ice pack across Raquel's forehead. "That's right, dear. Lay still."

"No... Don't try and get up," Lola said, rubbing Raquel's feet. "You'll be OK. Close your eyes. Breathe deeply. Meditate. I know you'll be all right soon. Don't worry about anything. I'll do your next appointment. Just stay right here and don't move. If you don't feel like doing Jennifer's blow-dry, Derrick or I will do that, too. Put everything out of your mind. Just look forward to tonight's dinner party, and Francois."

"Can I get you anything?" Derrick asked.

"A glass of water, and please dim the light," Raquel said. "I'm feelin' a tad bit better. I need a little more time, though, to muster up some energy."

"Sure, babe, anything you want." Derrick gently held Raquel's hand and kissed it. "Please accept my apology. I've been a real jerk today and I'm sorry. Please believe me when I say that. Your friendship means a lot to me. I value our good times together."

"A wise person forgives; a fool forgets." Raquel looked him in the eye.

"You'll forget, tiger." Derrick squeezed Raquel's hand.

"No I won't. Not this time."

"Yes you will."

"No I won't."

"Face it, you love me." Derrick kissed Raquel's hand. "You can't stay mad at me."

"Yes I can."

"No you can't."

"You're a dreamer."

"I love you."

"How can you not?" Raquel said. "I'm every man's dream."

"You're right."

"You two are something else," Lola said, shaking her head. "It's unbelievable how people choose to communicate."

"Hey, Raquel," Derrick said, feeling the bald spots in his hair.

"What?"

"Thanks for not breaking my nose."

"The day's not over yet."

Lola was relieved to see the hard edges of tension soften between Raquel and Derrick. She looked at the clock and wished she could forward it to closing time. Thinking of having dinner with Craig gave Lola strength to finish her day. She let out a deep sigh, then went on with her work.

Chapter 15

Lola wiped the tile in the shampoo area and lined up the bottles of hair products, her mind floating away to the serenity of her favorite exquisite Japanese garden in Tokyo.

"I've got to get out of this zoo before I go bonkers," Nattie said. "I'm going on a fast shopping spree next door, that always makes me feel better. I'll be back soon." She belted out "The Impossible Dream" while leaving the salon.

"To be willing to march into hell for a heavenly cause," Nattie sang.

"Nattie loves those show tunes," Lola said. "She really should have been an entertainer."

"Who said she isn't? She's spiced up our lives plenty," Mimi said. "She's got her odd ways, but you've been lucky to have had her all these years. God knows she's good in an emergency."

"She's helped me an awful lot, was with me at the hospital when my mother passed away. We had sat for hours," Lola said. "She wouldn't leave my side. Nattie comforted Dad more than I could have."

"It's amazing how people's exteriors sometimes hide what they're really like on the inside."

"Yeah, Nattie's a good example of that."

"Yes, she certainly is," Mimi said.

"Nattie makes people earn her friendship, but when you've earned it, you've got it for life."

"You've brought her joy and true friendship, Lola."

"Thank you, but a relationship or business deal is good only when both sides benefit."

"Yes, most definitely."

"This is the first calm minute I've had since early morning," Lola said, finishing Mimi's permanent. "It baffles my mind to think of what I've lived through today. Hopefully, the rest of the day will flow smoothly. I'm really glad Raquel's client didn't show up."

"It's so rude for people to not phone and cancel their appointments. It leaves you hanging in the air."

"I know... Emergencies do come up. I accept that, but what really gripes me is when I do someone a favor and book a real early or late appointment and they don't show. I've learned to give selfish people one chance, and if they blow it, I won't book them anymore. Now, Raquel and Derrick book them again; then they charge them double."

"Free will. It's a person's prerogative how they choose to handle a situation."

Lola told Mimi about the joke she and Raquel would play on Derrick at 5:30.

"Samson will pretend he is the husband of one of Derrick's married lovers."

"I hope Samson doesn't rough Derrick up too much. He's already had quite a day. The knots on his head may take awhile to go down."

"We've all had quite a day. Anyway, a little laughter will be good."

"Derrick asks for trouble. Anyone who dates a married person has problems within. Someday, sometime, somewhere down the road, they will have to deal with it."

Lola's mind flashed back to the afternoon in Rick's back office when she caught Rick with another woman. The deep hurt was still in her heart. She had never felt so forsaken in her life.

"I've never dated a married man, and I never will. There's no future in it. Plus, I would never betray another woman. Dating Rick, I was on the receiving end too many times, and it didn't feel very good."

"People who practice infidelity forget reality by wallowing deeply in the muck of false love. From my experience in life, I've seen that what goes around, comes around. It keeps me in tow."

"Me too. It seems that as life gets faster, the retribution comes more quickly."

"By the way, how is Debbie? I was saddened to hear about the fire."

"She's slowly making progress. Burns are dangerous. Luckily the doctors have the infection under control."

"That's reassuring. I was so sorry to hear about her accident. She's such a beautiful girl, inside and out. I wish her well. Be sure to give her my love."

"Yes, I will," Lola said. "Randy doesn't deserve her. And he's too immature to handle what's happened."

"It seems that way, but we shouldn't judge him," Mimi said. "Only God knows why two people are together. People are attracted to each other because they have certain lessons to learn from each other. They'll work it out in their own time. We all do, sooner or later. Patience is one of the greatest virtues any of us can attain."

"I'd still like to give Randy a piece of my mind," Lola said. "He hasn't been to the hospital once. He's been down at Mama Corelli's for three days, drunk as a skunk. Huh! As if booze will bury his sorrows."

"It will for a while. Then he'll wake up and do what is best."

"I hope so, for Debbie's sake. She's asked me about him and I encouraged her by saying that he'll be in to see her soon. She desperately wants to believe that he'll be there for her. She's afraid to face him, knowing that her physical beauty may be gone."

"Debbie's full of love. No matter what, she will always radiate beauty."

"Yes, and he won't. I hate him for that, for being so selfish and self-centered."

"Don't hate, Lola; for whatever you hate, you will become. Hate can destroy a person. Hate disconnects a person from God. Love is the magnet for goodness. Love, and you will become love."

"I know you're right, but sometimes I can't help myself."

"You'd better help yourself, for your own good."

"You make it sound so futile. Why?"

"A beautiful person is created in more ways than one. As a youngster, I attended school with two very pretty girls. They were sisters, extremely talented and creative. Even though they were identical twins, their personalities were as different as night and day. Their mother dressed them smartly with a sophisticated flair and styled their long blonde hair into rag curls that hung to their waist. Evidently their mother, like most of us, had a good and a bad side. Throughout the years, the fault-finding, negatively critical sister chose to dwell on her mother's negative side, spitefully hating her mother's shortcomings and blaming her own misery on her mother. The warm-hearted, kind sister chose to love her mother's positive traits and overlooked her mother's deficiencies. The sister who loved her mother grew up to be a lovely, charming socialite who maintained her beauty, enjoying life fully. The other sister, consumed by hate, lost her beauty at an early age and lives a miserable, sickly, lonely life. It was an individual thing, stark in truth. One mother, two daughters, and each twin took a different path. Each girl chose her own fate and face with what was in her heart."

"So... We destroy ourselves with hate."

"Definitely. We see in others what we are ourselves. Her hate caused her to place stumbling blocks in her own progress. Of course she denied it and blamed her self-made misery on others, and especially her mother."

"What a damnable trick to become what we hate," Lola said.

"Yes, it is."

"How are the sisters today?"

"They look so different, you'd never know they were even related. Their lifestyles are worlds apart. Hate is ugly. Like fear, it keeps a person away from virtue."

Lola's mind flashed back to her ten-year high school reunion when she was surprised to see that an overly-jealous cheerleader's face had become distorted with droopy lines and ugliness of expression.

"Mimi, this world has been your playground for years. You've had the opportunity to see it all, first class. What impresses you most?"

"I'm impressed when I see people being good to each other because they want to and not because they have to, or because they want something in return. And I appreciate it when a person gives me quality time, relates heart to heart and mind to mind, even if it's only for a moment, at a bus stop or in a line at a restaurant."

"I can identify to that. Too many people don't listen when they're being spoken to because they're too busy thinking about what they'll say next. Unfortunately, it seems like common sense and civility have flown out the window."

"Consciously or unconsciously, no matter what or where the upbringing, every human being has natural instincts to know the difference between right from wrong," Mimi said. "I feel it's something we are born with."

"I agree. I'm noticing more and more, as life gets faster, that many people are living in denial."

"It's frightening they've chosen denial as their safety mechanism."

"Hmmm..."

"Yes, dear?"

"Mimi, tell me something wise."

"Think with your heart. Feel with your mind."

"That's deep," Lola said.

"Yes, and it works."

"It must, because everything you touch turns to gold. You live what you are, Mimi. Thank you for inspiring me," Lola said, continuing her work. "We're just about finished with your haircut."

"It feels better already. I'm so relieved to get this done before my trip," Mimi said. "You asked what else impresses me?"

"Yes."

"The magnitude and beauty of Mother Nature overwhelms me. The mountains, the sea, the waterfalls, the forest, the rivers, flowers... It's all so glorious and grand. I can never get enough of the good feelings and richness nature gives. My favorite is to stand and face a full spring waterfall and be showered with mist. I innately go to nature when I need to be replenished with healing energy."

"Yes, there is a divinity and perfection in it all. I hope the day will come when people show reverence and respect for this earth again."

"They will, great leaders are emerging. People are more than ready to follow someone who is wise and just."

"Mimi, when you were young, did you ever wonder what your destiny would be?"

"Oh, my, yes. I had great desires and goals. Then life happened."

"Did it turn out similar to what you had envisioned?"

"No, not at all. I don't think a person knows their real destiny until they are old. By then, it's been done."

"I guess we think we know certain things."

"Yes, fate plays a big part, so does free will. Every choice we make affects the rest of our life. It's all relative. But don't get me wrong, I'm not disappointed at all. Years ago, as a young woman, I read in a philosophy book that by the time a person dies, he will have done everything he came to do on this earth. That rang true to me and I've flowed with it ever since."

"Sounds good to me."

Lola and Mimi discussed Bertha and the lease. Admitting her frustration, Lola told Mimi her fear of losing her salon.

"I always remember the horrible stories my grandfather told me of the great depression days, losing everything and having to start over, their house burned down, they had to live in their neighbor's barn. I guess it's put the fear in me."

"Don't take on another person's fears," Mimi said. "If things don't work out with the salon, you can come and stay with us in Switzerland for as long as you want. Anyway, it's wise to take a break before starting a new chapter in your life. Be kind to yourself. You're young, healthy, beautiful, and well loved. Let the jewels of life fill your heart."

"Thank you. I plan to. Mimi, you've always been so encouraging."

"Life is full of starting over again. Look at me at this age. I'm starting over again, only without André this time. The two of us were like one, a real team. He was my dashing gentleman, so full of fun and surprises. We cherished each other. In a way I feel like I'm starting over as half a person."

"I know, and that saddens me."

"I owe it to my loved ones to remain strong. André would have wanted it that way."

Lola thought of her mother. Tears welled up in her eyes. It was still too soon. Her emotional wounds had not healed into scars yet.

"Why the tears, dear?"

"I miss my mother so much," Lola said, wiping her eyes. "A day doesn't go by when I don't think of her. Sometimes I go to the telephone to call her. Then I remember that she is gone. I try to endure but it's just so hard."

"Know that her love is with you." Mimi brushed a tear from her cheek. "Life... We don't have to like everything that happens in our lives, but we must learn to accept, remember the special moments, and go forward. Never, never look back. André and I had a wonderful marriage. We lost our first fortune because of a crooked business partner, but we pulled together and made another one. Our goal was not to make a lot of money. It was to enjoy our family and work and serve people well. I am satisfied and content with what we accomplished."

Lola brought Mimi a hot cup of tea and a brownie.

"Thank you," Mimi said. "By the way, how is your father getting along?"

"Fine. He won't come out and say it in plain English, but I know he wants me to move home with him. Supposedly he needs help on the horse ranch for a while." Lola reached for the curling iron. "He's starting a new chapter in his life, too. I know it's lonely for him without my mother, but he has lots of good friends to keep him company, plus he's thrown himself into rebuilding that 1932 Model A Ford. Mimi, I love living in a big city. Santa Inez Valley is beautiful, and I do miss the ranch, but I'm not ready for that quiet lifestyle yet. I do go visit almost every week, or he comes here. The drive up there along the ocean is therapy for me. I usually leave Saturdays after work. Each sunset is different, each beautiful in its own way."

"He loves you so much. I think he wants what you want."

Lola smiled, knowing Mimi was right. Lola knew her father would be all right. Tall and handsome with fiery eyes, he looked to Lola more vital and happy each time they were together.

A short, slight, elderly twig of a man sporting a white goatee entered the salon and stood within four feet of Lola. Looking like an unborn bird, he shifted his weight from side to side. His hands were clenched behind his back.

"Well, hello there gorgeous," he said, his voice shaky from age. "My o my, you look ravishing today."

"Dr. Charles Hanson, what brings you into town again?" Lola nodded, speaking in a cool tone.

"I'm giving a seminar at the University. I happened to be in the area, so I thought I'd stop in to say hello and invite you to be my guest for dinner tonight."

"Thank you, but I have plans. You must excuse me, Dr. Hanson. I'm very busy and I can't visit with you now."

"No problem. I understand." He whipped out his business card and put it on her work station. "Here's my number."

"Unfortunately, I already have your number."

Walking to the door, he said, "Keep in touch, chickie. We'll get together another time."

Lola thought that it would be a cold day in hell before she would ever call him.

"You sure know how to pick the winners," Derrick laughed. "For someone who has such an organized life, you end up in the damnedest situations."

"I didn't need that. Just shut your big mouth or I'll shut it for you. Better yet, I'll get Raquel to shut you up."

"My lips are sealed." Derrick threw his hands in the air. "That won't be necessary. Raquel damn near killed me. I'm bruised everywhere. Just look at the holes in my hair! I've never had a worse headache in my life."

"What's all this about?" Mimi asked. "Who was that dear, sweet little old man?"

"Old is the only word you got right. Dear and sweet are hardly the terms to describe him. In the beginning he had me fooled, too."

"Tell me what's happened, and don't leave out one juicy detail."

"A couple of weeks ago, I had a client cancel her appointment for a permanent. That gave me a couple of empty hours so I went down to Mama Corelli's for lunch. All the local characters were there. I joined ten of them at the round marble table on the garden patio. Talk was in the air about Susan's tea party that next afternoon. She had invited sixty artsy people, which was a guarantee of an outrageously wild fun time."

"Somehow you always manage to get invited to the exciting parties. I've sure enjoyed some of them along with you. Now... Go on."

"This Dr. Hanson walks in. He's a ninety-seven-year-old friend of Susan's, and he had just driven down from San Francisco."

"That's a long drive for a man his age. Why didn't he fly?"

"He's a world-renowned scientist. *Who's Who in America*. He wanted to stop along the way to gather specimens from the seashore."

"Fascinating."

"Well, for hours his quick wit and compelling stories added quite a flair to the conversation. His knowledge of world travel was food for my soul," Lola said. "You know how I love Europe and the Orient. Visiting with him warmed my heart too because he reminded me so much of my courteous, sophisticated Uncle Marshall from Massachusetts, who many a time spent special holidays with my family at the ranch."

"I think it's so wonderful how your family lavishly entertained so much. I give credit to your mother for extending herself and working so hard to create a loving environment for everybody to enjoy."

"Yeah, house-guests were a way of life for us. Mom received so much pleasure from seeing everyone happy. Our kitchen was like a restaurant. So when Susan told me that Dr. Hanson was going to sleep on her hard sofa, I automatically offered him my guest room."

"Of course, dear. After all, your family brought you up to respect the elderly. You were thinking of his comfort, I'm sure."

"A lot of good it did me."

Lola explained to Mimi how Susan had dropped Dr. Hanson off at her apartment at 9 p.m., and Susan had agreed to join them for breakfast at eight the next morning.

"We enjoyed our evening, laughing, eating strawberry shortcake, and sharing stimulating conversation until 2 a.m. Then I showed him to his room, laid fresh towels out in the guest bathroom, told him to make himself at home, and I went to bed.

"It must have been satisfying to communicate with a talented universal man," Mimi said.

"Yes, it was delightful and motivating... Until daybreak."

"No! What happened?"

"That old fool is a mule-headed piece of bark."

"Why?"

"Well, I wasn't quite awake. I lay still, soaking up the early morning sun. I'm not much of a real early morning person, but I managed to open one eye and look at the clock. It was 5:00 a.m. I rolled over and lay in that calm state between sleep and slumber. Then an eerie feeling covered me like a smothering blanket. I felt as if penetrating eyes were piercing my being. I opened my eyes, and lo and behold, Dr. Hanson stood next to my bed, quivering as if cold, his gnarled fingers up and ready to grab at me. His glazed eyes scanned my covered-up body with lust. I lay there totally vulnerable."

"Oh my! What were you thinking at that moment?"

"I was totally, I mean totally taken aback. Within seconds, this supposedly sweet adorable old man snatched my comforter with his twisted hands, threw it to the floor, and literally dived into my bed, landing on me. Huh! Can you beat that?"

"Oh, no, dear. How dare him! That bird needed a few feathers plucked."

"Yes. Then get this... He did the dog paddle with his hands near my face."

"What?"

"It was so odd, I had never seen or experienced anything like it in my life. I was too mad to laugh. Then, the twerp had the audacity to try to kiss me with the rim of what had been his lips. His bony chicken legs continually moved in the motion of a swimming frog. I was bewildered, just couldn't grasp what was happening. It all happened so fast, felt unreal."

"You must have been mortified."

"I was until I realized I was twice his size. I'm five-eight. He's barely five feet tall. I've handled horses and worked on classic cars all my life. The lame brain didn't know what he was in for. Adrenaline surged within me. I grabbed the collar of his nightshirt, clenched it in my fist. I threw that old fogey into the air and rattled his scrawny body with all my might."

"Good grief. Serves the creep right. Well, I hope for your sake that he had underwear on."

"No way! No such luck... We're talking crepe and drape here. He had no balls, literally, just a crinkled sack of skin dangling back and forth like a pendulum."

"Ugh," Mimi said in a disgusted tone.

"If I'd had my scissors, I'd have clipped the old bird. He's lucky I didn't break his arms."

"I hope you've erased that terrible sight from your mind."

"It took a while." Lola continued her story. "I didn't realize my arms were so strong. I shook the hell out of that old buzzard. His glasses fell off and his tongue hung out like a thirsty dog's, but his dangling limbs still did the dog paddle. That was a new one on me."

"Ha! Ha! He was swimming with nowhere to go," Mimi giggled. "Please forgive me, dear. I realize this was a harrowing experience for you, but it's so funny. Your discussion is so visual. I just can't help myself."

"I bellowed out loud enough to make the old fossil's ears ring for a week. Then I said, 'You'd better shape your little ass up Charles, or I'll kick your shriveled butt out of this bed so fast you won't know what's happened.'"

"What did he say to that?"

"You're not going to believe this one."

"We'll?"

"That old coot had the nerve at that moment to ask me to call him 'Chuck.' Then he added, 'You're so beautiful. It's only natural for me to desire you. I am a man and I do have feelings.' That statement put me into a rage. I said 'not with me you don't, Buster.' Violently shaking him again, I told him that if he didn't behave like a civil gentleman, I'd knock his teeth down his throat."

"You would, too."

"Yeah, you're darn right I would. Now listen to the kicker. As I shook him again, his false teeth fell out onto my chest, slimy drool and all."

"Ugh! Such vulgarity... So revolting... That's a queer thing to happen. I'd have been livid by then."

"I was. It made me want to throw up. I threw him sailing into the air, and like a loony bird he hit the wall and fell to the floor. Out cold, he lay comatose. I thought I had killed the creep; then I noticed faint erratic breathing."

"My Lord! What did you do?"

"I called the paramedics. He was still out when they arrived, and that's the end of the story."

"Bravo. He certainly got what he deserved."

"Then I called Susan and told her what had happened. She was mortified, to say the least. She said Dr. Hanson had been a complete gentleman the fifteen years she had known him. Even though I laughed about this incident, I still felt violated."

"Of course, birds peck at the best fruit."

"I didn't dare tell Dad because he'd come with his double-barreled shotgun and shoot the bastard. I phoned Rick, thinking he would console me. He made matters worse by laughing at me and asking, 'what did you expect'?"

"Men are men," Derrick said. "What did you expect?"

"Huh! I expected him to be a gentleman like my sweet Uncle Marshall."

"How else would we learn tolerance if idiots didn't come into our lives?" Mimi sighed deeply.

Lola noticed Nattie walking to the salon from across the street. Her arms were filled with shopping bags. Lola hoped Nattie felt better. She knew that the loss of Nattie's dear friend Dorothy would leave a big void in her life.

Nattie whipped open the door and strutted down the center of the salon, kicking like a high-heeled show girl. She was dressed in a multi-gemstone-studded gold lamé bustier and white short shorts with her cheeks hanging out. Her black fishnet stockings clung to the curves of her shapely legs. With the freedom of an eagle in flight, Nattie sang her favorite show tune. Lola knew that music and singing was the way Nattie chose to deal with her feelings. Nattie's facade looked happy, but Lola could feel her deep hurt.

"Hello Dolly, well hello, Dolly. It's so nice to be back where I belong... I'm looking swell, Dolly... Can't you tell, Dolly? I'm still glowing, I'm still growing, I'm still going strong..."

Nattie sang as she walked toward Lola. Laughter was everywhere. Lola, amazed at Nattie in her skimpy tight-fitting clothes, thought she had really flipped out this time and feared that Nattie was just about to go over the edge. Lola realized that their hectic day had taken its toll on all of them.

"Never a dull moment with you around, Nattie," Lola said. "Are you OK?"

"Never been better, and nothing like shopping to shake the blues." Nattie slung her purse and shopping bags onto the table. "I was born to be wild. I'm going to work in this sexy outfit the rest of the day. Great color. Makes my skin tone look creamy and touchable. The gems are so bright, you may want to wear your sunglasses."

"You're my inspiration," Raquel said, blow-drying her client's hair.

"I'm glad I've already had my lunch," Derrick said. "Your boobs aren't covered, let alone your veranda. You have four wrinkles under your cheeks. You need your buns bobbed, Nattie. Someone may turn you in for indecent exposure."

"Let them. It won't be the first time I've entertained down at the police station. I'm a sexy senior citizen. And don't you forget it!" Nattie took her client, who had been waiting, back to the shampoo bowl. "Let me give you the shampoo of your life. It'll send you into orbit. Literally, I'm serious. There's something very special about me and my shampoos."

Lola put finishing touches on Mimi's hair, then collected money for her services. Embracing warmly, Lola said, "I'm going to miss you, Mimi. Keep well, have fun, and enjoy your flight."

"I'm sure I'll be thinking and laughing about today's experiences all the way to Switzerland."

"It's been a funny day, but the tragedy with Dorothy overshadows everything."

"Poor Dorothy. I'll say a prayer for her soul," Mimi said. "That old geezer was the topper, and to think he looked like such a sweet man. And that Timmy guy. Ugh! Looks can be so deceiving. Imagine! Those men have no face. They're not ashamed of anything they do."

"Why should they when they had nothing to lose?"

Mimi handed Lola a set of keys. "Here you are, dear heart."

"What's this for?" Lola was perplexed.

"For you."

"Why? What are you talking about?"

"They are the keys to André's Mercedes. It's our to gift to you. My lawyer will contact you to sign the papers. It's parked across the street."

Stunned, Lola could not believe what she was hearing.

"This is too generous of you, Mimi. I can't accept a gift like this."

"You can't afford not to. You cannot deny a dying man his wish."

"What do you mean?" Looking into Mimi's eyes, Lola asked, "What are you talking about?"

"André adored you. He wasn't an overly demonstrative man, but you must know that you were the apple of his eye. He considered you to be the daughter we never had. It touched him so that you loved unconditionally and gave so freely of yourself and your time, especially when he was dying. Many of our friends weren't emotionally developed enough to come and spend time with André when he was withered and in pain. It hurt them too much to look at him, just laying there. Plus, I don't think they've faced their own mortality."

"I know that too well. It's all so heartbreaking. People did the same thing to my mother." Lola felt her throat tighten, she fought back tears.

"You touched him, not only his heart, but his body. He so loved the facials, manicures, and pedicures you gave him when he was bedridden, and you read him his favorite poetry. Many a time you drove him, in his car, to chemotherapy when I wasn't well enough. André knew you loved driving his car and he admired how you handled it," Mimi laughed. "He always said you'd be a great race car driver."

"I would." Lola looked directly into her eyes. "Mimi... I give because I want to. If anyone benefits from what I do, then fine. If they don't, then that's fine, too. Plain and simple... Loving makes me happy. I never look to receive when I give. I have much to be thankful for in my life. Daily I say that I am eternally grateful for the abundance that is divinely mine."

"You truly are a radiant light in people's lives, and your heart is kind. You have the gift to see goodness in all. I commend your parents for having an angel like you."

"It takes one to know one." Lola held Mimi's hands. "I will always be grateful to you for helping me through the rough times during my mother's sickness and death."

"We had each other, and that was enough." Mimi kissed Lola's cheek. "Joy holds you close. The beauty you see in others is a beauty you carry within yourself. You touch the hearts of more than you realize. Giving will never deplete you because you know your source of power is divine. André was a wise man. He loved you and recognized your worth. There were very few people André stood for when they entered the room, but he always stood for you. Please accept this gift. You know the pleasure of giving because you give charity to all. Do not deny us that same pleasure."

At that moment, Lola felt André's presence with Mimi. Overwhelmed with emotion, she cried tears of joy while hugging her dear, dear friend.

"Oh Mimi, since you put it like that, I will graciously say thank you from the bottom of my heart. I will treasure you, André, and André's Mercedes forever."

"You've made me very happy."

"Me too. Now let me drive you home."

"No thank you, dear. I'm walking down to the drugstore now to pick up a few things for my trip. They'll call me a cab from there. Now take care, and don't forget to come and visit us in Switzerland. I have an easel, paint brushes, oils, and canvases waiting for you, and a spacious French country bedroom with a cathedral ceiling and three walls of glass overlooking the grassy hills."

"Thank you. It sounds wonderful and inviting."

Lola fantasized about visiting Mimi in the countryside on weekends while attending art school during the week in Paris. She wondered if her long desired dream would ever come true.

"I'll miss you, Mimi."

"Me, too."

Lola knew that when people connected from the heart in times of pain, their strong bond would last forever whether they remained together or not.

"Good-bye."

"Good-bye for now, dear heart. Live in your wisdom and keep on having fun."

Chapter 16

Lola signed the tag and sent the UPS man out with a brownie. Sitting behind the reception desk, she took a moment to reflect on her meaningful friendship with Mimi. Overwhelmed with Mimi's generosity, she sat in awe. Staring at the stylish late model silver Mercedes, still not believing that it was really hers, Lola tingled with excitement and looked forward to playing with her new loaded toy. She could not wait to get behind the wheel and drive up the Mendocino coastline for a leisurely cruise with Craig to enjoy the spectacular view.

Looking around, Lola noticed that Marcie, the aspiring actress who never aspired, was in the beauty salon.

"Hi, Marcie. I didn't see you walk in."

"Oh, hi, doll. I'm the alley cat. Remember? I snuck in from the back." Marcie practiced smoking in front of the mirror, blowing billows up into the air Bette Davis style. "Hello show people. I'm here, ready whenever you are. Hi Derrick darling, you sexy thing." Puff, puff. "Great outfit, Nattie. I love that gold lamé. Now that's really Hollywood... Venice style. You're just so with it, Nattie baby. Love it."

Worse than Raquel, Lola figured Marcie's narcissism could wear out a mirror.

"Got any good parts lately?" Raquel asked.

"No, my agent's been out of town. I'm going to the plastic surgeon after I leave here, you know, to have a little added here and there. Then I'll be a big star. No one will be able to resist me then. Lola, do you think I should pluck my eyebrows some more?" Marcie asked, looking closely at her face in the mirror. "Are they too heavy? Shall I have my crows feet removed? Maybe I will again. What do you think?"

Lola was polite to Marcie but knew to keep the conversation short. It was nothing for Marcie to babble twenty minutes without stopping. After the events of the day, Lola's tolerance had run thin.

Mrs. Grant sat quietly, her hands arranged like a tent, finger tip to finger tip. The lines on her face told her history of times gone by. Lola was pleased, knowing that Mrs. Grant was a stable force for the salon when things got hectic. Many times she had answered the phone, filled shampoo bottles, and folded towels.

"Nattie will be a while," Lola said, walking over to Mrs. Grant. "How about a nice cup of cappuccino?"

"That sounds great. Coming here is the highlight of my week. You know I come in early for the entertainment, the high energy. I've never been disappointed yet. All of you treat me better than my children do, and you sincerely listen to me when I talk."

"You're so sweet. We appreciate that you listen to our stories, too."

"That's what life is all about. We share our lives, and I love you all. Do what you have to do, dear. Let me know if you need some help. I'll read this week's *Globe* and sip my coffee until Nattie's ready for me."

Lola knew that the lonely retired widow, abandoned by her cruel children and left practically penniless, came in an hour early every week to partake of the goings on. Mrs. Grant had told Lola that the salon was one place she still felt like a part of humanity, and with everyone doting on her, it made up for the companionship that her children would not give.

Lola watched Derrick put moves on Heather, a married woman who insisted on having a male hairdresser.

"Shall I make you look like a glamour girl or a jungle cat today?" he asked.

"Whatever you're in the mood to do, say, or squeeze," Heather giggled. "Meowwww... You know your smile melts me down and I can't say no. As long as I have a man's touch on this fiery skin, I'm happy. My husband's such a cold fish, you know."

Lola was relieved to see that Raquel was in full form again, recovered enough to chatter and continue her work on her next client.

"I met the man of my dreams today, he's so great. Bigger than life! And would you believe this guy? Oh sugar darlin', he gave me all his money. I haven't had an extra second to go out and spend it all. I'll have him take me shoppin' so I can model everything," Raquel said. "Boy! You should've seen Nattie in action, beatin' up a pervert and everything... Her fancy foot work was somethin' else, fiddle music couldn't have kept up with her pace. Here, now hold still. I'm gonna snip these bangs just a smidgen."

Lola noticed Elwood, a thin man with thick rimmed glasses, walk in through the front door. No one else in the salon saw him until he accidentally kicked over a plant.

"Forgive me, please."

"No problem, Elwood," Lola said. "Hey, whatcha got in the pretty box? More goodies?"

"I know you all love chocolate truffles, so I brought some." The bewildered, soul-searching man interrupted Derrick. "Excuse me. I don't mean to bother you, but a friend of mine has a medical problem. Would you, by any chance, know of a good doctor who treats impotence?"

"Not me, man. Not on your life. Ask Lola, she keeps a file on everything."

Minnie's eyes were fixed on Elwood's candy box. Drooling, she stood next to the dessert tray. Elwood walked over to Lola and handed her the fancy lace box of truffles.

"Sweets for my sweet."

"Thanks Elwood, you're always so thoughtful. I'll share these with Doctor Brown," Lola winked. "Over in Santa Monica on Wilshire Boulevard."

Nattie's client, whom she had nick-named Mooching Minnie, kept staring at the box of truffles in Lola's hand.

"Nattie," Minnie said, "I'm not in the mood just right now to eat a raspberry Danish. I'd could go for something a little chocolatey."

"There's brownies there," Nattie pointed.

"I'm kind of in the mood for some candy with a little chocolate in it."

Lola opened the box and offered them to Minnie.

"Just one will do it for you," Nattie said. "We all want a taste, too, you know."

"Thank you, Lola," Minnie said, grabbing three. "Maybe next week you'll have more apple turnovers. Would it be OK, dearie, if I wrap one little tidbit of a brownie and the raspberry Danish in a napkin and take it home? I'll enjoy it much more later this evening."

"Help yourself." Nattie shook her head and smiled. "That's what they're there for."

"Thank you. I love the goodies you have every time I come in."

Lola laughed to herself while watching Minnie, with her short, stubby fingers, snatch several of each kind of dessert, wrap them all in several large napkins, then insert her new found treasures into her enormous plastic purse. Grabbing a handful of tea bags and hot chocolate packages, she stashed them in her bag, too. Lola remembered the time Minnie had brought in a quarter pound of cashews to show off to everyone how charitable she was, and then proceeded to eat every last one of the cashews all by herself. The standing joke in the salon, Lola knew, was that Nattie always gave miserly Mooching Minnie a late afternoon appointment so there would be enough dessert and goodies for everyone else to share and enjoy. It amazed Lola how some of their wealthiest clients had the cheapest, stingiest, most petty ways, and how some of the poorest clients were the most generous with what little they had. Lola thought back to dear old Mrs. Yates, a gentle sweetheart who lived on a restricted pension. She always brought in homemade candy or fruit from her trees. The homeless people showed their gratitude for their free haircuts by sending their social workers and counselors into the salon as new clients.

Lola listened to Laurel and Marla, sitting in the waiting area sipping their tea, argue about the correct way to put toilet paper on the dispenser. Laurel powerfully shook her finger in Marla's face.

"My nanny taught me that the proper way is for the paper to roll out from the underside."

"Well," Marla retorted, riled, "your nanny taught you wrong. Everyone who knows any etiquette at all would tell you that the paper should roll over the top."

"Obviously, you're an over-paper girl."

"Yes I am, and you should be, too."

"No way."

"Anyone with a half a brain knows that over-the-roll saves tissue. When I am a house-guest or at a hotel, I always make sure that the toilet paper is on the correct way."

"Say no more. I know your kind. Why, I'll bet you eat your corn on the cob from side to side."

"Yes, and row by row."

Listening to the two women bicker, Lola thought people are starving all over the world; sickness is epidemic, millions of homeless people are everywhere, earthquakes happen every day, taxes are soaring, unemployment is up, pollution is an international problem, and countries are at war. Who cared which way the toilet paper went on? Nattie winked at Lola and she realized Nattie had read her thoughts.

"Different strokes for different folks, babe," Nattie said.

"That's what makes the world go around."

"And around, and around, and around," Nattie laughed. "Maybe that's why there are so many dizzy broads around."

Just then Janice walked in. Lola gasped.

"My God, Janice! Did your fiancé beat you up again?"

The battered woman walked into the salon dragging her leg. She stood slumped while cradling her arm, holding back the tears.

"Yes, early this morning."

Lola felt compassion for Janice when she looked at her blackened eyes and bruised arms. She remembered her own black eye and cracked ribs from when Rick had slapped her around because of his frustration at work.

"I'm so sorry for you, Janice. Oh... Those bruises. They'll heal soon."

Lola reached for her.

"Don't give me pity," Janice said, backing away. "It perpetuates suffering, and there's nothing noble or righteous about suffering."

"But..."

"No buts about it. Against my better judgment, I stayed too long. I was a fool to allow him to drag me into his vortex of conflict."

Wordlessly, Lola moved forward and put her arms around Janice.

"Well... Tell me what's happened."

Janice's dark eyes grew large, filling with tears.

"I gave him the wrong fork to eat his breakfast."

"What do you mean?"

"I gave him a salad fork instead of a dinner fork. He went into a wild rage and started swinging. The apartment is still a mess."

"Oh, Janice, that's terrible."

"We've only lived together two months, and this is the third time he's done this. I forgave him the first two times, but this beating was the last straw. He doesn't think I'm capable or confident enough to leave him, but he just threw me away."

"He sure did."

"I'm going to hold myself strong. I owe it to myself to learn how to be a healthy survivor."

"Yes, you will. Promise me you're really going to leave him this time. Don't put up with this abuse. You deserve better. He's violated you beyond imagination."

"I know... I have to leave. I was torn in the beginning, but now I know my life is at stake. I love him so much, but my patience for the injustice is gone. He's killed my joy for wanting to be with him. I'm not willing to go down the tubes with him. He's threatened to kill me. He needs professional help, and I'm not trained to give it to him. I can only help him if he's willing to help himself. Unfortunately, he can't seem to come to terms with his abusive childhood. I've sure learned some hard lessons out of this deal."

"Please, let me call a client of mine who works at the Women's Center. She'll give you good direction. You can stay with me until you get settled."

"You've always been so helpful. Thank you, but I've already made arrangements. They won't let him out of jail for a few more hours." Janice wiped her hand over her forehead. "Earlier today I sold my car to a friend. Another friend bought me a ticket in her name. I'll be on my way to Oregon in two hours and start a new life with my distant cousins. He'll never find me there."

Lola thought back to what Mimi had said earlier about life being full of new beginnings and how true it was that life forces things in its proper timing whether we are ready or not.

"Thanks for squeezing me in today, Lola. I really appreciate it. I wanted to see you and have my last memory of Los Angeles be a good one."

"Aren't you sweet. Thank you. I'm giving you a good-luck haircut. Make all the wishes you want... And Think Big."

"I'm tired of learning my lessons the hard way. From now on, I will try to learn wisdom with grace and harmony."

"That's a good one, and be sure and pray for guidance in your dreams," Lola said, finishing Janice's haircut. "You've been a dear friend and client. Whenever you think of me, know that best wishes and warm feelings are coming your way. Please keep in touch."

"I will, and thanks again."

"I hate these ugly things in life. Like war, abuse continues. Hopefully, some day, people will learn how to be good to each other."

"Yes, let's be positive and know that it will be some day soon."

"It's time for justice, for everyone, everywhere. People should think before they speak, and when they do speak, they should speak with love in their heart. Then people would want to stay around them." Lola warmly embraced her friend. "I'll miss you."

"Me, too."

"Ugh! Another illusion popped."

"Why?"

"I thought we'd continue to laugh and share our lives and be friends for a long time."

"Life in the 90's. Be prepared for change. Nowadays, it's the only thing that is for sure." Janice wiped a tear from her eye and took a deep breath. "I never say good-bye. I just say I'll see you later."

"Then I'll see you later," Lola said, giving her one last hug.

It broke Lola's heart to watch Janice limp out of the salon, but she was reassured that Janice was determined to build a good life for herself, a life filled with the love and joy she richly deserved.

It was 5:15 p.m. Lola shampooed her last client, Patricia.

"You're just about due for a tint touch-up."

"I know," Patricia said. "That time rolls around too fast. Next time."

"Are you ready to go gray yet?"

"No way. I told my dentist today that if it wasn't for him and Lady Clairol, I'd be a toothless, gray-haired old maid."

"Ha! What did he say to that?"

"He thanked me for putting him before hair color."

"You're in great shape."

"That's because of racquetball and long walks on the beach. Helps the stress level."

At the bowl next to Lola, Nattie shampooed Mr. Jenkins.

"You're in good hands, Jake, and your scalp's a little tight," Nattie said. "There's pizazz in these digits of mine, so let me press a few things and relax you a little."

"Sounds good to me."

From the sounds of Jake's soft murmuring, Lola could tell that Nattie was giving him one of her super-duper shampoo jobs. Lola watched Nattie brush her large breasts onto Jake's cheek while shampooing his head.

"Feel better, Jake?"

"Oh, yes, much better. I'll bet you have a delightful bedside manner."

"Oh, you bet I do. Later, baby, you can squeeze me a little and give me a thrill."

Derrick greeted his client, kissing both cheeks.

"You have no idea how I've looked forward to seeing you today."

"Oooooo... Thank you." Diana fluttered her long, luxuriant eyelashes and flashed her big, brown eyes. "What's on our menu today, hot stuff? Dessert?"

"Appetizers today, babe. I'm short on time," Derrick said, putting his arm around her waist and guiding her to the shampoo chair. "We'll do the whole nine yards another time."

"Promise?"

"Of course. You know you're in my dreams when I'm not with you."

"I should hope so," Diana said, dazing deeply into his eyes.

Lola saw that Raquel, a figure of perfect elegance while working on her last client of the day, was energized from talking about Francois and the day's events.

"My new honey bunny is a Frenchman. Let's trim these ends and give you a pretty French braid today. Somehow, I'm in the mood for French. I do extra special work when I'm in a happy frame of mind."

More than ever before, Lola welcomed the end of her work day. Still in awe over some of the days happenings, she continued shampooing her long time client and friend, Patricia.

"You're overdue for a haircut, too."

"Just a fancy do for today. I have a blind date tonight. Dinner at Mama Corelli's."

"Great! We're all having a party there after work. Join us. We'll welcome your new boyfriend into our sane, normal world."

"Sounds good. He's a writer, too. And an artist."

"Then he'll understand us," Lola teased. "Glad you finished and sold your screenplay."

"Such a relief. It was a marathon, but I love what I do. I'm an obsessed writer. I can't seem to pull myself away from that computer until the story is complete," Patricia said. "You look a little frazzled. How's it going today?"

"Girl... You can't imagine what a day it's been. Trust me on this one."

"Like last New Year's Eve day?"

"No, no. Worse, much worse."

"No! How could anything be worse than that day? When I'm depressed, I think of that day and thank my lucky stars and immediately feel better."

"It's like this salon has been in the eye of a hurricane."

"That bad, huh?"

"For starters, Nattie's half naked. Check out Derrick's bruises and bald spots on his head, arms, and chest. The paramedics have been out several times. Dear, sweet Dorothy died. The old fossil popped in again. See that lime-green dildo? Nattie beat up a sleazy pervert with it." Lola rolled her eyes. "Those are just tidbits."

"Want to talk about it?"

"No, I don't have a large enough vocabulary, but I'll show you the video later."

"Great, I'll look forward to it," Patricia said, while looking around. "Hey, what was that crackling noise?"

"Oh, that's just Bertha up there, flushing the toilet for the thirtieth time today. Try to ignore it. We do."

The front door swung open. Randy stumbled in drunk and slithered towards Lola at the shampoo area. Slovenly and unshaven, the sight of the cowardly man disgusted Lola. She was annoyed with him for abandoning Debbie while she lay suffering alone in the burn ward at Mercy Hospital.

Nattie pushed Mr. Jenkins towards her styling chair.

"Wait for me, babe, I'll just be a second." Nattie sprayed air freshener around Randy, hissed at him like a snake, then spat at his feet. "Wallow in your weakness, pig. You have the emotional level of a frog. Your wife is a jewel, and you're a chickenshit loser. Shame on you. Who the hell are you to hurt Debbie, or anyone?"

"But..." Randy looked frightened. "Lola, help me."

"It's an inside job," Lola said. "Only you can help yourself."

"You can run, Randy, but you can't hide. People who stick their heads in the sand get their butts kicked. From the looks of you, you'll have to reach pretty high up to touch bottom." Nattie walked over to Mr. Jenkins and began his haircut. "I've never seen a selfish, lazy person get respect. You ought to give this jerk lessons on how to be a good husband."

"You're a real woman, Nattie." Jake kissed her hand. "My kind of gal."

"Aces are high and I'm wild," Nattie winked. "Maybe we could play a little strip poker tonight."

"I love your outfit. If you wear that, I'm sure to win."

"We'll both win, and thank you, darling. I love a man with good taste."

With mixed feelings of anger and empathy, Lola questioned how she would treat Randy.

"Good-by, Lola," Randy cried out with slurred speech. "I came to say good-by to you."

"Good, I hope you're on your way to the hospital."

"No... I'm going to commit suicide."

Lola did a double take. Her mind flashed to Debbie lying in pain in the hospital alone, needing comfort.

"What on earth are you talking about?"

"I wanted to see you before I killed myself."

"No! No you are not going to kill yourself. You are going to march over to that hospital and say hello to Debbie, hold her hand, and tell her you love her," Lola said, exasperated. "You wimp, I'm so furious at you, I'm livid. Debbie's been waiting for you for three days, and all you've done is guzzle booze down at Mama Corelli's."

"I've wanted to go but I can't handle what's happened to her," Randy said, staring at the floor. "I don't want to face her. I just can't."

"Our love should give us strength to face what we don't want to. If you really love her, you'll go."

"I love Debbie," Randy cried, in agony. "I know you're right, but I'm scared. I've tried, but I can't."

"Then you'd better try a little harder and not let fear get in your way. Now go home, freshen up, and get over to the hospital."

"I can't take it anymore." Randy stood like a broken man, sobbing. "I'm going to kill myself."

"No you aren't, you sonofabitch, not until you go see Debbie," Lola yelled. "She's always been there for you when you've needed her, even when she's busy with the kids and her acting career, and taking care of your sick mother. You're a poor excuse for a human being and you're not worth one hair on Debbie's head."

"I want to end it all," he wailed, shuffling his feet. "I want to die."

With shampoo on her hands, Lola grabbed Randy's collar and pulled his face to hers.

"Stand up straight, take a deep breath, and look me in the eye when I talk to you."

He refused to look Lola in the eye, so she shook him hard until he did. Randy's pistol fell out of his pocket and to the floor. With her foot, Lola swished it towards Derrick. He quickly picked it up and put it in his drawer.

"Let me tell you about suicide, Randy," Lola said. "It's a coward's way out. Nothing's going to end for you, and it won't get any better. You're going to continue up there right where you left off here on earth, only without your body. Your spirit will stay suspended in limbo until the day you were destined to die. You will be faced with what you've left unfinished here and it will drive you more mad than you are right now because you won't have a body to finish your work. You'll be an outcast up there."

"That's a lie," he said, pushing Lola away. "It'll be peaceful in Heaven. I need to rest with the angels. They'll make everything OK."

"Debbie's an angel. Go love your wife. Be strong for her. Why, I ought to slap you silly, maybe that would help you get your act together. Don't be so damn self-absorbed and self-centered."

"I'm not. I just hurt real bad," he said, moving away from Lola.

"Jealousy, fear, and worry disturbs the mind, and the cause behind it all is selfishness."

"I'm not selfish," Randy insisted in a tone which faltered through the vehemence of his emotions.

"Prove it then. Walk out of here right now and do what you have to do. If you really love Debbie, you will."

"Do you love me, Lola?" he blubbered. "Huh? Do you?"

"Sure I care about you, but I despise what you are doing."

"I need a hug." Looking like a pained, over-grown three-year-old child, Randy stretched his arms out towards Lola. "Give me a hug?"

Angered, not wanting to touch him, Lola hesitated.

"Listening to him is no walk in the park," Derrick said. "Give the guy a hug and let's get this ordeal over with."

Randy looked at Lola with misty doe-like eyes.

"Please," he begged. "Hug me?"

Lola thought Randy was a pathetic weakling and did not want to hug him but she felt she must. With deep compassion, Lola contemplated the agony which Randy seemed to suffer. She pulled him to her bosom and he laid his head on her shoulder and wept uncontrollably. Lola patted his back like she would a hurt child.

"Do you feel better now?"

"Yeah, I do."

"Good. Then get out of here, walk home, and clean up. I'll be calling the hospital in two hours. If you haven't visited there yet, you're going to hear from me. I mean it. It's time you put yourself aside and start thinking of others for a change."

"I will. Thanks, Lola." He wiped the tears from his eyes on his shirt sleeve while leaving. "I love you, Lola. You've been there for me more than once. I love you. I'll tell Debbie you said hello."

"Randy..." Lola said, "You deserve to live... We all do."

"Thanks. I needed to hear that. I love you."

Randy stumbled out of the salon. There was a sorrowful stillness in the air. Nattie grabbed a big pillow from the love seat and handed it to Lola.

"Holler bloody murder into this and don't hold anything back. Try to scream as loud as Raquel did with Francois."

"That pillow doesn't give me the same motivation," Lola laughed.

Burying her face in it, Lola screamed as loud as she could, then noticed that everyone was laughing and screaming to release their pent-up tension, too.

"Making memories," Nattie said.

This April Fools' Day was ending up to be more than Lola had ever encountered in the salon.

"Let me finish your shampoo, Patricia. I'm sorry to have left you lying like this."

"No problem. It's so sad. Randy's a perfect example of the crazy world we live in. Situations like this are epidemic."

"He comes from a long line of family abuse, plus his strength of mind is inferior to most. I used to fix his mother's hair. I know I should be more tolerant, knowing the type of environment he came from and all, but sometimes I just lose it," Lola said. "I wouldn't know where to begin to tell you about today. You're a writer. I'll give you a book."

"Where did you get those words on suicide?"

"Oh, I don't know. They came from somewhere out of the blue. Come to think of it, they were kind of scary. But, evidently it worked. Hey! Whatever works. It did sound pretty good."

"Too good. It's a frightening thought, enough to make a person think twice about ending it all."

"I used think I wanted to be a psychologist. Now, especially after today, I'm sure glad I'm not."

"Who says you aren't?"

"My bank account, that's who."

Sadness for Randy and Debbie filled Lola's heart. She wished them the best and hoped they would resolve their situation soon.

Her mind flashed to Craig. Contented, she smiled, knowing that he did not have a selfish bone in his body and that he would be a nurturing man who would be there to comfort her in an emergency.

Chapter 17

Lola brushed Patricia's long amber-colored hair with a wooden boar-bristle brush. It felt like silk running over her fingers and was as fine as Patricia's virtues.

"I know you really want to grow your hair longer," Lola said, "but these split ends really do need to be trimmed."

"Next time," Patricia said. "Lola, what time is it?"

"A hair past a freckle."

"When will Samson be here?"

Lola looked out the window.

"Any time now," she whispered, not wanting Derrick to hear.

"Where's that crackling sound coming from?" Patricia asked, glancing around the room.

"That's the second time you've said that. What sound are you talking about?"

"Listen." Patricia pointed to the ceiling. "Looks like more of the plaster has cracked."

"This old building's full of creaking noises. No big deal. We live with it and accept it as a natural part of life."

"This sound is different than the usual creaking this old wood makes. Can't you hear it? This cracking sound has a dull thud to it."

"You must be hearing things. All I hear is Bertha puttering around upstairs and flushing that darn toilet again and again. She spends more time in that bathroom than she does anywhere, including her kitchen."

"Does she still eat a lot of chocolate?"

"You've got it. Boy... What a memory you have."

"That's why I'm such a good writer. In fact, I'll be teaching my first writing class soon. You ought to join. It's great fun to write. Good therapy, too."

Lola thought back to earlier that morning when the mysterious Oriental woman had told her that she would write.

"I may just take you up on that."

"Terrific," Patricia said. "In a way, writing is similar to painting. You know your dynamic paintings touch people's private space and make them feel deep emotion. If you write like you paint, you'll surely be a success."

"Thanks. I try to create from the heart and paint what I feel. It's nice to be appreciated."

"Creative writing is a picture with words. I wouldn't have four of your paintings in my condo if I didn't know fine art. Mother's tried to get Father to bring home your seascape from his office, but he won't part with it. Somehow, in that particular painting, you seemed to have captured the essence of the ocean's fiery passion."

"How could I not at Carmel-by-the-Sea?"

"Oh... Beautiful Carmel, surrounded by the magnificence of Mother Nature. That unique art community possesses a passion to create," Patricia said, dreamy eyed. "Having freed myself to let my mind wander into realms of joy, I daydream into a turquoise sky misted with lavender radiance, into fluffy clouds of white visions, into cypress trees that hold emerald lights and sparkles from the stars from the night before, and into the splendid, rushing sea, filled with sapphires, pearls, and aquamarines."

"In the early morning mist, while walking on Carmel's shore, I step in the foot prints of others before me and squish the sandy granules beneath my toes," Lola said, continuing to create from where Patricia left off. "I then extend more free will and place my own footsteps in the white, cool sand in a path of my own volition."

"Just listen to us silly girls," Patricia laughed. "We need a vacation."

"Yes... To Carmel, God's gift to California."

Lola thought back to that thunderous day in Carmel when she had painted that picture she had sold to Patricia's father. Sunshine had burst through the mauve and salmon colored clouds, and winds fiercely spiraled through cypress trees while she stood at her easel on an enclosed redwood deck overlooking the ferocious sea. It had been a loving time in her relationship with Rick, a romantic weekend filled with tenderness and kisses in front of a toasty fireplace. An amiable feeling of love enveloped her. The sadness of accepting that Rick was gone for good almost made her cry. Lola chose to remember the good, and knew that more jewels of life were awaiting her.

"Where are you?" Patricia asked, looking into Lola's face.

"Somewhere very nice."

"Let me guess? Painting in an open field of wild flowers in the south of France."

"Paris comes before the south of France," Lola said, smiling.

"Life is interesting."

"Never a dull moment. Sometimes I'd like one, just to see what I'd do with it."

"I know what you mean. By the way, did Bertha sign the lease yet?"

"No. I'll zip up there after I finish your hair. She'll sign it then," Lola stated. "She's got to. Time's run out. She can only enjoy dangling me for just so long."

"But what if she doesn't sign?"

"Then you'll be the last client I do in this salon."

Feeling melancholy, Lola finished curling Patricia's hair with the iron, then watched Raquel put the crimping iron to her client's long hair.

"Wait until you meet Francois," Raquel said. "Girl, you'll just love him so much. My folks are thrilled."

"A man that's actually tamed you down? Unbelievable. I've got to meet this guy."

"You will, cissy. We're goin' out to dinner at Mama Corelli's. Francois will be here at six. Bring your hubby and come and join us." Raquel wiggled her eyebrows. "We're gonna have a lot to celebrate tonight."

"Thanks for the invite. We'll be there. We love to party with all of you wild and crazy hairdressers."

Knowing that there would be much laughter and good feelings, Lola looked forward to Mama Corelli's that evening, and Craig.

"Hold still, doll, and get ready to hand me the pins one at a time," Derrick said, blow drying her long red hair.

"Anything you say, honey-babes," Darla cooed. "I love to watch the way you move your fingers."

"And I love the way you love the way I move." Derrick held his hands up. "I'm a miracle worker."

Through the window Raquel saw Samson, then glanced and winked at Lola. In anticipation of the next episode of the day, Lola took a deep breath and let it out slowly.

"Show time," Raquel said. "This is it."

"What's it?" her client asked. "What do you have up that Southern sleeve of yours this time?"

"Just hold on," Raquel assured. "The action-packed entertainment is commencin' to begin."

"We're going to need a few drinks before din-din, darling," Nattie said, rubbing Jake's shoulders, "so we can relax enough to digest our food."

"Anything you say, Nattie. Whatever you want."

Samson flung open the door so rapidly that it rattled; its multi-colored stained glass cracked into prisms.

"Grrrrr..." Samson said, standing six-three, like a colossal grizzly bear on his hind feet, eyes bulging.

Massive in size, his tightly gripped fists pumped up his muscular arms. With his square jaw clenched, his eyes fierce with rage, Samson again growled ferociously. His loud roar made Lola shiver and shrug her shoulders.

"Who's this Derrick guy? Where's the bastard who's fooling around with my wife?" Samson bellowed, grabbing a towel and twisting it hard. "I'm going to start in on Derrick by wringing his neck just like I'm wringing this towel," Samson hollered, the cords protruding from his neck. "There's nothing I hate more than a womanizer, especially when my Lily's involved."

"Gulp... I... Uh.. I..." Derrick began to shake. "What in the hell is going on?"

Lola watched Samson and observed that everyone in the salon was gaping in amazement, too. The silence and stillness was intense except for the beat of the disco music that added to the thumping in Lola's heart.

"I want him. Now..." Samson competently spoke in his stage voice, loud and distinct. Pointing his finger towards Derrick, he said, "You're the one!"

Derrick, eyes opened big as a saucers, trembled like a leaf in a hurricane. Like a guilty mole, he looked for somewhere to hide. Lola saw the fear in Derrick's eyes, and she hoped that this experience would drive Derrick into a psychologist's chair to get professional help for his deep-seated problems.

"I'm outta here," Derrick squeaked. "There's no way I'm a match for this guy."

"So... You must be Derrick," Samson roared. "It's too late to hide, man. I've got you now."

Lola did her best not to laugh and interrupt the joke. It was more of an effective prank than she had originally thought it would be.

Raquel, smiling broadly, grabbed the camcorder and began to film.

"What a day! What a film. Look out, Derrick, your comeuppance just came up."

"He's the culprit, Samson." Nattie pointed her finger at Derrick. "Go at him, big guy. Teach him a lesson or two."

"Please Samson! No!" Derrick pleaded. "You've got it all wrong. I'm innocent. I'll swear to it. I don't even know a Lily." Derrick pointed to his client. "Honest. This is my girl friend. Tell him, Darla. Please!"

"You're a damn lair. I hate a lying fool." Samson ran towards Derrick. "I'm gunna fix it so you won't touch another woman for a long time."

"Lola, do something," Derrick squirmed, pleading for help. "Please! Now!"

Derrick was no match for Samson. Lola, starting to feel uncomfortable and question what was going on, stood in awe.

"Fine friends you are," Derrick said. "I'm innocent. How can you turn on me?"

Raquel kept the camcorder rolling. Samson seized Derrick, wrapping his long fingers around his neck. Picking him up off of the floor and leaving his legs to dangle, Samson shook Derrick hard enough to rattle his bones.

"This will teach you not to mess with another man's woman," Samson threatened.

"I won't... I promise... I swear."

Derrick dropped his blow dryer. Still blowing hard, the dryer spun around on the floor in the same direction as Samson twirled.

"Ugh..." Derrick gasped for air. "Call the cops, Lola," he begged. "This monster's gone mad."

"Wow! What a day!" Nattie cackled uncontrollably while slapping her leg. "I couldn't have had a grander finale for my retirement if I had staged it myself."

"Did you say retire?" Jake sat up straight.

"Yes I did, lover boy. You heard me right."

"I'm glad you like to sail and play poker."

"We'll do plenty more than that," Nattie said. "We'll roll on the high seas, baby, just you and me."

"You bet we will, honey. We're going to have a great time."

"I'm feelin' real good. Justice is bein' done," Raquel said, still filming. "Nothin' like being in showbiz."

"I hate you, Derrick," Samson said, a ferocious look on his face. "You're dog meat!"

Lola saw that Derrick was having a hard time breathing. His face had turned a chalky shade of gray. It surprised Lola to see violent rage in Samson's expression, an anger she thought must have come from his ex-wife and their divorce. Overwhelmed like the rest of the clients, Lola stood rigid in the commotion. Terrified, heart beating rapidly, she tried to call out to Samson to stop, but her voice froze in her throat. Arms feeling like lead, Lola slumped in her chair. Feeling helpless in a state of timelessness, she could not move. A surrealistic feeling enveloping her, Lola stared as if looking at the situation from another time in space.

"Grrr..." Samson said. "Hey, Derrick, how does it feel to be in the arms of your married lover's husband?"

"Like hell," Derrick said, terror in his voice. "Lola, get this goon away from me. Nattie, get your green weapon and start slinging. Put me down!" Derrick demanded, almost starting to cry.

"What?" Samson shook him again. "Does the crybaby want to get down?"

Soft-hearted Lola wanted to call Samson off of Derrick. After seeing the horror in Derrick's face, she realized the joke had gone far enough.

Before Lola could say anything, the front door flung open, rupturing and sending shattered wood and splinters of glass flying through the air. Lola watched three masked hoodlums barge into the salon and wave their guns. With silencers on their pistols, they shot a round of bullets into the ceiling, mirrors, and hanging pots of ferns.

Lola, in shock and feeling detached, thought she was watching a movie in slow motion. Her eyes open wide, she saw splintered wood and glass spray through the air, hanging plants swayed side to side, and larger particles of plaster fell from the ceiling.

Strategically, the criminals took their stand in the middle of the salon, aiming their guns at everyone. The tallest thug mumbled in a volatile baritone.

"This is a hold-up! Put your arms in the air!"

"April Fools', Derrick," Raquel said. "Your guys showed up just in time to save you from Samson."

Dangling like a sack of potatoes from Samson's shoulder, Derrick looked bewildered.

"What are you talking about, Raquel? My guys? Get real!"

"April Fools'... You know."

"No I don't know!"

The leader of the pack, standing like a football player ready to tackle, pointed his gun towards Samson and Derrick.

"Drop everything!" he demanded.

"Hey, man, what's going on here?" Samson said, easing Derrick to the ground.

"What's it look like, you stupid idiot?" the robber hollered. "All of you get in a tight group. You five, lay on your stomachs." He waved his gun, saying to Raquel, "And you, pretty baby, stand with the rest of the bimbos. And can the camera before I blow it up."

Raquel, moving with precision, quickly threw the camera on to the sofa. Dazed, Lola watched in amazement. Still in shock, because of the complexity in everyone's actions, she could not quite figure out everything that was going on. Intimidated into fright and silence, fear and wonder rendered Lola powerless.

"C'mon! Move it!" the head thug said.

"What about her?" the robber hollered, pointing to Lola.

"She's out of it," he said. "She can't cause no trouble."

The two robbers pushed everyone else together, manhandling them.

"You heard the boss. Now, move it!"

"Cut the joke, guys," Samson butted in. "This prank's gone far enough."

"It's never far enough." The thug shot two bullets at his feet. "No joke, dancin' fool. These bullets don't know or care how big you are, so don't go tryin' anything dumb or the next round of bullets will sleep in your heart."

The robber's eyes scanned the salon, and he shot several more bullets into the ceiling. More plaster fell.

"You're the joke, big guy. Do what I say or you're dead."

Lola, startled but still thinking this was one of Derrick's April Fools' Day jokes, tried to stay calm. She knew Derrick was more than capable of coming up with this. It was dead quiet. Bertha's booming footsteps from her bathroom above cut through the silence. Lola heard loud creaks from the wooden floor above when Bertha sat down on her toilet seat. Lola watched as more bits of plaster fell on the checkered linoleum floor.

Shaking her head to break away from the numbness she felt, Lola heard the words leap out of her throat.

"My God! What is this?" Lola exclaimed. "Enough is enough, Derrick. Call your geeks off. This joke has gone far enough."

Lola's heart throbbed violently as she tried to catch her breath. Derrick stood like a wax figure; he could not speak. She ran towards Derrick, got to the edge of the group where he was huddled, and hit his arm before the thug could stop her.

"Hurry and make them stop," Lola shouted, every nerve in her body tensed. "They're hurting us. How could you pull such a morbid stunt and put our lives in danger like this?"

"It's no stunt," Derrick stuttered. "I swear. I forgot to tell you that Max from the Sheriff's Office called after you left last night, warning us of three robbers running the beauty salon circuit. Just hope they don't rape anyone like they have before."

"Rape?" Lola gulped, looking like a raccoon staring at truck headlights.

From Derrick's facial expression and the tone of his voice, Lola knew he was telling the truth. Defenseless, she became terrified and shivered from fright. She could not speak. Her April Fools' Day had turned into a horror-ridden flick. Endearingly, she looked at her loving friends, terrified and trembling, and she prayed for safety.

"You two idiots, shut up!" the giant thug shouted.

A panicky feeling enveloped Lola. Distraught, she had never in her life felt so unprotected. Terror-stricken, she felt her heart would stop beating. Her life flashed before her. Standing like a petrified tree, she feared this would be her demise. She looked at her friends, her extended family, and tears ran down her cheeks. Totally vulnerable, Lola knew she and her loved ones stood open to attack, like helpless ducks in a shooting gallery. Panicked, Lola watched the robbers fire more bullets into the ten-foot-high ceiling. Everyone was frozen in fear.

"The rest of you get up and take your jewelry off," the villainous gunman screamed out, "and hand it over with your wallets and purses."

Out of fear for their lives, Lola and her friends obliged. Lola, with care, handed over her diamond studded locket with her parents' picture in it, then unpinned her sapphire and ruby studded broach which had been her great grandmother's. Recklessly the robber threw her valuables into the sack. She had treasured these precious gifts for years but now that her life was at stake, she willingly gave them up. Speechless, Lola had never been so terrified in her life.

"This should bring a pretty penny," the pudgy criminal said, yanking a diamond and emerald necklace from Patricia's neck. "This jewelry looks like it's from Rodeo Drive."

"Bind 'em up with those chains." The thugs collected the valuables and stuffed them into a burlap sack. "Hurry up!"

"You assholes line up next to each other." The gunman, waving his pistol, harshly hollered out in his gravely voice, "One wrong move from any of you jerks, and you're dead. I'm not gonna take any crap off of any of you!" he threatened. "You hear? Easy does it and we're outta here."

Lola heard a crackling sound come from the ceiling directly above the largest robber. Gun in hand, he brushed the plaster pieces from his face. Lola nudged Derrick's arm and motioned for him to look up at the fractured plaster hanging from the ceiling.

In a split second, the cracks in the ceiling suddenly parted, making a wide opening as splinters of wood fell. Lola watched Bertha's toilet fall down through the opening, leaving a ragged-edged hole in the ceiling the size of a tire.

"Look out!" Lola screamed.

The loud crash vibrated through the shop. At that split second, the toilet hit the head robber on his shoulder near his thick neck, knocking him to the floor.

"Ahhh..." he screamed in pain, his gun falling to the floor.

Lola focused her eyes and tried to relate to what she saw. The toilet had smashed to smithereens, spreading pieces of shattered porcelain everywhere.

"Ugh!" he said, eyes dilated, not knowing what had hit him.

The gunman rolled his eyes, shook his head, turned over, then slowly dragged himself up to his knees. He turned before passing out and falling into a state of unconsciousness and lay sprawled on the floor like a defenseless, beached whale. Quickly, Samson lunged at the paunchy gunman.

"Gotcha!"

Lola gasped in amazement while she watched Nattie quickly flick her cigarette lighter into a stream of hair spray, sending an orange blaze of wild flame toward the other criminal's handgun.

"Ouch!" he screamed in pain, shaking his burned hand as his pistol fell to the floor.

"Sonofabitch!" Derrick and Patricia quickly tackled the robber. "Hold on Patricia."

"Don't think I'm not! I didn't learn karate for nothing."

Lola watched Samson and Derrick smash the two thug's heads together, knocking them out cold. While rubbing the goose bumps on her arms, she took deep breaths to calm herself. Head spinning, Lola felt like she had been in a disastrous tornado.

Like a reporter ready for action, Raquel quickly grabbed the camcorder and held it to her eye.

"I can point and shoot anywhere," Raquel exclaimed. "It's all good stuff. Unbelievable! Just look at that slimy slob layin' there. And he thought he was such a tough guy with a big gun in his hand."

"He's a slab of dense meat now." Derrick was so scared that his voice squeaked like a nervous old lady.

Lola looked up and saw Bertha's corpulent derriere, looking like two over-stuffed bed pillows smashed together, squeezed through the rotted circle of wood where the toilet had been. The rest of Bertha's body was still upstairs in her decayed bathroom. Lola heard Bertha's plea and felt compassion for her miserable landlady.

"Save me!" Bertha screamed. "Help me!"

"Gross," Raquel said. "Will you look at that! Ugh!"

"Oh my God," Lola said. "Seeing is not believing."

"Help me!" Bertha's terrified, trembling voice sounded far away. "I'm hurt and I can't get up! Ahhhh..." Bertha screamed and sputtered, saying nothing coherent. "Yeowwww..."

"Holy shit!" Derrick said. "It doesn't even look like an ass. I wouldn't take a picture of that if you paid me. It would probably break my camera."

"Bertha sounds like a snortin' pig stuck in a hole," Raquel said.

"She *is* a snorting pig stuck in a hole!" Nattie pointed towards Bertha's derriere. "Unreal."

"You guys are terrible." Lola shook her head in disbelief. "Someone's got to help her."

Tying the thieves' wrists from behind with the cords from the blow dryer and curling iron, Samson explained to Derrick why he was in the salon.

"Sorry, man. It seemed a funny thing to do at the time."

"Good thing you were here, Samson. Thanks. You did give me a scare, though."

"I'll remember this joke for a long time."

"I think we'll all remember today whether we want to or not." Derrick pursed his lips, then smiled while shaking his head and feeling his bald spots. "Women and their conniving minds. Today's been a real bitch... A bitch of bitches. A relaxing warm sauna sounds pretty appealing right now."

Raquel kept the film rolling towards Bertha's rear end.

"Boy, talk about a Kodak moment! This is great. It's a shoe-in. For sure I'll win the $10,000 on *Funny Home Videos*."

"Yeah you will." Nattie pulled a set of handcuffs out of her purse. "Let me in there so I can snap these suckers on the creep." Straddling the groggy thug from behind, with expertise, Nattie pulled his arms together and handcuffed him, then kicked him hard in his crotch.

"Don't tell me you keep those steel bracelets in your purse?" Derrick laughed out loud. "Nattie, you are one classy broad."

"Emergencies, you know," Nattie giggled coyly, winking at Jake. "Kind of like today. Are you into jewelry, Mr. Jenkins?"

"Why, yes I am. I have quite a collection myself." He wiggled his eyebrows. "Please, Nattie... Call me Jake."

"My pleasure."

Jake smiled and his eyes sparkled. Lola saw that Nattie and Jake were already getting very friendly.

"What other goodies do you have in that purse of yours?" Jake flirted.

"Surprise, surprise!" Nattie whipped her purse around above her head. "I've saved the best for later."

Lola looked up at Bertha's rear end. It was disheartening to see Bertha in this ridiculous position.

"Quick! We must do something to help Bertha. Someone help me."

"I'm stuck! Please rescue me! Nattie... Lola... Ugh!" Bertha screamed and cried out in excruciating agony. "Help me! I'm wedged in this damn hole and I can't get out."

Lola listened to colorful expressions exchanged while everyone roared with hysterical laughter.

"My God!" Nattie hollered out, holding her stomach from giggling. "I've never seen an uglier sight in my life. I thought her face was ugly."

"It is," Raquel laughed, "but not as butt-ugly as that. Ugh! Just look at it, cratered with dimples like the moon and all. Gross! Gravity does weird things."

"Looks to me like about four ax handles across the butt." Nattie, shaking with laughter, reached for the heated curling iron. "All right, cowboy!"

"Nattie, how dare you! Perish the thought!" Lola exclaimed, angered. "You've gone too far this time. Don't even think such a horrible thing!"

"But every cow's got to be branded."

"Not this one! The poor woman's in a big enough mess without you adding to her misery. You stinker, now put that iron down."

The belly laughs continued. Feeling faint and out of control, Lola was outraged by what was going on.

"Lola, are you all right?" Raquel asked.

"I think so."

Lola felt she must get a hold of her emotions and be strong. She shook her head again and still could not believe what was going on in her salon. Thoroughly disgusted with everyone's behavior, she saw unconscionable sides of people's personalities she never dreamed existed, and it frustrated her.

"It's a massive target," Nattie blurted out. "I wish I had my slingshot. What a bulls-eye I could hit."

"Nattie, the woman is in a compromising position," Lola said. "Have you no reverence for human life at all?"

"No, not for mean ol' Bertha. She's gotten what she deserves, been due for years. This is great. Wild!"

"Retribution," Raquel said, still filming. "This video will definitely go down in history. I'm gonna show it at the next hairstyle show in Las Vegas."

"I would have never believed this if I hadn't seen it for myself," Patricia said. "If the rest of your day has been like this, I'll have my next book. Conversation at tonight's dinner should be very interesting."

"Count on it," Lola said, brushing her forehead. "I'm glad you're joining us. You're one person who has a calming effect on me."

"Now I know where that crackling sound came from," Patricia said.

"Unbelievable," Raquel said. "Bertha's rear looks like a planet up there. I'll bet she wishes Scotty would beam her up."

"Whatever, it's a sight for sore eyes," Derrick said. "I may skip dinner, but not the champagne. A bottle should do it."

Lola telephoned the local precinct.

"Hi Max... Yeah, it's me. Send the squad cars over to pick up the beauty salon robbers." She listened, then replied, "Yep, we've got them good. They're passed out and tied up tight. One kind of wakes up every now and then, but Nattie takes care of that. Please hurry, you couldn't get here too soon to suit any of us." Lola laughed, listening to Max. "It's kind of hard to put into words, Max. You'll have to see the video to believe it all. Hey, you and Anna come and join us for dinner at Mama's... OK. You're on."

Lola dialed 911, knowing they would be able to get Bertha out of her predicament.

"Hi Butch..." Lola paused. "Yeah, it's me again. Send the firemen this time, and tell them to bring a big net, an extra sturdy one. Bertha's toilet has fallen through her floor into our salon, and it hit the robber and knocked him out cold, and Bertha's caught in the hole. Her rear end is hanging through the ceiling. Unbelievable, must hurt real bad. Yeah, I'm serious... I don't have the kind of imagination to make this stuff up. Come yourself this time. You've got to see this."

"Lola, c'mon." Nattie grabbed the lease from the marbled vanity. "Lets get Bertha to sign it now, before help comes."

"You've got to be kidding? I can't do that. Not now, not after what's happened."

"Oh yes you can. What better time to do business than now? Let's get her when she's down."

"Nattie, have you no scruples?"

"No! Not for things like this." With all the speed in her power, Nattie dashed up the stairs. "C'mon, hurry."

Lola followed, feeling guilt for what she and Nattie were doing. "I can't believe I'm actually going along with you."

Nattie entered Bertha's bathroom, Lola behind her. Seeing poor Bertha was the most pathetic sight she had ever seen.

"Need some help, Bertha?" Nattie barked.

"Nattie... Oh Nattie," Bertha cried out in a trusting tone, gasping for air. "Please help me. I'm so dizzy. I think I'm going to die."

"You're not going to die," Nattie said. "You're too mean to die."

Even though Lola was upset with Bertha, she still had empathy for her.

"Of course we'll help you."

"Sanders," Nattie bellowed, "this is the worst I've ever seen you. Talk about a beaver... It's downright disgusting and shameful what you've done this time."

Lola saw that Bertha, her face bright red, was ready to pass out. She hoped Bertha would not have a heart attack. That would be more than she could bear.

"The hell with you," Bertha moaned. "Just call the fire department to come and get me out of here."

Lola stood behind Nattie while she handed the lease to Bertha. "Sign it. Then I'll call the firemen."

"Nattie, how dare you even think you can threaten me at a time like this," Bertha said, whimpering like a caged rhinoceros. "I was going to, but no way now! I'm getting out for good. This finalizes it."

"Sign it," Nattie demanded, pushing the lease and a pen into her bloated, crimson face.

"Nattie," Lola said, "Please... You've gone far enough."

"The carpenters can fix this place in no time flat. In a few days, this incident will be history... Forgotten."

"No way!" Bertha screamed. "I'll never forget this!"

Lola heard the hot water heater gurgling in the hall. Boom! Lola jumped at the sound of the loud explosion. She saw the water spray from the door-less closet, shooting water out of the pipe like a fire hose. Getting wet like a car in a car wash, Lola watched in amazement as water gushed everywhere.

"The supply line must have broken," Lola said, massaging her temples. "Ugh! Tell me this isn't happening!"

"Let's just hope it doesn't overheat and blow this place up," Nattie said. "With old buildings like this, you just never know."

"Help me," Bertha begged. "I've been rotten to you, Lola. I'm sorry. I'm so sorry. I was going to sign. I swear... This is no time to hold a grudge."

"Just hold on, Bertha. You know I'm not one to hold a grudge, especially at a time like this. We'll get you out of this mess." Lola heard the fire truck arrive. "Listen... The firemen will be up here in no time flat."

"I'm so scared. Yesterday wouldn't be soon enough for me." Bertha's fat jiggled as she sobbed. "Oh... I'm dying..."

"C'mon up, boys." Nattie directed the firemen where to go. "The porker's in her pen. Needs a little help. Finally got a bath, of course the fabulous hair-do I gave her is long gone. It's all history now."

"We have no choice, men," the fire chief hollered above the noise from the water heater. "We have to use the net. There's no time to try to cut her out carefully. That water heater can blow at any second. You know how bad the plumbing is in these flammable old buildings. One spark could ignite everything. Move carefully and swiftly."

Lola, filled with anxiousness, asked the fire chief what she could do to help.

"Go downstairs. Get everyone out of the building."

"I'm out of here." Nattie beelined it to the stairs. "Baby, it don't take a fool to read the writing on the wall."

Lola followed Nattie down the stairwell and yelled for everyone clear out of the building.

"Everybody split! The water heater may blow up any second and catch this place on fire. Spread the word."

Lola watched everyone grab their valuables and scurry out. The phone rang while she ran through the front door. Compelled to answer it, she turned back. For sentimental reasons, Lola just had to say Contemporary Hair Design one more time.

"Don't, babe," Derrick said. "It's too dangerous. Let's get the hell out of here."

"Go on... I'll be OK."

"Women!" Derrick said. "I'm not leaving you. I'll wait."

"Thanks, but I just have to answer."

"It's your choice, babe."

"Ugh! My salon!" Lola ran her fingers through her hair. "Go on, Derrick. I'll be right there."

Derrick ran out, following the others through the front door. Lola quickly grabbed the receiver. It was Sam, the film maker. Standing more straight, Lola perked up and spoke.

"Yes... I sure can, Sam." More excited by the second, she said, "Yes, I will, and thank you so much. I'm kind of in a rush right now. I'll see you at the airport next Friday. Yeah... I'll get details later. I've got to run. This place might blow any minute."

Lola ran out and stood across the street with her friends. Knowing they were out of danger, she relaxed a little and sighed a deep sigh of relief.

Lola heard the sounds of more sirens fill the air. Police were everywhere, their cars blocking the street. Business people from the neighborhoods ran to join the gathering crowd.

Shocked, Lola gazed at her salon. Etched windows, framed with hand carved wooden designs, had been finely crafted by artisans generations ago. Brick planter boxes filled with ferns, lobelia, geraniums, and azaleas circling the lamp posts added splashes of color in front of the brown rustic building. Sheer lace curtains blew gently in the wind. Lola felt an emptiness in her heart when she stood and watched her salon become a part of history.

Watching the police put the hand-cuffed robbers into their cars, Lola felt more relief.

"Yea!" Nattie cheered. "Give me the camcorder, Raquel. It's my turn."

"Can you believe those guys?" Lola said. "Robbing a beauty salon?"

"There was over one hundred thousand in jewels and bucks in that bag." Derrick wiped the perspiration from his forehead. "Damn! I hope to God that I never again experience the likes of today. I'm beat!"

"For once Bertha dropped in at a good time," Raquel said. "Those thugs will get what they deserve. To start with, Nattie's abuse damaged them plenty."

Lola stood in awe and watched the firemen and paramedics at work. Memories of her salon crowded her mind. Feeling numb, her body limp, she worried for Bertha's safety.

Walking towards Lola, Craig's mouth gaped open. Gently he put his arm around her shoulder and pulled her into his chest. Lola welcomed his comforting touch.

"I'm so glad you're here," Lola said.

"God!" Craig said, looking across the street. "What's happened? I heard the sirens a mile away. Are you all right? Is everyone OK?"

"Oh, Craig," Lola cried, tears streaming down her face.

"You're shivering, honey." Craig held her close. "Don't cry, darling. What's happened? Why are the police and fire trucks here?"

"You won't believe this... Bertha's rear-end is caught in a hole in the ceiling," Lola sobbed. "The shop may blow up any time now."

"Say what? What do you mean she's caught in a hole?"

"And Nattie was going to brand her with the curling iron."

"With what? Why?"

"I don't even believe what's happened today myself." Lola hung her head, weak from the trauma. "I'll tell you details over dinner. Plan on our conversation to be something else. You may not believe it but it's all on film. Unreal!"

"What's really happened with Bertha?" Craig questioned.

"Her rear-end is caught in a hole," Nattie said.

"Wait a minute," Craig said in disbelief. "In a hole? Did she ever sign the lease?"

"No, but she would have if all this mess hadn't of happened."

"What do you mean she's caught in a hole?"

"Just hug me for now, Craig."

"I'm so sorry for you," Craig said, embracing her tightly. "I know how much your salon means to you. If I can do anything to help you, let me know." Craig tenderly kissed her forehead. "I'm here for you. Believe me when I say that."

"Thanks, Craig. Thank you for caring. I guess it wasn't meant for me to continue in my salon. I tried so hard."

"You can't make things happen, babe," Nattie said. "I know you had good intentions, but force doesn't work."

"Starting over isn't so bad," Craig said. "I'll be by your side."

Tenderly touching her face, his lips met Lola's. For the first time, Lola felt good about starting over again. She squeezed Craig's hand, gazed into his eyes, and smiled a gentle smile.

"Thank God for good friends."

Lola basked in the comforting sensations of his warm embrace.

"We'll always be strong for each other," Craig assured her.

"Yes, we will."

"We have everything on film, Craig." Nattie popped her bubble gum and waved the video camera in front of them. "Wait till you see the craziness! Jake baby, do you have a VCR on that luxury yacht of yours?"

"I sure do... Big screen, too."

"Good, because loverboy, you're in for a real treat tonight."

"I'm sure I am." Jake wiggled his eyebrows, and smiled joyously. "For years I listened to the wild stories my beloved wife told me about all the characters in your salon. I'm absolutely thrilled that I'm finally a part of it all."

Lola laughed knowing she knew in more ways than one that she, Nattie, Raquel, and Derrick had earned reputations as colorful, fun, creative designers, action people filled with the spirit of living life to the fullest.

Lola noticed Francois in the distance walking towards them. Smiling, she motioned to Raquel, then gave her the OK sign.

"Oh, here's my honey," Raquel said, waving grandly at Francois. "This video will surprise him. I just can't wait to tell him just everything."

"Looks like someone needs a good lawyer." Francois put his arm around Raquel's waist. "What's going on here? Why all the police?"

"Oh, Francois!" Raquel said, batting her long eyelashes and dramatically swishing the hair from her forehead. "It's been such a horrifyin' day, filled with trauma and excitement to the max!"

"Tell me about it, sweetheart."

"I'm so shook up, darlin'. For now just please hold me and calm me down," Raquel cooed in a heavy Southern accent.

"Things will turn out, darling." Kissing her cheek, he surrounded Raquel with his arms. "Just relax, love. Lay your head on my chest and tell me what's happened. I'm here now. Take your time."

Lola was pleased to hear the sincerity in Francois voice as he spoke to Raquel. She felt a contentment in her heart that her dear friend Raquel and Francois would be able to build a loving relationship, one filled with joy, laughter, and happiness.

"Hey, Lola! Who called?" Derrick asked. "Was answering the telephone worth the risk?"

"Yes, yes, yes!" Lola exclaimed. "Sam called."

"Well," Raquel said, "what did he want?"

"Oh... He gave me my dream," Lola said in a heavenly voice. "Life is so beautiful when good stuff happens."

"Well?" Raquel said.

"Get ready for this," Lola said. "Sam's regular make-up artist broke her arm, and he wanted to know if I would fly to Paris with him and the crew Friday to film for eight weeks."

"How exciting!" Nattie said. "What did you tell him? Yes?"

"Yes! Of course. What else? When something falls in my lap, I go for it. The great part of it all is that I will only work fourteen hours on Saturdays. They don't need me for rehearsals during the week."

"Let me guess what you'll be doing during the week," Derrick said, smiling with delight.

"Yes! Yes!" Lola exclaimed, hoping up and down. "Dreams do come true. I'll enroll in art school and paint five days a week. Oh... I'll be a great artist yet."

"Honey, I'm happy for you." Craig hugged Lola tightly. "I'll miss you terribly, but you can be sure that I'll be waiting for you with open arms at the airport when you return. But, then again... If you want someone to do Paris with you in style, I'll fly over. I'm the one."

"Craig, yes... I was hoping you'd say that. I'll look forward to it."

"Me, too."

With love in her eyes, Lola looked deeply into the hearts of her dear friends, the wonderful people who shared her life. A warmth came over her as she recalled special memories of their togetherness. All of their vacations together had been memorable. They had always encouraged each other while performing at hairstyle shows throughout the world. They were loyal to each other in times of sadness and in times of joy.

"I'm so grateful that I have all of you," Lola said. "I love you so much. C'mon. Group hug. Thank you for sharing my good fortune and my life. Ah... Paris in the Springtime."

"Oh, sugar, I love you, too," Raquel said. "I'm just so happy, I could cry."

Nattie burst into song, singing her favorite French song. Lola joined everyone in their laughter.

"I love Paris in the springtime..." Nattie sang. "How about you, Jake?"

"Name any place in the world, Nattie, and it will be my pleasure to take you there."

"You're my kind of guy!"

"Maybe Raquel and I will come to visit you in Paris," Francois said. "I'll be flying there for Mother's Day."

"Oh, yes," Raquel said, jumping with delight. "I'd love to meet your family."

"And they will love to meet you."

"You kids go and have a good time," Nattie said. "As of right now, I am officially retired. Jake, let's you and me sail into the sunset."

"That's fine with me, Captain. You chart the course."

"What about you, Derrick?" Lola asked. "What are you going to do?"

"I didn't get a chance to tell you earlier, but I'm flying to London to do a layout and photo-shoot for Lorieann Designs."

"Lucky for you I didn't kill you earlier," Raquel said.

"Fabulous! Lorieann Designs is big stuff. We're all having new beginnings. I worried all this time for nothing. Oh," Lola said with joy, "I am eternally grateful for the abundance in our lives."

"Look!" Nattie pointed across the street. "They're bringing big Bertha out on a gurney."

"Thank goodness they got her out safely," Lola sighed in relief. "Bertha actually has a smile on her face."

"That's history for Bertha," Nattie said. "She's the only heavy person I've ever known that was not jolly with a good disposition."

Bertha waved as the paramedics put her into the ambulance. Lola watched as they drove down the street, and prayed that Bertha would have a wonderful new beginning in her life, too. Dazed, still safe in

Craig's strong arms, Lola stared at the building. Fondly, she had remembered her first day of work at Contemporary Hair Design. Bouquets of flowers and boxes of candy and balloons had poured in from all of her family and friends from all over the world, wishing her well. Mimi had been her first client. Patricia was her last. Lola accepted her salon may be gone, but she knew deep in her heart that her quality friendships would endure for a lifetime.

Lola, basking in memories, reminisced the good times. Suddenly, in less than a split second, the old, wooden building exploded into flames. Loud noises pierced Lola's eardrums. Holding her ears, gasping, she watched the flames skyrocket. Heat filled the air, brushing her delicate skin with its fire.

"Oh, my God!" Lola exclaimed. "That explosion sounded like a space shuttle going off."

"Gas line must have overheated," Craig said. "Thank God no one got hurt. That decrepit building was a real fire hazard."

Flames soared into the clear, blue sky. Within minutes, the entire building fell to the ground and burned to ashes. Blinking her eyes, Lola felt an empty feeling in the pit of her stomach. As easy as wiping chalk off of a blackboard, she knew her salon was gone forever.

Lola, remembering her fiery nightmare from the night before, thought back to the mysterious Oriental woman who had told her that by the end of the day she would understand the meaning of her dream.

"Run into the light," Lola said. "Raquel, do you remember what I said about my dream?"

"Yeah... I sure do, sugar darlin'."

"So do I." Lola nodded, smiling confidently.

"My mama always told us kids to listen to our dreams," Raquel said. "They tell a story."

"Run into the light," Lola repeated. "I love being in the light."

"Me, too," Raquel said. "White is my favorite color."

"White's not a color," Derrick said.

"Yes it is," Raquel insisted. "Tell him, Lola. You're the artist. You know for sure."

"No it isn't." Derrick stood straight. "White is *not* a color."

"Yes it is," Raquel quipped. "I just know so."

"Don't you two ever give up?" Lola said.

"Give it a rest, kids," Nattie said. "Boy! Some things never change."

Derrick pointed to the bald spots on his head and chest. Lola, in amazement, had not noticed that the spots were so big.

"Look at this, Francois," Derrick said. "Look what your Raquel did to me! Man... You've got to know you're dealing with a tigress."

"How well I know," Francois laughed, smiling broadly, his eyes dancing in the light. "*My* dream has also come true. Today is a very special day to celebrate."

Wonderful memories of days in her salon flashed through her mind. Melancholy, Lola knew she would miss working closely with her co-workers. They had been a great team. Taking comfort in her success, Lola was satisfied that she had worked hard, long hours and had reached her goal to be a talented, prominent salon owner, one with international recognition. Feeling sentimental, Lola cried.

"I can't believe it's all gone. The book just closed on this chapter of my life. All the years I put into the business, and within minutes, it's vanished right before my eyes. Poof... All gone."

"No one can take your memories away from you." Craig held her close to him, kissing her cheek. "It's out of your hands now. Be open to the goodness ahead. We'll enjoy it together. I look forward to it. Promise me you won't look back."

"Oh, Craig... I won't. I'll be too busy looking to our future."

A gentle calm came over Lola. Somehow, she did not mind the salon was gone. It was OK. Standing straight, she felt strong and optimistic, as though something marvelous, another exciting chapter, was in store.

"I'm ready for my new beginning. In fact, I'm razzed and jazzed and ready to go!"

"Look out world," Raquel said. "Cissy's got her lil' ol' mind set and I can see in her eyes that there's no stoppin' her now."

"That's my girl. No matter what, you've got to know that the best is yet to come," Nattie said. "Party time... C'mon, let's go to dinner. I'm starving."

"Mama Corelli has nine bottles of champagne on ice for us, plus cracked crab, fancy appetizers, and more," Francois said. "We have much to celebrate."

"Let's drink to our futures," Lola said. "They're going to be spectacular."

"And let's drink to love." Francois tenderly kissed Raquel. "It's what makes the world go around."

"And let's drink to my next novel. I'll call it *Hot and Hairy*," Patricia said. "Gee, I sure love hanging out with all of you. Artistic talent is limitless. Creative people is where the fun is at."

"All right! Let the good times roll!"

In the midst of the smoke, sirens, and firemen, Lola intertwined her arms with Craig and Nattie while walking towards Mama Corelli's.

"It's hard to believe the salon's gone," Lola sighed, glancing back at the burning ashes. "Just a memory now."

"Yeah," Derrick said, "but what a memory."

"Just remember, kids, the joy is in the journey," Nattie said. "Isn't that right, Jake?"

"Yes, dear. As one day ends, know the richness of another is on its way. Life's ocean waves, they are a constant, and it's all good."

Without a care in the world, free as a bird in a bright, sunny sky, Lola continued walking closely together with her friends. Thrilled over the possibilities in her near future, she felt a new excitement in the air. Having no boundaries, her mind ran rampant thinking and dreaming of attending art school in Paris, traveling the globe with her work, and most importantly, her growing more deeply in love with Craig. She squeezed his hand, then kissed it.

"You make me happy," Craig tenderly said.

"This is just our beginning."

"My brother is a jeweler."

"Diamonds?" Lola raised her eyebrows.

"Yes," Craig smiled broadly. "Wedding rings are his specialty."

Lola knew dinner that evening at Mama Corelli's would be a thrilling, stimulating, memorable occasion for everyone to share their feelings, crack jokes, and belly-laugh till the sun came up.

"What are you thinking, babe?" Nattie said, with love in her expression.

"Talk about twists and turns!" Lola answered. "Life is full of surprises. This is all blowing me away. Today was more than something else! I'm still in shock."

"Besides being in shock, cissy," Raquel said, "what else is in that pretty lil' ol' head of yours?"

"I have never felt freer or more excited in my life." Lola ran and jumped for joy and reached high in the sky. "I'm red-hot and ready to tackle life in a new way. I can hardly wait for the next episode to really begin. If new beginnings are all this wonderful, I want more of them. Oh... Paris, here I come."

"And?" Nattie grinned.

"I'm glad we got today on film," Lola said. "This made a spectacularly great finale for all of us."

"Dynamite, babycakes... But what are you *really* thinking?"

"The same as you, Nattie." Shaking her head, Lola laughed. "I know you too well."

"Yeah you do. Say what's in your mind, Lola. I want the confirmation."

Lola giggled, then screamed out, "What a crazy way to make a buck!"